Also available from Susan Mallery

And watch for a special Fool's Gold holiday book, coming soon!

A Fool's Gold Christmas

SUSAN MALLERY

All Summer Long

ISBN-13: 978-1-62090-264-6

ALL SUMMER LONG

To the one who makes every writing day wonderful. You keep me company, tell me every page is brilliant and remind me it's always a good idea to stop every now and then and take a well-deserved nap. To my own little princess. My sweet Nikki.

Also, a special thank-you to Bill Buchanan for all the technical help on the volunteer firefighters. He was brilliant, and any mistakes in this story are mine. (Yes, Bill, you really do have to share the dedication page with my poodle.)

All Summer Long

CHAPTER ONE

"DON'T TAKE THIS wrong, but seriously, a cat of your size needs to keep all four paws firmly on the ground."

Charlie Dixon continued up the ladder, aware that Daytona was watching her with serious contempt in his large, green eyes. The black-and-white cat was about twenty-six pounds of attitude. His climbing skills might be excellent, but his ability to get down a tree left much to be desired. At least once a month he got his big furry butt to the top of Mrs. Coverson's sycamore and yowled to be rescued. About an hour later, the old lady would panic and call the fire department. Daytona, named for Mrs. Coverson's love of all things NASCAR, glared and hissed and threatened, but in the end, he submitted to being safely carried to the ground.

"Come on, you," Charlie said, climbing the last two rungs of the ladder. "You know you're getting hungry and I'm your ride down to your food bowl."

On cue, the cat flattened his ears and gave an impressive growl.

"Cheap talk, big guy," Charlie said, then reached for the cat. Daytona took a swipe at the back of her hand, but the movement was halfhearted at best. He was already inching toward her, then allowed himself to be picked up and held against her.

"Don't worry," someone called from the sidewalk. "I've got your ladder."

Charlie sighed heavily. "Civilians," she muttered. "How do they always find me?"

Daytona didn't offer a response.

Charlie looked down and saw some guy hovering by the base of her ladder. "I'm fine," she yelled. "Step back."

"Someone needs to hold the ladder," the dark-haired man insisted.

"Not really."

Charlie tucked Daytona securely under one arm and started her descent. She went quickly, aware that Daytona's attention span was often shorter than the trip to safety. When he started squirming, they were both in danger of tumbling. This time she cut it a little too close.

Daytona pushed all four paws against her, then twisted in an attempt to climb down the rest of the way by himself. Charlie hung on. Not only didn't she want to fall herself, there was no way she was going to face old lady Coverson with a less-than-perfect Daytona beside her.

"Stop it!" she told the cat.

"Need me to come up?" the guy asked.

Charlie briefly wondered how much trouble she would be in for kicking him with her steel-toed boots and if it would be worth it. Some of her best friends were civilians, but honest to God, there were people who totally lacked common sense.

"Stay back," she yelled. "Step away from the ladder and don't interfere."

"I'm not interfering. I'm helping."

Before Charlie could respond, several things happened at once. Daytona gave one final push for freedom. Charlie leaned over to make sure she kept a grip on the squirming cat. The ladder lurched, the idiot below started up and everyone had a moment to rediscover the power of gravity.

Daytona fared the best. He used his claws to dig in to the side of the tree, then scurry down. Charlie came in second. She was maybe six or seven feet from the ground. It came up fast, but instead of hitting the sidewalk or even the grass at the base of the tree, she slammed into the guy who'd been trying to "help."

As she lay on top of the idiot and sucked in air, Charlie watched Daytona stroll over and give a last annoyed hiss. The cat stalked away, his tail high. Charlie rolled off the guy, aware that at five-ten and well-muscled, she weighed a whole lot more than was considered fashionable. No doubt he'd had the wind knocked out of him. With luck, only his pride was hurt and then she could lecture him on why it was never good to be stupid. At worst, she was about to have to call for an ambulance.

"You okay?" she asked, shifting into a kneeling position and glancing at the man for the first time. "Did you hit your head and—"

Crap and double crap. This wasn't some random stupid person, she thought, taking in the perfectly shaped jaw, the firm full mouth and, when his lids slowly opened, the dark eyes fringed by long lashes. This was possibly the best-looking man on the planet.

Clay Stryker, model, movie butt double. His ass had been flashed in magazine ads, calendars and on the big screen. He had a killer body and his face was even better. He was the kind of man for whom, on the promise of a smile, the earth would change its rotation.

She'd met him a couple of times. At her friend Heidi's recent wedding to Clay's brother, for starters. Plus, Clay lived at the ranch where she boarded her horse. They'd nodded at each other over stalls and hay bales. But she'd never seen him up close before. Not in the flesh, at least. Had never been so near to a flawless human.

Reluctantly, she had to admit, it was a little unnerving.

One corner of that perfect mouth turned up. "Hey," he said. "I saved you."

Charlie snorted. "Not likely. Did you hit your head? Because if you did, I'm hoping it knocked some sense into you."

The slight curve became a smile. "You're welcome." He sat up.

Charlie put a hand on his shoulder. "Hold on there, hotshot. Are you injured? You were at the bottom of our pileup. Make sure nothing's broken."

"My ego's a little bruised that you don't appreciate what I did for you."

"You knocked me off the ladder and nearly killed us

both. No, you don't get a cookie." She stood, then held out her hand to help him up. "Can you stand?"

The smile turned into a grin. Damn, the man was pretty, she thought absently. Despite the fact that it had literally been a decade since she'd found any man attractive, there was something about his near godlike perfection that was appealing.

He ignored her hand and stood in one easy movement. "I'm good."

"Charlie, are you all right?"

"Fine, Mrs. Coverson," Charlie said, trying not to clench her teeth. Her dentist had warned her that she needed to stop grinding her jaw when she was annoyed. Which was much of the time.

Mrs. Coverson stood on the front porch, Daytona in her arms. Behind her, Michelle Banfield, who worked with Charlie, stood with a half-eaten brownie and a look of guilt in her eyes.

"I was coming back out to help," Michelle mumbled. "Um, but there were these brownies."

"That's okay," Clay told her. "I was here."

It was all Charlie could do not to smack him upside the head.

"Here is the one place you shouldn't be. It's illegal to interfere with a firefighter at work. You do it again and I'll have you arrested."

Instead of being appropriately intimidated, Clay grinned. "You're tough."

"You have no idea."

He stuck out his hand. "Glad I could help."

"You didn't—" She shook her head. "Whatever. Fine. Thank you. Now go away."

She shook hands with him, conscious of his fingers engulfing hers. And he was taller, by at least four inches. Interesting facts, but of no earthly use.

First of all, she had yet to conquer her manphobia and if she decided she wanted to, it wouldn't be with anyone like him. She would look for safe. Nice. Normal. Second, even if she was silly enough to be attracted to him, which she wasn't, there was no way in a million billion years that a guy like him would be interested in a woman like her. Men like him fell for supermodels and…and…women like her mother. Well, back when her mother had been younger.

Charlie knew what she was. Strong and capable. She could wear the fifty pounds of gear her job required without breaking a sweat. She could haul hoses up ten stories of stairs, no problem. She was self-sufficient. She knew how to change a tire and fix a leaky faucet. She didn't need a man. Except maybe for one teeny, tiny thing.

"Ah, Charlie?"

"What?" she snapped.

Clay glanced at their still-joined hands. "Did you want me to leave? Because if you do, I'm going to need that back."

Damn. She released him instantly. "Sorry."

"No problem." He flashed a smile that would send a lesser woman to her knees. "I'll see you at the ranch."

The ranch, she thought blankly. *Oh, right.* He lived there; she boarded her horse there. They would run into each other. "Sure."

He waved at the two women on the porch. "Have a nice day, ladies."

They both nodded without speaking. As he strolled away, Charlie saw Michelle and Mrs. Coverson drop their gazes to his butt. Charlie allowed herself a quick look before heading toward the house and a freshly baked brownie.

Sugar was easy, she thought. Deliciousness followed by a blood-sugar spike. But men—not so much. And Clay was worse than most. Because for a split second, when he'd tossed her that last smile, she would have sworn she felt something deep down in her belly.

Not attraction. That was too strong a word. But a flicker. The faintest whisper. The good news was that part of her wasn't as dead as she'd thought. The bad news was she'd discovered that fact by being in the presence of a butt model with the face of an angel. A man who could have any woman he wanted, simply by asking. Or maybe hinting.

His world was ruled by those who were flawless. She was broken. Maybe not where anyone could see and she'd sure learned how to fake normal. But she knew the truth.

Still, progress had been made. A flicker today, a tingle tomorrow. Give her a millennium or two and she might find her way to being just like everyone else.

CLAY SECURED THE large screen that was the focal point of his presentation. He'd worked hours on synthesizing the information down to a few easily understood graphs and charts. He had stacks of research to back up every number.

Now, in the living room of the old farmhouse where he'd spent the first few years of his life, he prepared to share his proposal with his two brothers and his mother.

Given the choice, he would prefer to face a thousand restless stockholders. Sure, family was supposed to be supportive, but Rafe and Shane were both successful businessmen. They wouldn't be swayed by emotional connections. If anything, Rafe would be tougher on him.

Clay didn't remember much about his father. The man had died before Clay had turned five. But Rafe, his oldest brother, had tried to step into the void their father's death had left behind. He'd felt responsible for his siblings and had sacrificed for all of them. He'd wanted Clay to follow a more traditional path—college, then a safe, secure job. Having his baby brother run off to be a male model had grated on Rafe and he'd made it clear he thought Clay was wasting his life.

Now, over a decade later, Clay was ready to take his older brother's advice and settle down. Only he wanted to start his own business, and it involved the whole family.

Clay hadn't made this decision lightly. He'd spent over a year playing with different business ideas before settling on the one that made the most sense to him. He knew what he wanted—to be close to those he loved, to do something with his hands and to get involved with a community. This idea offered the opportunity for all three, and a healthy profit margin. He hadn't seen a downside. Of course, if there was one, Rafe would be happy to point it out.

Rafe, Shane and their mother, May, walked into the living room. Clay had positioned the sofa in front of the screen. He pushed a couple of keys on the laptop keyboard to load the presentation.

"Have a seat," he said, motioning to the couch. When nerves threatened, he reminded himself he'd done his research and he had a damned good idea. If his brothers weren't smart enough to see that, he would go somewhere else with it.

He pushed a key and the first slide flashed onto the screen. It showed a family on a picnic. "As our daily lives revolve more around technology, many people are looking for a way to reconnect with simpler pleasures. Over the past few years, there has been a growing trend in a new kind of vacation travel. 'Haycations' offer a way for families to spend time together in a comfortable environment, while rediscovering how life used to be. They work on a farm, get back to nature and unwind."

He clicked the second slide, which showed a husband and wife riding a tractor. "The average family wants value for their money, comfortable accommodations and a place where parents and kids can explore without having to worry about deadlines, crime or the latest tragedy on the news."

He went through several graphs showing how much families spent on vacation each year, then moved into the main part of the presentation. He proposed buying two hundred acres on the other side of the Castle Ranch. There he would grow hay and alfalfa for the horses and other animals on their ranch and Shane's. In addition, he would grow organic fruits and vegetables. The operation would be overseen by a farm manager, with much of the labor being provided by the "Haycationers."

Rafe was already building vacation homes, where the Haycationers could stay. There was plenty to do in town, when the visiting families wanted a taste of modern life. With horseback riding, a community pool and the perfect Fool's Gold summers, they would become a destination vacation.

"There are the obvious advantages to the local economy," he continued. "In addition, I've spoken with the middle- and high-school science teachers. They would all very much like to have small gardens for their students. It would give them a chance to have class projects involving agriculture."

He finished with projections on costs and the income stream. He figured they would break even the second year and be profitable by the third.

When he was finished, he turned off the computer and faced his family. May, his mother, jumped to her feet and embraced him.

"That was wonderful," she said. "I'm so proud. You did all that work. We should do it." She turned to her other sons. "Don't you boys agree?"

Shane and Rafe exchanged a look Clay couldn't read. He kissed his mom on the cheek. "Thanks for the support."

May sighed. "Yes, I know. I'm your mother. I love everything you do. All right. You boys work it out." She turned to the older two. "No fighting."

"Us?" Shane asked earnestly. "Mom, never."

"Ha."

She walked out of the living room. Clay settled in the chair by the screen and waited for his brothers to speak first.

Rafe nodded slowly. "Impressive. Who helped you put together the presentation?"

"I did it myself."

Rafe's eyebrows rose.

Clay relaxed into the chair, knowing he was going to enjoy this. "I have a degree in business with an emphasis on marketing. From New York University. I also completed an apprenticeship in farm management in Vermont a couple of years ago." He shrugged. "There's a lot of downtime in modeling. I didn't waste mine."

Diane, his late wife, had encouraged him to get his degree. The apprenticeship idea had come later, after she'd died. He'd needed to get away and hard physical labor had provided a way to heal.

Rafe blinked. "Seriously?" He turned to Shane. "Did you know about this?"

"Sure."

Rafe returned his attention to Clay. "You didn't want to tell me?"

"I tried a couple of times."

Rafe shook his head. "Let me guess. I didn't listen."

Clay shrugged. "Growing a successful company takes a lot of time."

He could have said more but in the past few months, Rafe had done some serious changing. The once-strident, meddling bottom-line-only mogul had become a person. Thanks to his new wife, Heidi. Love had a way of shifting a man's priorities. Clay had learned that lesson a long time ago, and in the best way possible.

With Rafe, Shane and their mother all settling in Fool's Gold, Clay had wanted to move close, as well. It was the perfect location for his Haycation. The strong sense of community was an added bonus. While his business was important to him, it wouldn't take all his time. Leaving him with the opportunity to get involved with the town. He had a few ideas about that—one he would discuss with a certain firefighter the next time he saw her.

Rafe flipped through the hard copy of the presentation that Clay had printed out for both of them. "You have a lot of information here."

"I did a lot of research."

Shane looked over the crops list. "I like the idea of having a say in what's grown."

Shane bred and raised racehorses. After years of breeding Thoroughbreds, Shane had bought his first Arabian stallion.

"You think people on vacation will really do work?" Rafe asked.

"Who doesn't want to ride a tractor?" Clay grinned. "If they don't do enough, we can hire local teenagers and college students. There's also a community of agricultural workers in the area. I spoke to them about hiring on if we need them."

Shane looked at him. "Mom will come at you with a list of what she wants."

May had been thrilled to be part owner of the ranch and she had immediately started collecting old and strange animals no one else bothered with. There were elderly sheep, a few llamas, and Priscilla, an aging Indian elephant.

"I've already done research on what Priscilla would most enjoy," Clay said easily.

They talked numbers for a while longer, with Rafe digging into the details on what the vacation bungalows would rent for and what it would cost for the extras, like a swimming pool. They debated providing lunch as part of the deal—barbecued hamburgers and hot dogs or sandwiches. Finally Rafe rose.

"You did good, kid," he told Clay. "I think we should go for it."

Clay stood. Satisfaction and victory had been a long time coming. There was hard work ahead, but he was looking forward to all the sweat required.

"I'm in," Shane said, joining them.

The three brothers shook hands.

"Everybody comfortable with Dante drawing up the paperwork?" Rafe asked. Dante was his business partner and a lawyer.

Clay put his hand on his oldest brother's shoulder. "No problem. As long as you don't mind me having my lawyer review every word."

"You don't trust me?" Rafe asked with a grin.

"Sure, but my mama didn't raise no fool."

CHAPTER TWO

CHARLIE CHECKED THE saddle one last time, then patted Mason's side. "Ready?" she asked her horse.

He snorted, which she took to mean *yes,* then led him out of the barn.

The morning still had a touch of coolness, although it would climb to nearly ninety later in the afternoon. The sky was blue and she was going on a ride. It was already shaping up to be a good day in a pretty good life. She had a job she liked, friends she could depend on and a place where she belonged.

From the corner of her eye, she saw movement and turned. Clay Stryker strolled toward her.

"Heading out?" he asked with an easy smile. "Want company?"

The word that came to mind was *no.* She didn't want company. She wanted to ride alone because she preferred it that way. But he was new in town and what with one of her best friends marrying one of his brothers, not to mention her other best friend getting engaged to another Stryker brother, she was going to be seeing a lot of him. It was simply the nature of living in Fool's Gold.

She eyed his body-hugging jeans and idly wondered if they cost less or more than her monthly house payment. "You know how to ride?"

The smile turned into a grin. The flash of amusement in his dark eyes gave her the answer before he spoke. "I think I can figure out how to hang on. Give me five minutes."

He turned toward the barn. She found herself staring at his butt, which was as spectacular as it had been the last time she'd seen him. Being physically perfect must be interesting, she thought, leaning against Mason and scratching behind his ears. Clay managed to get her attention, which was something of a trick. Maybe if she spent the afternoon with him, she would feel that flicker again. As her goal was to solve her "man" problem, having a source for flickers and maybe even tingles was a good thing. If he could get her fired up for normal guys, all the better. She would be healed and able to get on with her life.

He returned within the five minutes, a saddled horse walking behind him. She took in the long legs and perfect face. He sure was easy on the eyes.

"I recognize speculation in that look," he said as he approached. "Should I be worried?"

"Not about me."

She stuck her foot in the stirrup and swung up and over, landing lightly in the saddle. Clay slipped on sunglasses, then did the same. His graceful movements told her this wasn't his first rodeo.

"Nice day," he said as the horses fell into step with each other.

She settled her hat more firmly on her head. "You're not going to talk the whole time, are you?"

"Is that a problem?"

"Yes."

"You say what you think."

"Not as often as I should. Like the other day. You weren't helping."

"I broke your fall."

She rolled her eyes. "I wouldn't have fallen if you hadn't gotten in my way in the first place."

"You're welcome."

She held in a groan. It had been three minutes and the man was already making her crazy. She told herself to ignore him and instead focus on the beauty around her. The Castle Ranch was west of town and south of the new casino–hotel being built. Maybe a thousand undeveloped acres with plenty of trees and shrubs. Years ago, old man Castle had run cattle on the land, but when he'd died, the place had been abandoned.

She and Mason had a route they usually followed. It skirted the fence line and took them past the property Clay's brother Shane had bought for the racehorses he bred, around the back of the ranch and down by the main road.

As soon as they cleared the corrals, Mason picked up the pace. She touched him lightly with her heels and he started to trot. They moved together, familiar with each other's expectations. He broke into a canter and then galloped full out for a quarter mile or so. She let him set the pace, waiting until he eased back into a steady walk.

Clay had kept up through it all and now moved his horse next to hers. "You two have been doing this for a while."

"We have an understanding." She took in his comfortable seat and the way he held the reins. "You've obviously spent some serious time on a horse. Be careful. Shane will put you to work exercising his."

"There are worse ways to spend a day." He turned his attention to the horizon. "I grew up here. We moved when I was still a kid, but I remember liking everything about this place."

Charlie knew the story of the Stryker family. May, Clay's mother, had worked as old man Castle's housekeeper. The miserly bastard had paid her practically nothing, all the while promising he would leave her the ranch when he died. When he finally passed, May had discovered the ranch had gone to relatives back East. She'd taken her children and left.

A few months ago, unusual circumstances had brought May and her oldest son, Rafe, back to the ranch.

"Are those memories why you're here now?" she asked.

"Some. I wanted to be close to family." He glanced at her. "I'm starting a business. Haycations."

She'd heard the term. "Families spend a week on a working farm. Living like it was 1899."

He grinned. "I plan to offer indoor plumbing and internet access."

"That will make their kids love you." She thought about the vacation rentals Rafe was building and the riding horses Shane had recently bought. "Fool's Gold is a tourist destination as it is. This is going to bring even more visitors. That will make you a popular guy with the city council."

"I hope so. I meet with them Friday."

"Haycations aren't an intuitive leap for a male model."

He shrugged. "I had to do something with my life. I'm thirty. Being a butt double is a young man's game."

She felt her mouth drop open. "I honest to God don't know what to say to that."

Clay chuckled. "Trust me. No one wants to see some old guy in his underwear."

Charlie was sure that was true, but Clay was light-years from anyone calling him "an old guy."

"You're quitting before they ask you to leave?" she asked.

"Something like that." He pointed to the stream that cut through the north end of the property. "Want to have a seat?"

"Sure." She drew Mason to a stop, then slid to the ground.

They left the horses in the shade and walked to the bank of the stream. She was aware of Clay beside her. Taller, which was nice. Broader through the shoulders. They settled on the grass, next to each other, but not too close. He pulled a pack of gum out of his shirt pocket and offered her a piece.

She took it and slowly unfastened the wrapper. "You lived in New York before?"

"Uh-huh."

"Fool's Gold is going to be an adjustment."

"I'm ready for the change."

She glanced at his profile. He looked a lot like his brothers, but with the added patina of perfection. She knew almost nothing about his personal life, but would guess he didn't lack for female attention. Too pretty for her tastes, she thought absently, sticking the gum in her mouth. A man that flawless would scare the hell out of her.

To be honest, nearly any man would scare the hell out of her if she thought he was interested in sex, but no one had to know that. Still, she was determined to conquer her lone, lingering weakness. Just as soon as she found the right guy.

"How long have you been a firefighter?" he asked.

"Nearly nine years."

"All of them here?"

"No. I started out in Portland." She smiled. "Oregon, not Maine. Stayed there about three years. I was on vacation when I found Fool's Gold. I went by one of the stations while I was here and introduced myself. Three days later, they made me an offer."

"The town seems to have more female firefighters than most places."

"The town has more women in traditional male jobs

than most places," she said. "Until recently, there was something of a man shortage."

The slow, sexy grin returned. "I hadn't heard."

"Yes, you had and I doubt you care."

He leaned back on his elbows. "You're assuming I always get the girl."

"Don't bother trying to convince me I'm wrong."

"I wouldn't try to convince you of anything."

"How did you become a model?"

He moved his sunglasses up on top of his head. His dark gaze looked past her to the horizon. "I was discovered at a mall." He glanced at her. "Swear to God."

"I thought that only happened in the movies."

"Me, too. There was a fashion show. I went because hey, pretty girls parading around in what I'd hoped were short dresses. One of the male models hadn't shown up. They were frantic. I was his size. They shoved me in his clothes and told me to walk. I did. After the show, an agent came up to me and talked to me about becoming a model. I moved to New York a week later."

"Lucky break."

"That's what I thought. I'd just graduated from high school and didn't have any idea what I wanted to be or do. I started working right away. Within a few months, I had landed a couple of campaigns."

Ah, a man with a charmed life. She supposed she shouldn't be surprised. "Fame and fortune followed?"

"I'm not so sure about the fame, but, yes, I did well. During an underwear shoot, there are a lot of changes. No one bothers going behind a curtain. Somebody saw my ass. A few days later my agent got a call asking if I wanted to be a butt double in a movie. At the time it was a little embarrassing, but they were willing to pay, so I said yes."

"Is it true you had your butt insured?"

He chuckled. "Not anymore, but, yes, I had insurance on several parts of my body. Along with limitations. No sports that can disfigure. I had to maintain a certain weight and build, no tan lines. No tattoos."

A lifestyle she couldn't imagine. "What happens now? You gain fifty pounds and get 'Mom' tattooed on your butt?"

"I doubt I'll do either. I'm ready to settle down."

"Won't you miss the groupies or whatever they're called?"

"Nope. I gave them up years ago."

"After the first couple of hundred, it gets boring?"

"Something like that."

Casual sex. She'd heard about it, of course. Didn't understand it, which was part of the problem.

"I'm not sure you're going to be comfortable here," she said. "We're pretty traditional. Family friendly, lots of festivals."

"I like festivals. Besides, I've seen the rest of the world already. This is what I want."

He looked at her as he spoke. There was an intensity to his voice and his gaze. For a second, she felt that tingle again. An awareness of his long legs and the muscles in his chest and arms.

She reminded herself that being attracted to Clay

hardly made her a special snowflake. She would be one of a million and expected to take a number.

"Good luck with settling in," she said and rose. "I need to get back."

She walked toward Mason.

"Charlie?"

She turned back to Clay and waited.

"I want to talk to you about the volunteer firefighters. I hear there's a class starting soon."

He stood there, bathed in sunlight. The pose was powerful, his body well-defined. He looked like a model in a shoot. Probably not a stretch for him. He'd spent the past decade looking good. No doubt his idea of a hard day was having to get spray-on tan *and* a haircut. Pretty but useless, she thought.

"I don't think so," she told him. "It's a rigorous process."

One eyebrow rose. "You're saying I can't handle it?"

"I'm saying no."

The humor faded and his expression became unreadable. "We don't want your kind?"

"Something like that."

She didn't want to be rude to her best friend's brother-in-law, but this was different. Life-and-death different. Charlie took firefighting very seriously—mostly because if she didn't, someone would end up dead. If Clay couldn't handle that, well, that wasn't her problem.

She swung into the saddle and rode away.

THE FOOL'S GOLD firefighters worked a nine-day cycle. In that period of time, they worked three twenty-four hour shifts. She did her cardio in the exercise room at the station, but she preferred the gym for strength training. Nearly every morning she was off, she started her day with a grueling workout.

By eight, the business people were long gone and the moms had yet to arrive. There was a lull and she enjoyed the quiet. She left the weight machines for others, preferring to use free weights. Her goal was always to challenge herself, to stay strong. Not just for her job, but for herself. Being strong meant being safe. Dependence was weakness, she reminded herself as she used a towel to wipe sweat from her face.

But today she wasn't able to find her usual centered place. Her movements were off, her concentration shot. She knew the cause, too. Clay.

She'd been mean the other day, dismissing him the way she had. She wasn't usually like that and couldn't help wondering if her reaction had something to do with her awareness of him. Being attracted to a man frightened her and when she got scared, she got defensive. Maybe not her best quality, but one she couldn't shake.

The crazy part was she knew she had to deal with her problem so she could move on emotionally. So feeling something close to sexual attraction should be a good thing. But her intellect was unable to convince her gut that all was well.

Knowing she had to figure out a way to have sex with a man was one thing. Actually doing it was going to be another. Gritting her teeth and thinking of England had been her original plan. Based on how she'd snapped at Clay, she might need to rethink her strategy.

She glanced toward the punching bag in the corner and wondered if she should try to take out her indecision on something less human. Before she could decide, the man in question walked into her gym and threatened to ruin her entire day.

She felt the subtle ripple go through the building before she saw Clay. A group of women leaving the aerobics room stopped as one and turned to watch him. He walked by the free-weight alcove on his way to the cardio equipment and everyone else in the gym turned to watch. Charlie found herself just as mesmerized by the long, muscled legs and strong arms.

He wore exactly what every other guy wore. Shorts and an old T-shirt. Yet he stood out. Maybe it was the way he walked or the power in his shoulders. Maybe it was that indefinable something that had made him so successful. Whatever, she would swear she heard every woman within two hundred feet sigh.

Clay walked to one of the treadmills. He put in earbuds and flicked on his iPod, then started the machine. Within a minute, he was jogging. Five minutes later, he set a pace that would have challenged her on her best day.

Charlie returned to the rest of her workout. As she finished up with triceps work, she was aware of him just out of view. The loud music in the gym meant she couldn't hear the pounding of his feet on the treadmill, but she imagined the steady beat and felt herself drawn to both it and the man.

She set the weight back on the rack and faced the truth. When it came to Clay, she'd made assumptions. People had done that to her all her life. They'd taken one look at her too-tall self, at her big feet and strength and thought they knew who she was. Especially after the rape.

She'd always prided herself on being better than that, on getting to know a person, but somehow she'd forgotten. Or she'd been blinded by his appearance. Presumed he couldn't do the hard work of becoming a firefighter because of *what* he was rather than *who.* In her world, those were fighting words.

Aware that there was only one solution, she wiped her face again and walked toward the treadmills. She circled around so she came at Clay straight on, her gaze meeting his.

He didn't look away. He also didn't smile. He kept running, his long legs moving with practiced ease, chewing up the miles. When she stopped in front of the machine, he straddled it and hit the stop button. Then he pulled free the earbuds and waited.

She cleared her throat. "I was, ah, thinking. About what you said before."

His dark eyes were like his brothers' but without the friendly welcome she usually got from Rafe or Shane. Guilt made her shift in place.

"Fine," she grumbled. "I was wrong. Is that what you

want to hear? I judged you unfairly. I don't usually but you're not like other people."

"Is that your idea of an apology?"

"Yes, and you should accept it because it doesn't happen often."

"I can tell. You need practice."

"Bite me," she growled, then winced when she realized he might take that wrong. "We are starting a class for volunteers," she added quickly, before he could speak. "It will cover CPAT preparedness. Oh, CPAT stands for—"

"Candidate Physical Ability Test. I've done my research."

"Good. Then you know you'll need to pass it before you can start training. I run the classes."

"Lucky me."

She couldn't tell if he was being sarcastic or not but decided not to ask. "If you're interested in applying, you should. I'll tell you that the volunteers are well prepared and we have high expectations. If you're willing to do the work and be dedicated, then there shouldn't be a problem."

"Do I get a break because you owe me?"

"No. I don't owe you and no one gets a break."

One corner of his mouth turned up. "Just checking."

"I can't be bought."

"Neither can I."

She huffed out a breath. "The applications are online. The class starts next week."

"Think you'll enjoy kicking my ass?"

She grinned. "Oh, yeah. I run a tough class. But over ninety percent of the candidates who complete my training pass the test." Her smile faded. "People probably assume a lot of things about you, don't they?"

"All the time."

"I'll do my best not to let it happen again."

"Taking me on as a project?"

"Hardly." He wouldn't need her help for anything. "I believe in being fair. Plus, I don't like it when people judge me. Like I said, you're welcome to apply."

"Thanks," he said and smiled.

The flash of thousand-watt attention caused a distinct clenching low in her belly. She mumbled something that she hoped sounded like "Goodbye" and made her escape.

Once safely in the women's locker room, she sank onto a bench and held her head in her hands. Even she knew that a clench was much, much worse than a flicker. She could only hope that Clay was a busy guy and totally forgot about applying. Otherwise, she was going to have to face him twice a week for the next eight weeks.

And not just in a "Hi, how are you" kind of way. They would be spending serious time together, working out together. There might even be touching.

Aware that anyone could walk into the locker room at any second, she refrained from banging her head against the wall, even though it seemed like the best plan on the table. Attracted to Clay? Talk about a stupid move.

She straightened and squared her shoulders. No, she

told herself. Being attracted to Clay wasn't a problem. The clench was a sign that she should get started on finding the man who would take her all the way to normal. Or at least seminormal. She would take a lover, do the deed, then get on with the rest of her life. Easy.

When she got home, she would start a list of potential instructional partners, then figure out how to tell some guy that she would very much appreciate it if he would teach her the finer points of the whole sex thing. Oh, and on her way to her place, she should probably stop by the liquor store because that conversation was going to require her to be more than a little drunk.

CLAY HAD PREPARED for his presentation to the city council. He'd never had to deal with a local government before, but his Haycation idea was going to change that. He wanted the business to be welcome and would use his time to show how tourists would bring plenty of dollars to the area. In return he was hoping for a few minor zoning changes and a little less trouble over permits.

Rafe had told him that Fool's Gold was business friendly, with Mayor Marsha Tilson taking a personal interest in what was happening in her town. Still, Clay wanted to be prepared. He was the new guy and more than willing to work harder than established businesses. It would be worth it. By this time next year, his Haycations would be going strong.

After setting up his laptop, he tested the spreadsheet program on the large screen in the room. Then he waited for the meeting to start.

By five to eleven, the seats around the long con-
ference table were filled. Charlie had mentioned that
women filled most of the jobs traditionally held by men
and he saw that was true in city government, as well.
Not one city council member was a man. The women
who had filed into the room ranged from their early
thirties to those "of a certain age." The mayor had to
be close to seventy.

Clay sat in the back of the room. The mayor's assistant had told him that while he was the star of the
morning, the council would need to do a little business
first. In a town as dynamic as Fool's Gold, there was
always something going on.

As he glanced around, he found himself thinking it
would be nice if Charlie were here. She'd surprised the
hell out of him the other day, when she'd admitted she
was wrong and apologized. He grinned as he remembered her practically biting the words as she said them.
She was tough, both physically and mentally. And fair.
Qualities he could admire. He found himself thinking she would have liked Diane, which was surprising. On a physical plane, they were nothing alike. Yet
inside, where it mattered, they had the same strength
of character.

The mayor called the meeting to order.

"While we're all here to listen to Clay Stryker's presentation, first we have an issue with parking behind
the library."

Mayor Marsha picked up a sheet of paper and slipped
on reading glasses. She wore her white hair in an up-

swept kind of bun. Despite the fact that much of the town subscribed to what Clay's fashion friends would call "California casual," she dressed in a tailored suit.

"As most of you know, there is a lower parking lot. It's used for overflow parking and backs up on several warehouses," the mayor began. "A few years ago we decided to plant trees to provide a visual separation from the more industrial area." She paused.

"No good deed goes unpunished," one of the older ladies announced. "You should know that, Marsha. We put in trees to make it pretty and now they're being used against us."

The mayor sighed. "While I don't agree with your theory about good deeds, Gladys, we seem to have inadvertently created something of a problem. The trees have given the parking lot a somewhat secluded feel. Local teenagers have decided to use the lower parking lot as a—" she paused and coughed delicately "—make-out spot."

An old lady in a bright yellow tracksuit leaned toward Gladys. "Think we could go there and get lucky?"

Mayor Marsha looked at the two women. "Eddie, if you interrupt, I won't let you sit next to Gladys anymore. I don't want to have to separate the two of you, but I will."

Eddie straightened and muttered something Clay couldn't hear.

"I've spoken with Chief Barns," Mayor Marsha continued. "She's going to make sure the evening patrols get down there more regularly. That should help."

"They have to do the wild thing somewhere," Gladys announced. "Give 'em a break."

Clay felt his mouth twitching as he tried not to smile. He'd always assumed watching government at work would be boring, but he was wrong. This was fun.

"Call me old-fashioned," Marsha told her, "but I would prefer to make things a little more difficult for them."

"Winter will help," another council member said. "As soon as it gets cold, they won't be able to stay in their cars for too long."

"Lucky us," the mayor murmured.

"Play music." Eddie shrugged. "I read online somewhere that teenagers can be driven off by playing certain kinds of music. The library has an outside sound system. We could turn on the speakers at the back of the building and use them to play music kids can't stand."

"Disco, perhaps?" Mayor Marsha said with a slight smile.

There was more discussion about the kind of music that turned off teenagers. Eddie volunteered to find the article and report back directly to the mayor.

Mayor Marsha glanced back at her sheet. "Under old business, we still have the issue of Ford Hendrix." She stared at them over her glasses. "I don't have to remind you that this is a sensitive topic, not to be discussed outside of this room."

Gladys shook her finger at Clay. "That goes double for you."

"Yes, ma'am."

The name was familiar. There had been several Hendrix brothers back when he'd been a kid, he thought. Sisters, too, but when he'd been five or six, girls had been less interesting to him.

"Ford has been gone nearly a decade," the mayor continued. "From what I've learned, his latest tour of duty ends next year. It's time for him to come home."

"I'm not sure we should get involved in this," one of the younger women said. "Isn't Ford's decision to reenlist or not up to him and maybe his family?"

Eddie sniffed. "You young people spend a lot of time with your heads up your asses, if you ask me."

Mayor Marsha's expression turned pained. "I don't believe anyone did ask you." She turned to the younger woman. "Charity, you're right. It's not our place to meddle. Normally I wouldn't, but Ford needs to come back to where people love him. Being in Special Forces takes a toll on a man. He needs to heal. And Fool's Gold is the best place for that."

There was a brief discussion on how to get the mysterious Ford back in the fold, so to speak. At the end of that conversation, the mayor invited Clay to make his presentation.

"Good morning," he said as he walked to the front of the room. "Thanks for inviting me to speak."

"We enjoy looking at an attractive man," Eddie told him with a grin. "We're shallow that way."

The mayor sighed, but Gladys gave her a high five. Those two must have been hell on wheels when they were younger, he thought.

He passed out the printed version of his business plan and then connected his laptop to the cord for the screen.

He clicked on the first slide and began to talk about Haycations. He showed pictures of the land he'd bought, a diagram of what would be planted where and a few stock photos of people driving tractors for general interest. He outlined the number of families he hoped to attract, extrapolating about how much they would bring to the local economy. He had a rough idea of what kind of advertising he would do, along with about how many local people he would be employing.

Twenty minutes later, he finished with a request for the three small zoning permits.

"Impressive," Mayor Marsha told him. She smiled warmly. "We all appreciate how you've taken the town's needs into account as you've written your business plan. I believe there are several local business owners who would like to hear about this. They might have some helpful ideas for you."

"That would be great."

"You'll be settling here permanently?" she asked, her blue gaze steady.

"That's the plan."

"We're not exactly New York."

Something Charlie had mentioned. "I'm ready for a change."

"You know," Gladys said, her wrinkled face bright with amusement, "if you really want to help the town, I know a way."

"Don't," Mayor Marsha said, her tone warning.

Gladys ignored her. "You could loan your butt to a campaign we're planning."

"Stop it right now," the mayor said forcefully. "That's not what we're here to talk about."

"He's got a famous butt. I've seen it in the movies. We all have. Work with your strengths, I say."

Clay was used to faking any expression a client wanted. It was why he'd become so successful. Now he made sure he looked amused rather than angry and uncomfortable.

Gladys slapped a tabloid magazine on the table. The headline was clearly visible. Famous Model Insures Butt for Five Million Dollars.

"Why waste money on something like a Haycation when you only have to flash the real deal to make a mint?" she asked.

The mayor winced. "Clay, I'm so sorry. There was some discussion about asking you to be in our campaign." She glared at Gladys. "We were going to use your face, however."

"A waste of resources if you ask me," Gladys mumbled. "Everybody would rather see his ass."

CHAPTER THREE

CLAY TOSSED HIS computer case into the passenger seat of the truck, then started the engine. But instead of driving away, he gripped the steering wheel with both hands and told himself not to take it personally. He'd been a model for a lot of years. He understood being talked about like an object rather than a person. He'd had his appearance dissected a thousand times before. He'd been told he was too tall, too short, too big, too small, too young, too old, too handsome, not handsome enough. When a client wanted a "look," he either had it or he didn't.

He'd made millions, he'd gotten an education, he'd invested well and he'd moved on. Now he was ready for act two. The problem seemed to be escaping what he'd been in act one. He hadn't expected to be blindsided by a bunch of old ladies.

"Hell," he grumbled under his breath, not sure what to do with the frustration boiling inside of him. He didn't want to go back to the ranch. Putting his fist through a wall would create other problems. Finally he put the truck in gear and drove out of the parking lot.

Five minutes later he pulled into Fool's Gold Fire

Station number one. He could see into the engine bay. The aid car and engine were gone, out on a call. As he watched the Quint—an all-purpose vehicle with a pump, a water tank and various ladders—started up. Seconds later, it pulled out, sirens blaring.

Clay followed, staying back far enough not to get in the way. He stopped at a light and watched the Quint turn into what he remembered as one of the older residential areas. When the signal turned green, he went north, and then east. Two blocks later, he could see smoke rising. As he approached the scene, he pulled over and parked.

A crowd had already collected. Clay joined them, watching several firefighters finishing up what looked like a garage fire. Hoses lay across the driveway. White smoke and steam escaped through the open garage door.

He studied the various firefighters. They wore turnout pants and jackets, and helmets. He was able to pick out Charlie right away. She was one of the tallest firefighters, but he also recognized her confident stride and the way she took charge.

On the other side of the driveway, a mother stood with two boys. They were watching anxiously and Clay figured they owned the house. He wondered if one of the kids had started the fire. If so, someone was going to be in big trouble.

Charlie and her captain approached the family. The woman listened intently. Suddenly her body relaxed and she smiled, nodding. *Good news,* he thought. A sedan pulled up at the curb and a man jumped out. He rushed to the woman and kids and drew them against him.

The cleanup went faster than he would have expected. Hoses were rolled and stowed, equipment picked up. Charlie continued to talk to the family. Finally she shook hands with everyone, had a word with one of the kids and started toward the engine.

Clay stayed back with the dwindling crowd as he considered what he'd seen. The idea of doing this— helping where it was really needed—appealed to him. He wanted to come in, make a difference, then disappear. Let the folks get on with their lives and forget he was ever there. He wasn't interested in being a hero. He wanted to get the job done.

Charlie and her captain walked toward the engine. The captain spotted him, said something to Charlie, then approached.

"You must be Clay Stryker," she said, holding out her right hand. She held her red helmet in her left. "I'm Olivia Fargo. Nice to meet you."

"Likewise."

They shook hands.

Olivia was probably pushing forty, with short red hair and blue eyes. She was tall, nearly as tall as Charlie, and had a no-nonsense air about her.

"I hear you're thinking about becoming a volunteer firefighter," Olivia said.

"I'm going to be putting in my application later today."

"There's a class starting soon."

"I heard."

She looked him over. "It's a lot of work. You might find the training too time consuming."

"I'm committed to doing what it takes."

"You really want to help out?" she asked.

He had a feeling he didn't like where the conversation was going to go, but nodded anyway.

"We're always short on money," she said. "We do a big fund-raiser for new equipment. The extras the town can't afford to provide." Olivia smiled. "We were thinking of a calendar this year. You could be in it. That would help a whole lot more. A lot of people can volunteer. Not that many have your..." She paused. "Natural talents."

CHARLIE STOOD BY the engine, waiting on Olivia. She could hear everything being said. Nothing about Clay's expression changed, but she would swear he wasn't happy. Not about Olivia's comments or the request he do the calendar. From their brief conversation the other day, she knew he was ready to put his old life behind him...so to speak. But there was a long road from being a model to wanting to put his life, and perfect ass, on the line fighting fires. Why would a guy like him want to take the risk?

There was only one way to find out, she reminded herself. That was to ask the question.

She walked over to the two of them. Olivia glanced at her. "I was telling Clay about the calendar. I don't think he's convinced."

Clay's dark eyes gave nothing away, but she felt the tension in his body.

Olivia pointed at the Quint. "You left a nozzle," she said. She turned back to Charlie. "Give me five?"

"Sure." Charlie waited until she was out of earshot. "I take it the calendar isn't your dream job."

"Not exactly."

"I'm covering a partial shift for a friend until noon." She glanced at her watch. It was twelve-thirty. "Once we get back to the station, I need to take a quick shower. I'll meet you at the Fox and Hound in an hour and you can tell me all about it."

CHARLIE LIKED TO go to Jo's Bar for lunch. They cooked her burgers the way she liked and the place catered to women without being too girlie. But she knew that showing up with Clay would lead to more questions than she wanted to answer. Which made the Fox and Hound more neutral ground and therefore safer for her.

She arrived right on time and stepped into the cool interior. It was late enough that there was only one person waiting.

Clay stood when he saw her, uncoiling his long, honed body. He wore gray trousers and a button-down shirt. *Sex god does business,* she thought, aware that after her shower, her total nod to fussing with her appearance had been to make sure her T-shirt was clean. At least she had on jeans instead of her usual baggy cargo pants. In honor of Heidi's recent wedding, she'd gotten a pedicure. She couldn't remember ever wearing polish before, but kind of liked the way the deep pink color looked. Yesterday she'd scrounged up a pair of sandals to show off her toes. She'd worn them to the station at the start of her shift, which meant she was wearing them now.

As testament to how screwed up she was when it came to men, she was actually torn between being pleased she at least had a decent pedicure to show off and being afraid Clay would think she was trying. Most likely the best solution would be years and years of therapy. However, she had neither the patience nor the bank account for that path. She would have to find another way to flirt with normal. A quest for after lunch, she told herself. She always problem solved better on a full stomach.

The hostess could barely keep her mouth from hanging open as she gazed at Clay. The college-aged woman batted her eyes at a rate that made Charlie wonder if she would need medical attention later for a muscle strain.

"Table for two?" the hostess asked breathlessly, flipping her long blond hair over her shoulder.

"Please," Clay said, then stepped back to let Charlie go first.

The polite gesture caught her off guard. Even more unsettling was the hand he put on the small of her back, as if helping guide her to the booth along the side of the restaurant.

She was aware of the touch, of his palm and every finger. Not in a oh-let's-have-sex kind of way. But just because she honest to God couldn't remember the last time a man had touched her like that. Or, excluding shaking hands, anywhere.

They slid onto the seats and settled across from each other. The hostess leaned toward Clay, offering a flash from her low-cut blouse. She smiled.

"I could give you my number," she whispered, although the words were still loud enough for Charlie to hear.

Clay didn't even look at her. "Thanks, but, no."

"You sure?"

"Uh-huh."

He picked up the menu, then put it down. "I thought I would be someone else when I got here," he said when the hostess had given him one last lingering look before flouncing off.

Charlie leaned toward him. "What are we talking about?"

"Sorry. I was thinking about the captain inviting me to be in a calendar to raise money."

"Not the girl?"

"What girl?"

"The hostess who practically stripped in front of you ten seconds ago?"

His eyebrows drew together in confusion. "I didn't notice."

"She offered you her number."

He shrugged.

The gesture was so casual, so dismissive, Charlie had to believe Clay honestly hadn't been paying attention. Because it happened so much, she thought.

"Phone numbers are the new rose petals," she said absently, picking up the menu and wondering if she should order the London chicken wrap or try something new.

"Phone numbers are what?"

She put down the menu and grinned. "Sorry. I was thinking out loud. Rose petals. You know, like in Roman times. Throwing petals before the emperor. Now you get phone numbers thrown at you. All Hail Caesar. Or Clay." She wrinkled her nose. "Not exactly the same ring to it. You might want to change your name to fit in a classic 'all hail' better."

"I'll suffer with people stumbling through it," Clay muttered. "What's good here?"

"Everything," Wilma said. She'd appeared at the side of their table. Wilma was at least sixty, was a champion gum snapper and had worked at every incarnation of the restaurant since it had first opened its door decades ago. Now she stared at Clay, her penciled brows raised.

"So you're the pretty one everyone's been telling me about. Nice. I saw your ass in that movie a while back." She looked at Charlie. "You with him?"

Charlie did her best not to flush or choke. "We're friends."

"Too bad. You make a cute couple. Not as cute as me and my Frank, but that's a high bar." Her friendly gaze sharpened. "You eat, right?" The question was addressed to Clay. "If you're not going to eat, then don't order."

Charlie opened her mouth, then closed it. Apparently, Jo's Bar would have been a safer choice.

Wilma turned back to Charlie. "Diet Coke?"

Charlie nodded.

Wilma faced Clay. "And you?"

"Iced tea."

She scribbled on her pad. "Charlie usually gets the London chicken wrap. It's more a Baja wrap but what with this place being called The Fox and Hound, that would look stupid on the menu. It's good. Get that."

Clay handed her the menu.

"Fries?" Wilma asked no one in particular.

"Yes," Charlie told her, passing over her menu, as well.

The older woman patted Clay on the shoulder. "You'll never be as good as my Frank, but you're not half-bad, kid." With that, she walked away.

"Sorry," Charlie said when they were alone. "I'd forgotten how Wilma could be."

"Bossy and outspoken?"

"That's a nice way of putting it."

Clay surprised her by smiling. "I like her. She seems like she suffers no fool."

"She's an institution. This restaurant has gone through several changes and Wilma has been here for every one of them. She's one of the first people I met when I moved to town."

Wilma returned with their drinks, slapped them down on the table, then left.

Charlie pulled the paper off her straw. "You're not happy about the calendar thing," she began.

"No, but it's how my day has been going. I met with the city council this morning. I told them all about my Haycation idea."

"They must have been happy. It's going to bring in money. Every town wants more of that."

"The mayor seemed interested. Some of the others were more intrigued by the idea of me being in an advertising campaign for the town. Starring my ass."

Charlie winced. "That sounds like Gladys."

"Are she and Wilma sisters?"

"No, but they share some personality traits. Sorry."

"Not your fault. I expected this to happen in New York. Given what I do, it was inevitable. I thought it would be different here."

Charlie studied him. "I guess I'm like everyone else. I would have assumed your life is perfect."

A muscle in his jaw tightened. "Right. Shut up, cash the check and be grateful. I've heard that before." He leaned back in the booth. "Whatever. I can do the calendar."

"But you don't want to."

"No."

"Then don't."

He raised his eyebrows. "I'm trying to fit in. I want to be a part of what's going on in town. Get accepted into the volunteer program. Saying no isn't going to help."

"I agree, but the ultimate end is to have a successful fund-raiser. It's not to make you uncomfortable. Don't you have model friends? Couldn't you get a couple of them to be in the calendar?"

He stared at her. She had to admit that all that intensity was a little unnerving. That stomach-clenching thing returned and with it the smallest hint of pressure between her thighs.

She shifted on her seat.

Uncomfortable with the silence and her physical reaction to Clay, she found herself entering dangerous territory. That of speaking without thinking.

"The thing is," she told him, "if you want people to take you seriously, you have to take yourself seriously first. Agreeing to do the calendar yourself reinforces the stereotype. You're more than what they think you are. It's a cliché but you're going to have to work harder to prove yourself. It's a very strange kind of discrimination."

One she'd seen with her mother. People reacted to Dominique first because of how she looked and later because of who she was. Charlie had also seen the dark side of being judged on physical appearance. Most strangers staring at her with a "Really? You're *her* daughter?" look in their eyes.

Clay leaned back in the booth and swore softly. "You're right."

She blinked. "I am?"

"Yes. About all of it. I've had a manager taking care of the crap in my life for the past ten years. I've gotten lazy about taking responsibility for what I'm doing. Thank you for being honest."

"It's what I do best. Say what's on my mind. Give me thirty years and I'll turn into Wilma."

He gave her a slow, sexy smile. One that nearly turned her tummy upside down. "There are worse fates."

She grabbed her drink and gulped down some soda.

He leaned toward her again. "I'm going to call some guys I know about the calendar. I don't know how to fix things with the city council, but I can solve that problem, too."

"You might wait a little on the town issue. Mayor Marsha has a way of smoothing things out. I'm sure she's pleased by your Haycation idea."

He was staring at her again. As they hadn't eaten yet, she was fairly confident she didn't have anything in her teeth.

"What?" she asked after a couple of seconds.

"I just keep thinking that somebody I knew would have liked you." His expression turned serious. Almost sad.

Charlie felt the stomach clench again, but this time for a totally different reason. "Your girlfriend?" The one he'd left behind in New York and missed desperately?

"My late wife."

"You were married?"

The words burst out before she could stop them.

"Not a tabloid reader, huh?"

She shook her head. "I'm sorry. I didn't mean to sound so shocked. You just don't seem like the marrying kind."

She groaned and slapped her hand across her mouth.

He stretched out his arm and pulled her hand away. "It's okay. You can say what you think. I won't be offended."

Wilma appeared with lunch. Charlie grabbed a French fry, thinking that maybe her blurting problem was because of low blood sugar. Perhaps in addition to food, the best solution would be not talking so much.

"Tell me about her," she said, then reached for the first half of her wrap.

He picked up a French fry, then put it down. She could practically see the tension leaving his body as he relaxed. Something she wanted to call contentment softened the sadness in his eyes.

"She was brilliant and funny," he began. "A photographer." The smile returned. "She hated models, especially male models. She used to say we were all vapid and useless." His smile broadened. "We met at a party and she was not into me."

Charlie chewed and swallowed. "I would have liked her."

He chuckled. "She would have liked you. I couldn't take my eyes off of her. I was twenty...she was thirty-four and when I asked her out, she laughed for a good two minutes straight. I got her number through a friend of mine and wouldn't stop calling. She finally agreed to meet me for coffee, but only so she could tell me all the reasons it would never work."

She heard the affection in his voice, saw the pleasure

he took in the remembering. Lately her friends had been busy falling in love, so she recognized the symptoms.

"I convinced her to give me a chance at a real date. She surprised both of us by agreeing. At the end of that first night, I was completely in love with her. It hit me like lightning. It took her a lot longer to come around."

"The fourteen-year age difference would be difficult for most women," Charlie said. "It's stupid, but it's been pounded into us that the guy should be older."

He nodded. "She had trouble with the age difference, with the fact that I was so young, my career. But I was determined to win her." He paused. "I proposed six times before she said yes. We were married within a week. I didn't want her to change her mind."

Charlie laughed. "A man with a plan."

"I wasn't the only one. Diane talked to me about my future. She pointed out I couldn't be a model forever. She's the one who suggested I go to college. Think about my future." His smile faded. "She was killed five years ago in a car accident. I was on a shoot when I got the call. She was a force of nature and then she was just...gone. I never got to say goodbye."

"I'm sorry." Charlie put down the second half of her wrap.

"Thanks. I still miss her. The pain is different now. Not so sharp. But it's still there. She was the best thing to ever happen to me."

Charlie knew better than to offer some stupid promise that things would get better, or that he would be fine. Sometimes a person simply had to sit with the pain and deal. That was probably healthier than what she'd done, which was try to pretend it had never happened.

While loss and betrayal were different, they both left scars.

Clay picked up his wrap. "Sorry. Didn't mean to get into all that with you."

"I'm happy to listen."

Maybe it was an illustration of how twisted she'd become, but she almost envied Clay. At least he'd loved once. She never had and wasn't sure she wanted to. Loving someone meant engaging in a level of trust she wasn't comfortable with. But belonging like that sure sounded nice.

"Part of the reason I wanted to settle here when I retired was to be near my family," Clay said. "In the past couple of years, I've wanted to be closer to them."

Charlie couldn't help grinning. "Retired? You're what? Thirty?" She grabbed a fry then held it up in the air. "I know, I know. Being a butt model is a young man's game. You told me."

"Beauty fades."

She took in the dark eyes, the firm set of his jaw, the broad shoulders. His was still in full force.

Conversation shifted to more neutral topics. They finished their lunch arguing if the Dodgers would ever make it to the World Series again and whether or not the L.A. Stallions had a chance at a winning season.

"Stallions not Raiders?" Clay asked. He took the last bite of his wrap and waited.

"I know Oakland is physically closer, but I've always been a Stallions fan. I can't explain it."

Wilma appeared with the bill. Clay grabbed it before Charlie could.

"I've got this," he said.

"Make sure you leave a big tip," Wilma told him.

"Yes, ma'am."

The old lady grinned, then ruffled his hair. "You're not bad, kid. You can come back."

When she left, Clay leaned toward Charlie. "Does she really get a say in that?"

"This is Fool's Gold. There are very strange rules in play."

He'd left a couple of twenties for what she knew to be a twenty-five-dollar tab, then stood. "Thanks for lunch," he said.

"Thank you. With a tip like that, Wilma is going to be sending you personal invitations to return."

"The food was good."

She rose. "If you want, I'll go over the application paperwork with you. To make sure everything is correct."

"I'd appreciate that." He pulled out his cell. "Want to give me your number?"

She nodded and rattled it off, knowing the hostess would be spitting nails if she knew. The difference was, Charlie wasn't interested in dating Clay. But then maybe the hostess didn't want to date, either.

They walked to the front of the restaurant, then out onto the sidewalk. Her truck was parked in front.

"That's me," she said, pointing.

"Okay. I'll finish the application tonight and then call you."

She started to say that was fine, but before she could form the words, he leaned in and kissed her on the cheek.

"Thanks," he murmured and walked away.

She stood there, on the sidewalk, her cheek all tingly and her insides doing some kind of fertility dance. Even someone with her lack of experience got the message. She was attracted to Clay. Sexually attracted. Based on how quickly she was thawing, after a few more meetings she would be reduced to a screaming, sobbing groupie.

It was just her luck that after literally a decade of not having a single erotic thought, she found herself attracted to possibly the best-looking man on the planet.

A COUPLE OF days later, Annabelle Weiss slipped into the booth at Jo's Bar and smiled at Charlie. "I invited Patience McGraw to join us. Do you know her?"

Charlie watched the pretty brunette walk through the door and pause for a second before heading to them.

"Sure," Charlie told her friend. "Sometimes she cuts my hair." Out of the corner of her eye, she saw Annabelle glance at her short hair. Charlie rolled her eyes. "Stop it. Yes, I do get my hair cut professionally."

"And it looks adorable."

Charlie knew that *adorable* wasn't a word that could ever be applied to her, but she accepted the comment in the spirit in which her friend meant it.

Patience approached their table. "Hi, Charlie," she said, sliding into the booth.

Patience had grown up in Fool's Gold. She had a daughter, Lillie, and was divorced.

"Hi, yourself," Charlie said. "How's it going?"

"Good." Patience had big brown eyes and a sweet smile. "Were you waiting long?"

"I just got here," Annabelle said. "Charlie is always hungry, so she was early."

"I'm not always hungry," Charlie muttered.

Patience laughed. "I was dawdling, I'm sorry to say. There's this retail space I have my eye on."

Annabelle drew in a breath. "You're going to open your own salon? Does Julia know?"

Patience worked for Julia Gionni, one of the two feuding Gionni sisters. Neither woman was the kind to appreciate a valuable stylist breaking out on her own.

Patience laughed. "Don't panic. I'm not thinking about opening my own place. Sorry. I didn't mean to worry you. I was just daydreaming." She leaned forward. "I would love to open my own coffeehouse. Crazy, huh? I'll be twenty-eight in December. At the rate I'm able to save money, I'll be a hundred and seventeen by the time I have enough."

"I think a coffeehouse is a great idea," Annabelle told her. "Somewhere local to gather."

"Exactly." Patience smiled. "I have all these ideas. Do you know Trisha Wynn?"

"She helped me with a legal issue a couple of months ago," Annabelle said.

"I dated her son," Charlie announced.

Just then Jo came up and handed them menus. "We're trying a new salad. It's seasonal, with apples and fried chicken. You can get it with grilled chicken, but then I'll pretty much think less of you. I'm just saying."

"Can I get garlic bread on the side?" Charlie asked.

"My kind of girl. Of course you can."

Annabelle sighed. "I want to be tall like Charlie. Then I could eat what I wanted."

"I work out a lot, too," Charlie reminded her.

"Yeah, I'm less interested in that part," Annabelle admitted.

They placed their drink orders and Jo left.

Patience turned to Charlie. "I didn't know Trisha had a son. Things didn't work out?"

Charlie hadn't meant to blurt out the information, but lately she seemed to be blabbing far too much personal stuff. "It was no big deal. We figured out we were better off as friends, but Trisha was bugging him about finding someone, so he took me to meet her. She and I got along great." So much so that Trisha had been devastated when Charlie had finally come clean and admitted there wasn't any spark.

What she hadn't told Trisha was the lack of spark had come about because every time Evan had tried to "take things to the next level," Charlie had frozen. *Panicked* would be a better word, but why go there? Unfortunately for Evan, the next level had included kissing.

Now he was married to someone Trisha didn't like and Charlie always felt a little guilty. As if her and

Trisha getting along so well was a problem for the new wife.

"How is Trisha helping with your coffeehouse dream?" Charlie asked, thinking they should stop talking about her sad dating past.

"She taught a class at the adult education center. It was on how to open your own business. I took it and came up with my plan. All that stands between me and coffeehouse heaven is start-up money."

"You'll find it," Annabelle told her.

Patience nodded. "I'm thinking positive thoughts and buying lottery tickets."

"Hey, that can work," Charlie said. "That's how Heidi got the money for the down payment on the ranch."

Jo returned with their drinks. Iced tea all around. Decaf for the pregnant Annabelle. She took their orders. Charlie passed on the new salad, preferring her usual burger and fries. Patience and Annabelle both ordered the special, with the chicken grilled and no garlic bread.

"You're such girls," she told them when Jo left.

"Yes, and the poorer for it." Annabelle raised her glass of iced tea. "To Heidi, who flies to Paris in the morning. I'm both envious of her and delighted for her." She smiled. "The Paris part. Not that Rafe isn't great, but I prefer Shane."

"A loyal fiancée," Patience told her and clinked glasses with her. "To Heidi and Paris."

"To Heidi and Paris," Charlie said, joining them.

Like Annabelle, she wasn't all that interested in Rafe. To be honest, the city wasn't that thrilling, either. But being with someone, that had appeal. Because if she could do that—if she could be with a man, she would be healed. Or at least better. She was fine with scars—it was the open wounds she wanted gone.

Charlie looked at Patience. "Is Lillie excited about school starting soon or sad that summer is over?"

"Mostly excited. She's been taking dance classes and loves it." Patience wrinkled her nose. "I adore her. She's a great kid and I would throw myself in front of a bus for her." She glanced around and lowered her voice. "But she's a terrible dancer. She tries and just can't seem to find the rhythm. Her teacher is really patient with her, so that helps."

Charlie could relate to being a bad dancer. But in her case, she'd had to compare herself with her perfect, delicate, talented and famous prima-ballerina mother. Not a place she wanted to go again.

"In another couple of months, the girls will start learning their parts for *The Dance of the Winter King*," Patience continued. "Lillie can't wait."

"I love *The Dance of the Winter King*," Annabelle said. "It's wonderful."

Charlie nodded. "I like it, too." It was a Fool's Gold tradition and even with her mother-induced ballet trauma, she enjoyed the production.

Patience's phone chirped. She pulled it out of her pocket and glanced at the screen. "Oh, no. One of the stylists had to go home sick and Julia needs me to come right in."

Annabelle lightly touched her arm. "It's okay. We'll do lunch another time."

"Sorry," Patience said as she rose. "I'll cancel my order with Jo on the way out."

Charlie nodded. "What Annabelle said. Rain check."

"I promise." Patience walked toward the bar.

Annabelle waited until she was out of earshot and then leaned toward Charlie. "What is going on with you and Clay?"

Charlie had been drinking and nearly choked. "Nothing. What are you talking about?"

"He mentioned you about three times yesterday. You're helping him get on the volunteer roster or whatever it's called. You had lunch together." Her green eyes sparkled with excitement. "Are you dating Clay?"

"No." Charlie glared at her. "No. Stop it. We're friends. Barely. I don't really know him. Yes, I'm helping him because… I'm not sure why. Sometimes I can be nice. Just go with it."

Annabelle leaned back in her chair. "Interesting."

"No, it's not."

"You like him."

"I think he's pleasant."

Annabelle laughed. "And hot." Her mouth opened, then closed. "You're attracted to him."

Charlie groaned. "No. And keep your voice down."

Annabelle waited expectantly.

"Fine," Charlie whispered. "Maybe a little. But it's all an intellectual exercise. I'm not stupid. A guy like Clay isn't… I have issues I have to work through. So being attracted to Clay simply means I'm not as dead as I thought. That's a good thing."

"It's a great thing."

"Don't make this more than it is."

"You'd be a cute couple."

Charlie looked at her friend. "Don't think for a second I wouldn't kill you."

Annabelle grinned. "You love me too much and I'm not afraid of you. Clay's a sweet guy. You should totally go for him."

"Yeah. Because that's going to happen."

CHAPTER FOUR

"I THOUGHT THERE would be a pole," Clay said, looking up at the ceiling of the firehouse.

"A challenge in a one-story building, although there is a two-story fire station in town." Charlie led the way through the engine bay. "Honestly, they've done away with poles. Too many injuries."

"People slipping down the pole too fast?"

"No. People falling through the floor. These days, if a station is two stories, we take the stairs."

"Hard to be a superhero on stairs."

She glanced over her shoulder and grinned. "Tell me about it. I had to turn in my cape last week." She stepped through a doorway. "Administrative offices are that way." She pointed to the left. "Our living quarters are this way."

He followed her toward the living quarters. When he'd called Charlie to tell her he would be coming by to drop off his application, she'd offered to show him around.

She'd already explained the various pieces of equipment, including the difference between the engine and the Quint. Like most towns in America, the majority of the station's calls were about something other than a fire. Many involved medical emergencies, including car accidents. Here in Fool's Gold, more than a few were about things like Mrs. Coverson's cat.

"Self-explanatory," Charlie said, pointing at a large open area with several sofas and a huge flat-screen TV. Behind the sofas was a big dining-room table and behind that was the kitchen.

"The paid firefighters work twenty-four hours at a time so we take our meals here. As a group, we're responsible for our own breakfast and lunch." She walked into the kitchen and pulled open the door of a jumbo-size freezer. Inside, dozens of casserole dishes were neatly stacked and labeled.

"What's that?" he asked.

"Our glorious community at work. Thanks to the Casserole Brigade, there's a steady supply of dinners provided to all the stations in town. Precooked and ready to just thaw and heat. A few times a month, we'll get a call and someone will come by and cook us dinner. We also have a barbecue out back where we can grill hamburgers or steaks."

"Nice setup."

"It works."

She returned to the engine bay and pointed to another door. "Sleeping quarters, bathrooms and showers are over there." Her gaze narrowed. "Don't get any ideas."

"What?"

"Some guys assume they're communal showers and get excited at the thought."

Clay pictured a brief flash of Charlie in the shower and found himself surprised by his own interest, not that he would tell her that. "I'm pretty sure I can control myself."

She didn't look convinced, but moved on anyway. "Come on," she said, heading back to the engine bay. "I'll buy you a cup of coffee."

Five minutes later, they were seated at the kitchen table. They each had a mug of black coffee. Charlie's blue eyes were thoughtful as she studied him.

"You sure you want to do this?" she asked. "It's not going to be easy."

"Fool's Gold is going to be my home for a long time. I want to be a part of things." While he found the Haycations interesting and looked forward to the challenge of starting a business, he was going to have too much time on his hands. He was done with college and in a place where he wanted to put himself out there. "I'm used to people not taking me seriously."

She nodded slowly. "I would have mocked you before. It must be difficult being so special." She shrugged. "I'm starting to get that maybe there's something to it. You're going to have to work harder than everyone else."

"I'm good with that."

"You're really staying? You're not going to complain it's too difficult and head back to New York?"

He grinned. "I already sold my apartment. Nothing to go back to."

"You have friends there."

"I have friends all over the world."

He sensed she was asking about something else entirely, but he couldn't figure out what. If she was a different kind of woman, he would wonder if she was coming on to him. He was used to invitations. Most of the time he ignored them. When that was impossible, he gently said no.

He was thirty years old and he was willing to admit his heart had died along with Diane. There had been women. A night here, a weekend there. But it wasn't the same. The need for sex was biological. He didn't *want* anymore. Didn't need. Everything worked, but no one appealed.

He leaned back in his chair and reminded himself that this was Charlie. If she wanted him in her bed, she would ask. Or at least offer to arm wrestle him. She didn't play girl games. He respected that and her. He also found the idea of Charlie in bed intriguing. More so than any other offer had been in a while. Not that she was offering. But if she did...

"I'll do my best to make sure they give you a fair shot," she said, rising to her feet.

"Thank you."

He stood and took the hand she offered. They shook.

For a second he felt something. A flash of attraction. *Potential,* he thought, shocked that after all this time he could imagine anticipating being with a specific woman. Before he could decide if he wanted to pursue said attraction, she was escorting him outside and telling him he would hear from the Battalion Chief within a couple of weeks. Then he was standing on the sidewalk, staring at the fire station trying to figure out which was crazier. Him having to fight to put his life on the line for free or being interested in a woman who probably thought she could take him in a fight.

"I'M SORRY, I'm sorry," Pia Moreno said as she grabbed her handbag and car keys. "Don't hate me."

Charlie laughed. "I would never hate you and you're not imposing. Stop worrying."

"You sure?" Pia paused and sucked in a breath. "I'm so late."

"Go."

"The twins are asleep and—"

Charlie physically pushed her toward the door. "Peter will be home in the next few minutes. I'll explain what happened and stay here until you're back. He gets a snack. There are freshly baked cookies on the cooling rack. He can have two. Get out before I'm forced to hurt you."

Pia smiled gratefully. "You're a goddess."

"If I had a nickel." Charlie pointed to the door. "Out."

"Yes, ma'am."

Pia raced to the door. Seconds later Charlie heard her car engine start.

A little less than an hour ago, she'd received a call from a very frantic Pia. The town's festival planner had forgotten about a meeting with several vendors. As the salespeople had all come in from out of town, rescheduling had been impossible. Charlie had agreed to emergency babysitting.

Now she walked quietly into the twins' room and stared at the two sleeping girls.

They were on their backs in cribs. Wispy curls draped across foreheads. Rosebud mouths puckered slightly. Charlie studied them, allowing the longing to wash over her.

She'd always thought she was too grumpy a person to ever want children. While she liked the idea of family, she'd never thought she would have one of her own. But a few years ago, that had all started to change. She'd found herself watching mothers with their children. She'd volunteered to babysit a few times. She'd taken over the junior firefighter program at the station.

Earlier this year, she'd made the decision to have a child of her own. A husband didn't seem possible, but a child... That was different.

She knew that being in Fool's Gold had changed her. She'd been taken in and loved until she'd had no choice but to open her heart. With that action had come the realization she had a child-size hole that needed filling.

"I'm going to have to fix the broken parts first," she whispered to the sleeping girls. A couple of months ago her friend Dakota had pointed out that until Charlie was healed, she shouldn't take on a child. Charlie had wanted to be pissed, yet she'd known her friend was right. But after a decade of hiding, she wasn't sure how to start healing. Or she hadn't been until a few days ago.

Downstairs a door slammed. She left the babies' room and found Peter Moreno dumping his backpack on a kitchen chair. He saw her and grinned.

"Hi, Charlie." He crossed to her and wrapped his arms around her.

"Hey, kid. Your mom's not here." She hugged him back, then ruffled his hair.

"I guessed that when her car was gone."

"She had a meeting she forgot about, so she called me. She won't be long."

Peter was getting taller by the day. Skinny, with bright red hair, he was smart and athletic. Two years ago, he'd been a scared kid, abused by his foster father. Raoul and Pia had adopted him, despite the fact that Pia had been pregnant with twins. Now they were a loud, happy family.

"She takes on too much," Peter said in a tone that implied his father saying the same thing. "Women do today."

Charlie laughed. "You're a charming guy, aren't you?"

Peter grinned. "Dad says I get that from him and it's going to serve me well."

"I'm sure it is. Come on, let's eat cookies."

Charlie poured them each a glass of milk. Peter washed his hands and then put cookies on a plate. They settled at the kitchen table.

"How was your day?" she asked.

Peter grinned. "You sound like my mom."

"I'll take that as a compliment."

He told her about his second day of school. He was in seventh grade now, having to deal with going from class to class. They discussed optimal locker placement and how girls could get really pretty over a summer.

Charlie mostly listened. She liked how excited he was about math, how confident he was in his friends. She could feel his trust in Pia and Raoul and remembered the emotionally battered kid he'd been only a couple of years ago.

His birth parents had been killed in a horrible car accident. He'd been witness to the tragedy, trapped in the backseat. When Raoul and Pia had fallen in love, they'd never considered not adding Peter to their family. A lot for a newly engaged couple to take on. Especially considering the twins weren't their biological children, either.

Charlie wasn't sure she was as emotionally strong as Pia had been, but she liked to think she would have some of her friend's grace. She knew she wanted a chance to give to a child, to be a constant in a changing world.

Fixing herself first made sense. She needed to be emotionally whole, or at least on the road to being whole, before she took on the responsibility of a child. From what she'd been able to figure out, the slower route was the most sensible. Find a good therapist and work through the issues of her past. Deal with the rape, the way she'd shut down, the lack of justice. Grow emotionally over time. Healthy, reasonable and so not her style.

The alternative was more radical—tackling the lingering effects head-on, so to speak. If she had a fear of flying, she was the type of person who would book a flight to Australia and get it over with in one hideous seventeen-hour plane ride. But she wasn't afraid of flying, she was afraid of physical intimacy. More specifically, she was afraid to trust. Not men in general, but any man in an emotionally and physically intimate setting. Hardly something an online travel site could help her with.

The truth was, she could live with being broken. But being broken meant she was unlikely to raise a whole, healthy child. She didn't want to raise a kid who was afraid because Mom was. Which meant getting better.

She needed a professional, she thought as she listened to Peter. Or the closest thing she could find.

CHARLIE'S HOUSE WAS a lot like her. Practical, well kept and not the least bit flashy. Clay took in the neatly cut lawn, the well-maintained hedges, the unexpected flashes of color by the walkway.

She'd called him a couple of hours ago and asked him to stop by. He hadn't seen her since he'd gone by the station nearly a week ago. He wasn't supposed to start on the volunteer firefighter program for a few days, so he wasn't sure what she wanted to talk about. Still, Charlie was anything but boring, so he was sure he would be interested in whatever she had to say.

He climbed the three steps to the porch, then reached for the bell. The door opened before he could press it.

"Good. You're here. Come in."

She stepped back as she spoke, motioning him inside with her arm. As he passed her, he was aware of the tension in her body and the color on her cheeks. Not from makeup, he knew. Something else had her flushed.

"Are you all right?" he asked.

"Fine. I'm a little… Well, that doesn't matter. Sit."

It sounded like more of a command than a request.

He took in the comfortable oversize sofa, the extra chairs, all done in black leather. Color came from red and tan rugs over the hardwood floors and a few throw pillows. To the left was the arched entrance to a dining room and beyond that he would guess was the kitchen.

He walked to the sofa and sat down. Charlie settled across from him in one of the club chairs. She pressed her lips together, looked at him, then jumped up.

"Stay," she said, holding out her hand, palm to him. Then she dropped her arm to her side. "Sorry. You don't have to stay. What I meant is please don't get up. I think I need to pace."

Unease radiated from her. Something had happened— he'd guessed that much. "Are you hurt?"

She made a choking sound in the back of her throat. "Not in the way you mean. I'm fine. Everything is fine. Great, even. Sparkly." She stopped talking and walked to the end of the room. When she returned, she positioned herself behind the second chair, as if wanting a physical barrier between them.

She was dressed as usual in jeans and a T-shirt. Instead of the steel-toed boots she wore at the fire station, she had on athletic shoes. Her arms were toned and muscled, her short hair slightly mussed. She was exactly as he remembered, yet he would swear that everything was different.

He wanted to go to her, to give her a hug and tell her that he would help her get through whatever was wrong. Only Charlie didn't strike him as the hugging type. On a more practical level, who the hell was he to think he could solve any of her problems? Typical arrogant male response. That's what Diane would say.

"I want to ask you something," Charlie said, her hands gripping the back of the chair.

"Okay. What is it?"

"Background first," she said. Her gaze locked with his, then slid away. "My freshman year of college I had a crush on one of the football players. Senior guy, good-looking. He smiled at me and I was hooked."

"Lucky guy."

Charlie blinked at him. "He didn't see it that way. He invited me to a party…. I went. When he asked me up to his room, I said yes. I was young and stupid. I didn't realize he expected to have sex. I thought we'd…" She shrugged and looked away. "I wasn't thinking. Things went too far. I told him to stop and he didn't." She turned her attention back to him and pain filled her blue eyes. "I wasn't strong then."

Clay felt a rock hit the bottom of his stomach. "He raped you," he said flatly.

She nodded. "I fought, but he was bigger and he knew what he wanted. After, when I was crying, he told me to grow up, then he walked away." She drew in a breath. "You know, there really can be blood your first time. I grabbed the blanket and took it with me, then I went to the police. He was brought in and questioned. I could hear him in the next room. When they asked him what happened, he laughed. God, I remember that sound. He laughed and asked them if there was any way a guy like him would have sex with a girl like me unless she'd begged. And even then he'd had some trouble getting it up."

Clay considered himself an even-tempered guy. But right then he wanted to find the man in question and break every bone in his face.

He consciously controlled his breathing, his anger. Charlie had been through enough. She didn't need to deal with his reaction to her experience.

"I'm sorry." Stupid, but all he could think to say.

"Thanks."

"They believed him, right?"

She nodded. "Everyone did. Even my mother told me it was wrong to tease boys that way. I left college, ended up in Portland."

"Oregon, not Maine."

She managed a slight smile. "That's the one. I got strong. Now I can take care of myself."

More important to her, she was safe, he thought. No man would have the physical upper hand again.

"I want to tell you it's behind me, but it isn't," she said, staring down at the chair. "I haven't... I can't imagine being with someone."

He stared at her, digesting the meaning behind the

words. Charlie had to be close to his age. Which meant she hadn't been with a guy in over a decade.

"I want kids," she said quickly, meeting his gaze. "I'm not sure how yet. IVF, adoption, there are a lot of options. I want to have a family."

"You'll be a good mom."

"You don't know enough about me to be sure about that, but thank you for the support. The thing is I know I have to be emotionally strong as well as physically strong to be a parent. I don't like it, but there we are. Until I can make peace with my past, I shouldn't take on a kid."

She paused, as if gathering her thoughts. "I'm afraid I'll pass on my mistrust of men to any child I have. I don't want that. If I have a son, I want him to be proud of who he is. I want him to have male role models in his life, which might be difficult if I don't get over my problem. If I have a daughter, I want her to grow up with the idea that it's good to be open to love. I don't want to pass along my fear."

"You've thought this through," he said slowly, thinking that Charlie was brutally honest—even with herself. Something he admired and respected.

"I've thought about a lot of things. Including your problem."

He frowned. "I have a problem?"

"Getting accepted into the volunteer program. No one is going to take you seriously. It doesn't matter how well you do, they won't get past who you are and how you look."

A blunt assessment that was probably accurate.

Was she relating their situations? If so, what was she offering and what did she want in return? Sperm? A character reference?

"Deep breath," she said softly.

"Are you telling me or yourself?"

"Both of us." She swallowed. "I want you to help me get over my fear of being physically intimate. I want to be able to be with a guy without running screaming into the night."

"Is that what happens?"

"I've only tried a couple of times, but, yes. I freeze up. I panic. I run. I can't do that. I want to be over this. I want to be like everyone else."

"Being like the rest of the herd isn't all it's cracked up to be."

"So speaks someone who's perfect."

"I'm not perfect," he said automatically. Then the meaning of what she said slammed into him. Charlie wanted him to have sex with her. Not just sex for the night. She wanted him to help her heal.

Now it was his turn to stand, but once he was on his feet, he didn't move. Not toward her or away. He stared at her, watching color flare more brightly on her cheeks. He saw her vulnerability, her fear that he would say no and her terror that he would say yes.

"I'm not looking for anything more than sex," she whispered. "I don't want to fall in love or have a relationship. I just want to be normal enough to get on with my life. Figure out the kid thing. Be in a family." She drew in a shaky breath.

Clay knew Charlie well enough to understand that the one thing she would avoid at any cost was being in a weak position. Yet she'd laid herself bare to him, exposing not just her past pain, but her most secret hopes and dreams. He realized he respected her, so he respected her request, even as it confused him.

He was used to invitations, to numbers handed to him and suggestions made. But Charlie wasn't interested in a good time. Nor did she want to be able to say she'd been with him for bragging rights. This was real and painful.

"I appreciate you not breaking into hysterical laughter," she whispered.

"It's not funny. What I want to do is find that guy and beat the shit out of him."

One corner of her mouth turned up. "You're such a guy."

"Which makes me a decent candidate for the job." He shoved his hands into his jeans pockets. "None of this is expected. I need to think about it."

"Sure. Right. It's a lot to ask." Her grip on the back of the chair tightened.

He looked at her, at the shape of her face, the slight trembling of her mouth. She was nothing like Diane, yet she reminded him of his late wife. Diane had been blunt, as well. Tough, determined. She would have liked Charlie.

"I'll get back to you," he said at last.

"You know how to find me."

He nodded once and left. When he was outside, he headed for his truck. Honest to God, he had no idea what he was going to decide. So he wouldn't, not just now. Time had a way of making things more clear. Diane had taught him that, too. He'd learned all of life's most important lessons from her. The most significant had been how to love. A skill he had little use for these days.

CHAPTER FIVE

A TYPICAL DAY in Clay's New York life had included working out at the gym, getting a facial or maybe a manicure, a meeting with a client, a fitting for a future shoot or talking to his agent about upcoming projects. Despite the ongoing party scene, Clay had usually spent evenings with friends, and he'd often been in bed well before midnight.

Life on the ranch was different. Rafe and Heidi had left for Paris and their honeymoon, which meant someone else had to take care of her goats. Shane had agreed to take over the early morning milking, but when he was in town, staying at Annabelle's, the work fell to Clay.

It was barely eight in the morning, but Clay had already milked the goats, fed the horses, the elephant, the pony, the pig, the llamas and the sheep. Next up, he would paint the porch railing in preparation for winter. There were blisters on his hands and his spray tan had long since faded, replaced by a farmer's tan, earned through working outdoors.

This was better, he thought as he collected the sandpaper and scrapers. He draped a tarp over one shoulder. He liked getting up early and being able to point to what he'd done in a day. He was tired and sore when he fell into bed at night, but he'd done something with his time. As soon as escrow closed on the land he'd bought, he would start to work on preparing for his fall alfalfa crop. He had rented the equipment already and had interviews lined up for the farm manager. But for now, painting the railings at the Castle Ranch was going to be enough.

He spread out the tarp and went to work on the scraping. From inside came the sound of laughter. His mother and her new husband, Glen, were having a house built on the other side of the property. It would be finished by the end of the month and they would move into it. Until then, they stayed at the main house.

Shane was also building a house nearby. He and Annabelle would settle there while Heidi and Rafe stayed in this one. Everyone on the ark had paired up, Clay thought, except for him and his little sister, Evangeline. Which meant he was going to need his own place. While no one would kick him out, he wasn't exactly the party favor most new couples were looking for.

He added "get a house in town" to his mental to-do list. He wouldn't need much space. There was only him. For a second he allowed himself to wonder what Diane would think of Fool's Gold. She would like it here, he decided. Not just for the physical beauty of the mountains, but she would enjoy the people.

She had been the best part of him. Loving her had been easy—a lightning bolt. He'd surrendered to his feelings because he hadn't had a choice. Within a single date, he'd known she was the one he wanted to be with for the rest of his life.

After she'd died, the world had lost its color. Time had healed him, but he would always miss her. Need her. He wasn't interested in loving someone else.

He bent over the railing and scraped the peeling paint. As the bare wood was exposed he found himself thinking of Charlie and her unexpected request. Just as surprising was the fact he was considering what she wanted.

He liked being around her. He liked her toughness and competence. She wasn't like everyone else. He supposed he wasn't immune to being flattered by her request—her assumption that he could be the one to heal her. Which sounded great, but there was reality to deal with. Heal her? How? With his incredible magnificence?

He dropped the scraper and reached for a piece of sandpaper. The sun was warm, the sky blue. There were birds chirping and another burst of laughter from inside the house.

With Diane, he'd been unable to get enough. No matter how many times they made love, he wanted more. Wanted *her*. Since then, he'd gone through the motions but little else.

He tried to imagine touching Charlie and found the idea appealing. She wouldn't make it easy, he thought with a grin. Knowing her, she would make it difficult and yet that was okay.

She thought she needed to get over her fear of having

sex. He knew what she needed was to learn to trust. And he needed… He drew in a breath. He needed to care about someone again. Not love, obviously. But something. Right now attraction and compassion would be a step forward. Charlie wasn't the only one who needed a good healing, he thought. Maybe they could figure out a way to fix each other.

"I'M INTRIGUED," Dakota said as Charlie walked into her office. She smiled, amusement brightening her brown eyes. "As you requested, I've cleared my schedule for the whole hour. Now what is this about?"

Charlie had been friends with Dakota for years. She'd met all three of the Hendrix triplets within a week of moving to Fool's Gold. They were bright, funny women who cared about other people and understood the value of loyalty. While Charlie believed in the latter, she liked having added security.

She handed over a check for a hundred dollars.

Dakota took the offered paper, studied it for a second, then raised her eyebrows. "Is this what I think it is?"

"I'm hiring you as my therapist for the next hour. It's a onetime thing."

While Dakota didn't have a private practice, she was still a trained and licensed psychologist.

"If I'm your therapist, patient confidentiality applies," Dakota said slowly, motioning to the chair on the far side of her desk. "This must be important."

"It is." Charlie studied her friend. "It's not that I don't trust you," she began, aware that Dakota could take the whole check-writing thing wrong. They were friends. As such, Charlie should trust her. And she did. It was just...

Dakota leaned forward. "I understand," she said gently. "No explanations are required. You need the added security to feel safe so you can talk about whatever's bothering you. Of course I'll be your therapist for this hour and I will keep everything you tell me confidential."

Damn. While she appreciated the support, right now she was uncomfortably on edge. If she were anyone else, she might even admit to being emotional. But she wasn't, so that wasn't an option. Still, Dakota's support made her eyes burn. Which wasn't the same as crying. No way.

"Okay," Charlie muttered. "Thanks."

"You're welcome. Now what's this all about?"

"The baby thing."

Dakota already knew about Charlie's past and her desire to have a child. In fact, Dakota had been the one to point out that Charlie needed to consider curing herself first. Not advice she'd wanted to hear, but words that had made sense.

"You were right," Charlie told her. "About me getting better before having a kid."

Dakota leaned toward her. "I also told you I wasn't the person to take you on that journey. I do have the names of several trauma specialists. They're in Sacramento, so you wouldn't be dealing with anyone local. It's a drive, but more private."

"I may have to do that," Charlie said, then wished she was standing so she could shuffle her feet or pace. Sometimes, sitting still was difficult. "But first I'm going to try something else."

"Okay, and what is that?"

Charlie swallowed, squared her shoulders, then looked her friend directly in the eye. "I talked to Clay Stryker about having sex with me. Getting me, you know, ready. So I can do it without freaking."

Dakota's mouth dropped open. Charlie was pretty sure there was a rule that therapists weren't supposed to show emotion of any kind, let alone shock.

"Clay Stryker?"

"Yes."

"The underwear-model guy?"

Charlie nodded. "I've met him a few times. He wants to be a volunteer firefighter. He's more than a pretty face. We've talked a few times and we're sort of friends. So I asked him."

"Oh, my." Dakota cleared her throat. "He's an interesting choice."

"I don't care that he's good-looking. Or famous. I know what you're thinking. That I should have gone with somebody normal, right? It's just, he's nice. He was married before and when he talked about his late wife, there was something in his eyes." She pushed to her feet and started pacing. "That's why I'm here. Because I asked. Was it stupid? Am I an idiot?"

"You're a lot of things," Dakota said. "Stupid isn't one of them. Your plan is unconventional, but when you decide to face a problem, you jump in. So this isn't that surprising." She paused, as if considering her words. "You know the actual problem isn't about sex, right?"

Charlie sighed. "Yes, I know. It's about trust. Trusting a man. Trusting myself with a man. Being able to have men in my life in a serious way so my child can be comfortable with a male role model."

Dakota smiled. "You've been thinking about this. You're aware of the problem and taking steps to fix it. That's good."

"I hope so. I keep thinking if I can just be with a guy without freaking, I'll relax more and start letting men in my life," Charlie admitted. "Clay was nice about it. He didn't laugh or say no. He's thinking about it. I'm just scared he'll agree. And maybe scared he won't."

Normal seemed like such an easy goal—for everyone else. She'd always been on the fringes.

"You're attracted to him?"

"Have you seen him?" Charlie asked with a grin. Then her smile faded. "Ignoring the obvious, there have been a few tingles. Nothing huge, but more than usual for me."

She returned to the chair and sank down. "I'm not expecting anything like a relationship. I don't want that. I just want to get through whatever it takes to be in a place where I'm comfortable having a kid. Whatever form that takes."

"Understandable," Dakota said. "Okay, you have a plan and you've taken the first step. Now what?"

"I don't know," Charlie admitted. "That's what I want to talk about. What do I do if he says yes?"

"You let the man seduce you."

Charlie could feel her face getting hot. "I can't even think about that. It makes my stomach hurt. But assuming I can get through that, aren't there girlie things I should be doing? I don't know how to do this stuff. Is there a Dummies book?"

"No book required. Just be yourself."

"Being myself is the problem. Do I have to buy lingerie? Get a bikini wax?"

Dakota laughed. "I would pay big money to be in the room next door when some poor person tries to give you a bikini wax."

"You're not helping."

"Sorry. Look, you're understandably conflicted. Who wouldn't be? If he says yes, then shower, shave in the usual places and let the man do his thing. If he says no, I have the name of the trauma specialists to give you. How's that?"

"Good." She drew in a breath. "I'm on birth control. I have period issues and the pill helps."

"One problem solved. Oh, be safe and use a condom."

Charlie winced. "I hadn't thought of that."

"I'm sure he'll take care of buying them, but just make sure you have the conversation."

"Because that will be so comfortable."

"If you can't talk about protecting yourself with the man, how do you expect to have sex with him?"

"I thought I'd just lie there and think of England."

"He'll be so flattered to hear that."

Charlie told herself to keep breathing. After all, she didn't have to do it that second. And Clay could say no. Although now that she'd asked, she found herself hoping he would agree. Or maybe not. Maybe therapy was a better choice.

Dakota's expression softened. "Trust yourself. You have good instincts."

"I picked the guy in college and look what happened there."

"You didn't pick him. You were young and impressed by who you thought he was. There's a difference."

"I hope so."

"From what I know about the Stryker brothers, their mother raised them right. Keep breathing. Whatever happens, you're strong and capable. You'll get through this."

Charlie could only hope she was right.

WHAT CHARLIE DISCOVERED was that waiting could be its own brand of hell. She worked the next day and that was a nice distraction. Paige McLean, the station's former receptionist, had dropped by to talk about how happy she was with her new husband. The two of them had been in Australia and were heading to Thailand next. But once Paige left, Charlie had too much time to think. Worse, she was now off for twenty-four hours. She was jumpy and crabby and lots of other words ending in *y*.

In desperation, she attacked her hedges, deciding to cut them back before winter.

She'd been at it for a couple of hours. She was sweaty and hot, her sticky skin dotted with bits of leaves and smudged with dirt. She had just finished with the last hedge and was about to take her tools to the garage for cleaning when Clay strolled up.

He looked cool and fresh, his cotton shirt all smooth. His jeans were worn, with interesting creases at the hips and thighs. She couldn't see his eyes behind his sunglasses, but there were tiny reflections of herself on the lenses. Sweat, grime and debris were not her best look.

"What do you want?" she demanded, before she remembered that perhaps she might want to be nicer to the man she'd asked to sleep with her.

One corner of his mouth twitched. "Not a morning person?" he asked.

"It's two in the afternoon."

"I was giving you the benefit of the doubt."

She sighed. "I don't like yard work. I'm not good at it. Not the physical stuff—that's easy. But knowing what to do. I think my plants make fun of me behind my back."

"Because they respect you enough not to do it to your face?"

"Something like that." She looked at him, then away. Confusion made her uneasy. Should she demand he tell her what he'd decided? Or just withdraw the request and accept a year or two of therapy?

"We should go inside," he said, motioning to the front door.

As it was her house, she should do the inviting, but she decided to simply go with it. She put down her clippers and wiped her hands on the front of her tank top, wished her jeans were a little cleaner, then mentally shrugged. This was the real her. If Clay couldn't handle it, then sex was out of the question.

But as she led the way into the house, she realized she was filled with a queasy combination of anticipation and dread. He could agree or tell her to go to hell. To be honest, she wasn't comfortable with any of the possibilities.

She passed through the living room and walked into the spacious kitchen. The previous owner had updated it a decade or so ago, which had been more than enough for her. Appliances that worked, wood cabinets and a countertop where she could stack takeout was plenty. Annabelle had done a full five-minute lovefest on the six-burner stove she'd chosen for Shane's new house and an even longer soliloquy on the countertops. Charlie had listened with seeming interest because she wanted to be a good friend, but dear God. It was a kitchen. She simply didn't have it in herself to get excited.

The table and chairs by the window had been a garage-sale find. She'd stripped them herself and refinished them. Heidi had helped her pick out the cheerful red cushions. Now she pointed to the chairs.

"Sit."

The word came out as more of a bark than she would have liked. Clay removed his sunglasses, gave her an amused single-eyebrow raise, then did as instructed.

She sighed. Fine. She would admit it. The boy-girl thing was a complete disaster for her. At least she understood her limitations. Besides, she wasn't looking for a meaningful relationship. She simply wanted to get laid.

Sort of.

She pulled a pitcher out of the refrigerator. After filling two glasses with ice, she carried them over to the table, set the pitcher in the middle and then glared at Clay.

"Did you want something else?"

The amusement never faltered. "You get defensive when you're nervous."

"Shut up."

He chuckled. "Thank you for illustrating my point. Now you sit."

She plopped down and poured them each a glass of lemonade. After passing his to him, she happened to glance at her hands.

Dirt covered every inch and collected under her nails. Crap. She probably should have washed her hands before getting them drinks. Which she would have done if he hadn't been here. The man rattled her and not in a happy way.

"I'm not defensive," she snapped.

He picked up his glass and took a sip. His unsettling gaze swung back to her. "This is lemonade."

She rolled her eyes. "Most people would say the yellow color was a dead giveaway."

He reached his free hand across the table and placed

it on her forearm. "No claws required, Charlie. I'm not the enemy."

His voice was gentle, as was the pressure on her arm. She was aware of the warmth of his fingers on her skin. It all seemed easy for him. Because for him, the touching thing was no big deal.

She could touch, too, she reminded herself. She could carry a two-hundred-and-fifty-pound man out of a burning building, then give him CPR without blinking. But even she knew that was different.

She drew in a deep breath, ignored the warmth his fingers generated and then exhaled.

"Yes," she said carefully. "It's lemonade."

"You used sugar."

"Have you tried it without sugar? Do you know what a lemon is?"

His hold tightened slowly. She had a feeling if she were a stray cat or dog, he would be murmuring something like, "It's okay, girl. No one is going to hurt you."

"I was making conversation," he told her, his tone still tinged with amusement. "Most people don't use sugar. They use something without calories."

"Women," she said, snatching her arm away. "You mean women. I don't like artificial sweeteners. And if most women lived my day, they could afford the calories." She glared at him. "Are you saying I'm fat?"

He leaned back in his chair and picked up the glass. "Nope," he said easily.

"Good. Because I'm not. I have muscles. I'm strong." She eyed him. "I could probably take you."

"Not a chance."

"I don't fight fair."

"Neither do I."

That statement sent a shiver of undetermined origin rippling through her. She clutched her glass in both hands, not sure what to do next.

"Tell me about your family," he said.

She blinked. "Excuse me?"

"Your family. Who are they?"

An unexpected question. "I, ah, don't have any brothers or sisters. I lost my dad while I was still in high school." She thought about him and let herself relax into the memory. "He was great. A carpenter. He was a big guy and when I was little, as long as I was with my dad, I knew I was going to be okay."

She smiled. "We were a team." Mere mortals in the shadow of her glamorous and disapproving mother. Her smile faded. "After he died, I was devastated. My mother and I had never been close. That didn't change."

An understatement of award-winning proportions, she thought. But there was no reason to explain that her mother was world-famous ballerina Dominique Guérin. Even though it had been over fifteen years since Dominique had graced a stage, her career lived on in DVDs and PBS specials. And her ego was a life force that would live on for generations.

"You don't see her?"

"No, and I'm okay with that." More than okay. Delighted. But why go there?

"You're honest," he told her.

"Too honest. I tend to only be invited on shopping trips with my friends once. I don't get the whole polite-lying thing. Okay, sometimes, sure. But when you can see disaster coming? Why not say something? I'd want that."

Rather than reply, he just looked at her. His dark gaze was steady and, after a few seconds, unnerving. She found herself needing to fidget, although she wouldn't let herself.

"I like that you're honest," he said at last. "That you get defensive when you're scared, that you risk your life for people you don't know. I like that you're a good friend and that everyone in town has something nice to say about you."

She'd been uncomfortable with the compliments, but that last statement gave her something to hide behind. "You've been talking about me behind my back?"

"Unlike your plants, yes." He smiled at her. "I'll do it."

Do what? She hadn't asked a question and…

Thoughts filed neatly into subjects and the most obvious guesses of what he was talking about popped to the front of her brain. She opened her mouth, then closed it. A neat trick, considering her heart had come to a complete stop in her suddenly tight chest.

I'll do it, as in "it"? The big it?

She had a feeling she'd gone completely pale. Or flushed the color of a radish. Neither would be attractive. But there had to be some outward manifestation of her inward disbelief.

"Why?"

The word burst out before she could stop herself.

Clay grinned, then stood and walked around the table. He took her hands in his and pulled her to her feet.

"I like you."

She must have kept breathing, because she didn't pass out. But the world seemed to be spinning.

"You say that now, but you'll probably change your mind." About all of it. "You know, I shouldn't have asked. It was presumptuous. Too much, really. We barely know each other." She tried taking a step back only to realize he was still holding on to her hands.

She stared down and saw his hands were much bigger than hers. His fingers were longer, his palms broader. There were no tingles, no heat. Just a sense of incredulity.

"I'll get you where you need to go," he told her. "How did you describe what you wanted to be?"

"Normal," she whispered.

"Right. Normal."

"Thank you. That's very generous, but I'm taking it back. I'm okay the way I am. Really. Normal is highly overrated."

He released one hand. "You're scared." He rested his free hand on the side of her neck, his thumb on her cheek, his long fingers reaching to her nape.

She wanted to tell him she wasn't scared. That she laughed in the face of fear. Only she couldn't seem to stop trembling long enough to speak. Terror wasn't fear, right? She wasn't actually lying.

The need to run grew, only her feet weren't listening. Worse, Clay was moving closer. Like they were going to touch or something.

"You're not starting now, are you?" she whispered, wishing she were somewhere in outer Mongolia. He would never find her there and she was pretty sure she would like yaks. "This isn't a good time for me. I have grooming things I need to do and maybe I have to throw up."

She pressed her lips together, wishing she didn't sound like such a girl. She was strong, she reminded herself. Powerful. Safe. No one was taking that away from her.

"Don't worry," he told her, his dark eyes staring into hers. "Nothing will happen before you're ready. It's a process. I've been doing some research. We'll go as slow as you need."

Before she could figure out what to say to that, he leaned in that last little bit and kissed her.

She'd been kissed a few times in the past decade. Her sad attempts at dating had usually ended with a kiss. Then the guy expected more and she ran. Sometimes literally.

This was different, she told herself. Clay was practically a hired professional. She needed to trust him, to give herself up to him. Or at least endure.

That decided, she braced herself for the inevitable. The clawing sense of panic, the unease low in her belly, the overwhelming need to bolt. She curled her free hand into a fist and told herself to hang on. It would be over soon.

His mouth lightly touched hers. A quick brush, then nothing at all. He did it again. The third time his lips lightly pressed against her own, she found herself able to breathe. The sensation of dread faded a little.

He dropped his hand to her shoulder, then slowly slid it down to the clenched hand. His fingers pried hers apart.

"Relax," he murmured.

"Are pigs flying?"

"You're not going to make this easy, are you?"

"Where's the fun in that?"

He released her other hand, then cupped her cheeks. "I'm sorry for what that bastard did to you."

She immediately stepped back, moving until she was too far away for any contact at all. "You had nothing to do with it."

"I'm apologizing in general."

"Thank you."

He looked at her for a long time. She wanted to put more distance between them, like a table or a continent, but forced herself to stay where she was.

"I'm not going to give up," he told her. "Just so you know."

"I can't decide if that's good or bad."

He chuckled. "Like I said. Honest. That's a good thing." He stepped toward her. "I'm going to kiss you again. On the mouth. You're going to let me."

She waited for the rush of discomfort, the unwelcome

tightness. But as she watched Clay approach there was only mild concern. Maybe because she knew he would be gentle. Careful. Maybe because her desire to have a child was getting bigger than her fear. Whatever the reason, she hung on to the lack of terror and went with it.

When he was right in front of her, he paused. "Want to touch me?"

"Maybe next time."

He laughed, then leaned in and pressed his lips to her cheek.

She'd been expecting a kiss on the mouth, so the cheek contact was a surprise. A chance to relax. She took a breath.

He kissed her other cheek.

"How very European," she murmured.

"Chère," he said, in a bad French accent.

He kissed her nose, then her chin. Finally he touched his lips to hers.

Without thinking, she let her eyes close as she absorbed the feel of what he was doing. There was heat and firmness. He didn't move, didn't demand. It was a chaste kiss, but also kind of, nearly, almost… Nice.

She wasn't sure how long they stood there, lips barely touching. Seconds ticked by. Instead of getting more tense, she felt herself relaxing. An unexpected urge to raise her arms, to rest her hands on his shoulders had her starting to move. Only Clay stepped back and then he wasn't kissing her anymore.

"Lesson one," he told her.

"How many are there?"

"As many as it takes. This is going to be a full service seduction."

"Oh, my."

He gave her one last smile, then turned and walked out of her kitchen. She heard the front door open, then close and she was alone with the idea that maybe, just maybe this wasn't going to be too awful after all. Maybe she could find her way to normal.

Smiling, she, too, went out front, prepared to collect her gardening tools then head inside and shower. She'd just put the last of them in the garage and was walking toward the front door when a long, black limo pulled up in front of her house.

Limos weren't common in Fool's Gold. It was more of an SUV kind of town. So she immediately assumed the driver must be lost. That safe, happy feeling lasted until a powerfully built guy in a suit got out of the passenger side and walked around to open the rear door.

Even before the tiny foot in a ridiculously high heel touched the street, Charlie knew. Her gut twisted and the pressure in her ears increased. The world went silent. It was that last incredibly still moment before the tornado hit—when animals knew a storm was coming, but humans could only blink at each other in confusion.

A second foot joined the first, then Dominique Guérin stepped back into her daughter's life.

CHAPTER SIX

"CHANTAL!"

Charlie flinched at the sound of both her mother's voice and her real name.

"Mom."

Dominique walked toward her, arms outstretched. She moved with a dancer's grace, her body fluid and elegant, her head high. She wore a tailored suit and her gold-blond hair was in a stylish pixie cut that flattered her delicate features and large green eyes.

Dominique was pushing sixty but looked to be in her early forties. She was petite, maybe five-one or -two, but powerful. Charlie might have inherited her height and looks from her father, but she'd gotten her strength from her mother. As a child she'd watched Dominique practice for hours, working until she was drenched in sweat and her male partner nearly unconscious with exhaustion, and that had been after she'd retired.

As her mother approached, Charlie started to feel like a cartoon character who had been given a growth potion. She got larger and larger until she half expected her head to poke through the clouds. It was always that way when her mother was around. Charlie was the giant next to the tiny perfection that was Dominique.

Her mother stopped in front of her, arms still open. "Aren't you going to greet me?"

"What? Oh. Right." She bent down at the waist and awkwardly hugged the other woman. She then dutifully kissed both cheeks. The action was similar to what Clay had done to her, but the feeling was very different.

Charlie straightened and took a step back. "What are you doing here?" she asked.

"Can't I visit my only child?"

"You never have before."

Dominique sniffed delicately, then pointed to the house. "You can invite me inside."

Charlie wasn't sure if that was a statement of fact or a prod. Probably the latter, she thought.

"What about him?" she asked, pointing at the hunky guy in the dark suit still standing by the car. He wore sunglasses and kept glancing up and down the street— no doubt wishing he were protecting the president rather than an aging former ballerina.

"Justice is my bodyguard. He'll wait outside."

"Lucky him," Charlie muttered under her breath, then turned and walked into her house. Once in her house, she faced her mother.

Dominique took in the comfortable living room, probably finding fault with every piece of furniture. Charlie had bought for comfort and out of respect for her budget. As Dominique was more into how things

looked than how they functioned, she would no doubt
be horrified.

"Why are you dressed like that?" Dominique asked.

Charlie glanced down at her dirty jeans and sweaty,
smudged tank top. "I was working in the yard."

Her mother's eyes widened, although Charlie noted
that her brows didn't lift. BOTOX, she thought idly. One
of the advantages of never being even close to pretty
was not having to worry about getting older.

"Yard work? Like a peasant?"

Charlie managed a laugh. "Yes, Mother. Exactly like
a peasant. Later we'll all line up and the Lord of the
Manor will give us bread and wine."

Dominique's mouth thinned in disapproval. "I know
you think you're funny, Chantal, but you're wrong."

"It's Charlie."

"What's Charlie?"

"My name."

"I would never call my daughter that. It's a boy's
name."

"It's better than Chantal."

Dominique drew herself up. "You were named after
my grandmother."

"Your grandmother was named Ethel. Or Alice. De-
pending on which one you're talking about. You named
me Chantal because it's French and you thought I was
going to turn out like you and be a dancer. Sorry to
disappoint."

Charlie shoved her hands into her jeans pockets and
held in a sigh. This was a conversation they'd had many

times before. It never went anywhere, so why did she keep trying? Her mother wasn't interested in family— she wanted to be adored. Charlie had never been very good at the worship thing. Something nearly as unforgivable as being tall and gangly. All Dominique had wanted from her daughter was for her to be a perfect replica of herself. Charlie had failed at that from the second she'd been conceived.

"I see you haven't changed," her mother said, her voice tight.

Charlie felt the first soggy wetness of guilt. If she wasn't careful, she would be sucked under and drown. It happened every time they were in the same room.

"You came a long way," she said, trying for neutral ground. "There must be a reason."

Dominique walked over to one of the club chairs and perched carefully on the edge. "I wanted to see you. In the past few years, we've lost our special bond."

"We never had a special bond," Charlie blurted before she could stop herself. She sighed. "Sorry. Okay. Special bond. I'm not sure what you mean."

"Some mothers and daughters are close."

Charlie didn't like the sound of that. "You want to be close?"

"We're family."

"I haven't seen you in five years."

"That's my point."

"You don't like me very much. I'm nothing like you. I don't understand the greatness of your career, I'm a constant disappointment."

Her mother's chin lifted. "I never said that."

"You said it all the time. It was practically a chant."

Dominique rose. "I can see this isn't a good time. We can talk more later. I've come to Fool's Gold to rest and recover."

"From the never-ending grind of your fame?" Charlie asked, wondering if her mother would hear the sarcasm or accept the question at face value.

"Exactly. It is the price I pay for being who I am. That's why Justice is with me. To protect me from my fans."

Question answered. Charlie had a feeling there were a whole lot fewer fans than there used to be, but she wasn't going there. After all, Dominique wasn't intentionally cruel. She was simply self-absorbed.

"I'm staying at Ronan's Lodge. Will I like it?"

"It's not up to your standards, but you've always been very good at making do."

The words were in response to the growing sense of guilt. Charlie didn't know how her mother did it but in every situation Charlie ended up feeling like the bad guy. Right now she knew she should offer to let her mother stay in her guest room. She also knew she would never actually issue the invitation. She rubbed her forehead as a steady pounding began right behind her eyes.

"I will be in touch," Dominique said as she walked to the door.

Charlie followed her, torn between relief that the visit was ending and confusion as to why her mother had come in the first place. "It's nice to see you."

Dominique turned and stared. "We both know that's not true, don't we?"

She let herself out.

Charlie stood in her living room, awash in guilt and knowing there wasn't a damn thing she could do about it.

"Ms. Guérin, it is a great honor to have you at our hotel," the manager of Ronan's Lodge gushed as the bellman delivered Dominique's many suitcases into the suite. "In our town, as well. We don't get many celebrities of your stature here. If there is anything I can do to make your stay more pleasant, please, please let me know."

He pressed a business card into her hand. "I've written my cell number on the back. I would encourage you to call me anytime. Day or night."

Dominique took the card and the gushing with little enthusiasm. No doubt her assistant had called ahead and requested the staff be attentive. Back in the day, no preplanning would have been necessary. The manager, an average-looking man in his forties, would have been stuttering and shaking at the thought of being so close to her. Strangers would have stopped her in the hallway and on elevators to tell her how much they admired her. Men would have begged to buy her a drink, thinking they would attempt to seduce her.

Today she was simply a middle-aged woman who used to be someone.

Growing old was a bitch.

The manager finally left. Dominique crossed to the window and stared out at the view. She wasn't sure why Chantal had settled in this small town at the foot of the Sierra Nevadas, but she had. Now as she stared up at the snow-covered peaks, she shivered slightly. Her journey was like that of a mountain climber. First she would gather supplies, then she would make the ascent. Her goal wasn't physical, but emotional. Still, it would be grueling and she could fail.

She turned and glanced at her bodyguard. Justice Garrett carried himself like a man comfortable in any situation. He had military experience of some kind, was licensed to carry a concealed weapon and could probably stop a bullet with his bare hands. He was extremely well trained. He was the sort of man a person took into the most dangerous parts of the world. With his dark blond hair and deep blue eyes, he was handsome enough. But there was a wariness in his gaze. He was a man who carried ghosts, she thought.

Now he looked back at her, as if asking, "What next?"

As if she had the answer. She'd hired him only a few days before and they had yet to get to know each other.

"You must wonder why you're here," she said, returning to the living room of the suite and opening the minibar. "What possible danger could an old woman like me be in?" She closed the minibar and walked to the small tote that had been left on the coffee table. After opening it, she pulled out a bottle of eighteen-year-old Scotch.

She held up the bottle in invitation.

"I'm on duty."

She smiled. "We both know no one is after me."

"Then why am I here?" He gave her a slight smile. "I don't come cheap."

She opened the Scotch and poured some into two glasses. She picked up one and settled on the sofa. Justice came into the living room and stood by the window. He didn't even glance at the drink.

"Money isn't one of my problems," she told him, then took a sip. The smooth liquor went down easily. "I have enough for several lifetimes. It's the other things that are missing. Youth, love, family."

"You have a daughter."

"Technically. Biologically. She doesn't love me." Dominique took another drink, knowing the more difficult truth was that Chantal could barely stand her. "What did you think of her?"

"She's lovely."

Dominique laughed. "Hardly. Chantal is many things, but not lovely. She's capable and strong. She gets both of those from me. I am not the delicate flower you see before you."

She rose and walked into the bedroom. Justice followed her as far as the doorway. She motioned to the three suitcases by the dresser. A fourth had been put on a luggage rack.

"Would you please put those on the bed for me?"

He did as she requested and stepped back. She set her drink on the nightstand, then opened the smallest of the suitcases. Inside were several carefully wrapped pictures. She took the top one and removed the protective layers, then held out the framed photo.

"My husband," she said.

Justice took the picture.

She didn't have to look at it to see Dan. So tall and handsome. He'd swept her off her feet within a few minutes of meeting her. Her manager had arranged for Dan to put in shelves in Dominique's New York dance studio. She'd shown up unexpectedly to find him working. He'd turned around, smiled and she'd been lost.

They'd married two months later, much to the shock of her business manager and all her friends. But she'd never regretted the impulsive decision. They'd loved each other until the day he died. There had been other men in her life and in her bed. Before him and after he'd died. But no one else had ever touched her heart.

"He looks happy," Justice said, returning the picture to her.

She took it and placed it on the dresser. "He was. He had me and Chantal. He loved us both." Dominique had struggled with that, she remembered, wanting to be the center of her husband's universe. How he'd devoted himself to his daughter. Sometimes she'd been jealous. Foolishly, maybe. Wrong, perhaps. But true.

She offered another picture. This one of a three-year-old Chantal in a tutu. Even then she'd been too tall and far too awkward. She'd wanted to play with trucks instead of dolls and she had no patience or talent for any kind of dance.

"I wanted a daughter like myself. A dancer. Someone I could nurture and mold. What's that old saying? If you want God to laugh, make plans?"

Justice gave her back that picture.

"No advice?" she asked.

"Not in the job description."

"Were you a spy, Justice?"

"Nothing that exciting."

"I'm not sure I believe you. Do you think I'm attractive?"

Nothing about his expression changed. "Ma'am?"

She smiled briefly. "Don't worry. I'm not trying to seduce you. I used to be beautiful. A sheik once offered me a million dollars for a night with him. Just like that movie from years ago. It was before I met my husband, so I said yes." The smile returned and broadened as she remembered. "The next morning he sent me home with the million dollars and a diamond necklace. He wanted to marry me, of course. So many of them did."

She sighed, knowing the memories would be with her tonight. Sometimes they were just like her former suitors. Insistent. Determined.

"Well, Justice Garrett, I will see you in the morning. You have your room key?"

He touched his jacket pocket. "You never answered the question."

"Why I hired you?" She shrugged. "Isn't it obvious? With you around, I get to pretend that I still matter. That I'm still famous. That I have significance. None of which is true."

He looked at her for several seconds, then murmured, "Good night," and left.

When the door had closed behind him, Dominique picked up the picture of Dan and stared at his familiar face. "I would give it all up to have you back," she whispered. "You know that, don't you?"

Tears filled her eyes. As there was no one to impress, she let them fall. Smudged makeup didn't matter these days.

She pressed the picture to her chest and let the truth wash over her. She was alone. She had been for years, but she'd never allowed herself to see it. Being in that hospital room, waiting to find out if she was going to live or die, had brought that painful reality home. As she'd waited, she'd vowed that if she survived, things would be different.

Chantal was the only family she had left. Dominique refused to lose her. She was here to be a part of her daughter's life—however much Chantal might resist.

"PICK IT UP, people," Charlie yelled. "I'll make this a timed drill if I have to."

As she watched, the ten volunteer candidates finished running around the track. With the opening of Josh Golden's cycling school, she'd been offered a new place for her candidates to work out. As long as she didn't schedule training during cycling sessions, Josh had given her access to both the indoor and outdoor track, the weight room and an unfinished area she planned to use for various drills involving hoses and other pieces of equipment. She was a happy camper.

Now she waited until the last of the women ran up to join the group. Charlie blew on her whistle, the signal for everyone to race toward the large truck tires she'd had delivered. The concept was simple. Drag the heavy tires from one end of the field to the other. After running two miles.

She'd already wrapped ropes around the tires and provided gloves. But nothing helped the fact that the tires weighed about a hundred and twenty pounds. Each.

But instead of racing as instructed, two of the women smiled at Clay. One even flipped her hair. Charlie snorted in disgust. Sure Clay was the most fit person on the field, but he was a major distraction. Still, she would give him credit for ignoring their preening and grabbing the ropes of his tire. In a matter of seconds, he was dragging it across the field at a brisk pace.

The other two guys in the group did their best to keep up with him. Two of the women were only a few yards behind, but the other four were seriously struggling.

Charlie walked over. "What's the problem, ladies?"

The tallest of the women, the blonde, looked at her. "This tire is too heavy. Can't we do something else?"

It was the same with every class, she thought, having been at this long enough not to even be surprised. She let the question hang there a couple more seconds, giving herself time to get her mad on. Then she gave the woman the same smile she suspected bears used right before they snatched up unsuspecting salmon.

"There is a belief among many firefighters that women don't belong. Do you know why that is?" She paused.

All four of them shook their heads.

"Because some idiot wants it to be easy. It's not easy. A firefighter wears about fifty pounds of gear. Which means if the guy next to him goes down, you have to drag him plus fifty pounds out of a burning building. And by drag, I mean carry."

She stepped closer to the blonde, staring her in the baby blues and wishing she'd had onions on her burger at lunch.

"Either you're ready to do the job or you're not. Because I, for one, am not explaining to any family that Daddy isn't coming home because you weren't strong enough to save him. That tire weighs a hundred and twenty pounds. Assuming the average male firefighter weighs two hundred and his gear is another fifty, then you're responsible for carting around two hundred and fifty pounds. So don't whine to me about the damn tire."

When she finished, she wasn't shouting, but there was a whole lot of energy in her voice.

The blonde's eyes welled up with tears. "You're being a real bitch, you know that?"

"I know, honey, but it's only going to get worse. So this is probably a good time for you to find something else to do with your afternoon."

"You're right about that."

The other woman stomped off the field.

Charlie turned back to her group. She wasn't surprised to see that they'd stopped to listen. What did impress her was Clay standing on the other end of the field. He'd completed the assignment.

"Anyone else want to complain about the tire?" she asked.

There was a chorus of nos, followed by some serious tire moving.

Three hours later, everyone was dripping sweat and collapsed on the grass. Charlie made sure they each had a bottle of water.

"Good work, people. Michelle Banfield is teaching the next session. You'll see me at the end of the week."

She gave them what she hoped was a friendly wave, picked up her clipboard and started toward the parking lot. Clay fell into step beside her.

"Great workout," he said.

"I'm glad you enjoyed it." She kept moving, doing her best not to notice his muscled arms or long legs. Shorts and a T-shirt had never looked so good.

"You went easy on us."

She glanced at him. "How did you know?"

He shrugged. "It was the first day. You don't suffer fools but you're not mean. You didn't enjoy making Madeline cry."

"You know her?"

"She introduced herself to me."

Charlie might be completely inept when it came to the whole boy-girl thing, but she wasn't stupid. "She gave you her number."

When he didn't answer, she wondered how many of the other women had done the same.

"Must be nice to be you," she muttered.

"Not always. Besides, I'm otherwise engaged these days."

She stopped and stared at him. "What does that mean? You're dating? You've only been back a few weeks. I didn't think you had time to get involved. Look, if you're seeing someone I don't want to…" She paused, fumbling for the right phrase for what they were, in theory, going to do.

He faced her. He was taller than her, broader in the shoulder. She was used to being the same size or bigger than everyone in the room, so it was kind of strange to be smaller than Clay. Nice, but strange.

"I'm not dating," he said quietly. "I meant you."

"Oh. Okay. That's fine, then."

His dark gaze settled on her face. "Know any martial arts?"

"Not formally. I've taken self-defense classes, of course and I can have a mean left hook."

"I could teach you. We could spar sometime."

She held the clipboard against her chest. Not exactly like a shield. She sighed. Fine. Yes, exactly as if she were trying to protect herself.

"How would that be fun?" she asked. "Sparring with someone who doesn't know what she's doing? Don't you want to work out with someone better than you? Isn't that how you learn?"

"You don't think you could take me?"

"Not that way. I wouldn't know how to begin."

He took the clipboard from her. "Charlie, take a deep breath."

"Why?"

He raised his eyebrows.

"All right," she grumbled and did as he requested. "And?"

"That was flirting."

"Breathing?"

He grinned. "No. My offer to spar with you. Think about it. The two of us in a room, getting physical."

"I don't think that was flirting. I didn't flip my hair. Isn't hair flipping required?"

"Is that why you wear it short?"

"No." She grabbed the clipboard and held on to it with both hands. "It's more practical this way and I'm busy."

"Or you're doing your damnedest to deny your femininity."

She held in a snort. "Please. Have you seen me? I'm not the least bit feminine." Something her mother had pointed out endlessly when Charlie had been growing up. "I don't care about that sort of thing." She glanced around to make sure no one was within earshot. The other trainees had already left and Josh's next cycling class hadn't arrived. They were the only ones in the parking lot.

"What's this all about?" she asked. "I thought we were just going to have sex."

"This is having sex."

"No one is naked."

"Flirting is foreplay. You'll like it."

"I doubt that." Why did there have to be foreplay? Why couldn't they just get to it and get it over with?

"Then *I* like it. It's fun."

She hadn't thought of sex as being fun. To her, it was something to be endured for the greater good.

She sighed. "Why can't you be a regular guy and just want to get to it?"

"Because just getting to it is what hurt you in the first place."

The man saw too much, she thought, more impressed than annoyed. "So we have to flirt?"

"Yes."

"I don't know how and I don't think I'll be very good at it."

He flashed her another smile. "That's the can-do spirit that we all admire."

"Shut up or I'll hurt you with my clipboard."

"I'd like to see you try."

Humor flashed in his eyes. And an invitation.

Charlie swallowed hard, then said, "I could so take you. I'm tough and you can't possibly handle me."

She felt stupid and vulnerable as she spoke. Exposing herself like that. Because there were a thousand horrible things Clay could say. Something along the lines of "Why would I want to?" or "You're right. I couldn't handle a woman as big as you."

Instead he moved a little closer. "I'm good at handling."

She opened her mouth, then closed it. "I have no idea what to say. I suck at this."

He surprised her by leaning in and kissing her. His lips lingered for a second, before he straightened. "Don't worry about it. There's a path to seduction, Charlie, and we're going to walk every step. No matter how long it takes."

With that, he turned and walked away. She had a bad feeling she was standing there, slack-jawed. Looking as stunned as she felt.

When he drove off, she was able to close her mouth. A few seconds later, movement returned and she could walk to her truck. But it was nearly an hour before the tingles he generated faded. In her book, that was going down in the win column.

CHAPTER SEVEN

DOMINIQUE HAD NEVER been in a fire station before. She knew what they were, that there were large vehicles and equipment. Burly men with axes. She even understood that her daughter was a firefighter, but knowing and seeing were different.

After stepping out of the limo and onto the curb, she paused.

"This is a mistake," she murmured to herself.

Justice, wearing his usual dark suit and sunglasses, stood by her door. "Maybe not."

"Do you have a family?" she asked.

"No, but I know they can be…difficult."

She studied him for a moment. "I suspect you do," she said, then sighed. "Fine. Here goes nothing."

She walked up the wide driveway, toward the open garage doors. Fire trucks faced out. They were big and slightly intimidating. She couldn't imagine riding in one, let alone driving one. No doubt there were professional drivers who took care of that sort of thing. A woman in a uniform looked up as Dominique approached.

"Can I help you?"

"I'm here to see my daughter. Chantal."

The other woman, forty-something with drab skin and lines around her eyes, shook her head. "Sorry. There's no one here by that name."

Dominique braced herself for the unpleasantness and said, "Charlie. You would know her as Charlie."

The other woman's eyes widened in surprise. "Oh, sure. Let me get her."

Dominique smoothed the front of her jacket. In deference to small-town America, she'd dressed more casually. Tailored trousers, a silk blouse and a light jacket. She preferred a suit, but fitting in was important. She might be here awhile.

A door opened and Chantal stepped into the garage area. Dominique drew back when she saw her daughter's dark blue uniform. The pants were terribly unflattering and the short-sleeved shirt was boxy.

"Mother," Chantal said warily. "What are you doing here?"

"I came to see you. We need to talk."

"I'm at work."

"You don't seem very busy."

"I'm still at work. You're the one who always told me that without an excellent rehearsal there can't be an excellent performance."

"I'm amazed you remembered."

"I did and this is my rehearsal time. We can talk later. When I'm not on duty."

"When will that be?"

Before Chantal could answer, a horrendously loud

sound cut through the quiet afternoon. It was followed by a voice blaring out something about an accident, followed by an intersection.

Dominique found herself in the middle of frantic activity. People burst into the garage area from all directions. Chantal grabbed her by the arm, dragged her over to the wall and pushed her onto a bench.

"Stay here until we're gone," she commanded, then turned and ran.

Dominique bounced back to her feet. "Where are you going? You can't simply walk away from me like this."

Chantal took off at a run and didn't glance back. In what seemed like seconds, people in fireman coats and pants were climbing onto the biggest truck. The ambulance beside it pulled out and turned left onto the street. As soon as it was out of sight, she heard the siren begin.

Someone who looked suspiciously like her daughter opened the driver's door of the biggest truck and climbed inside.

"Chantal?" Dominique asked, unable to believe what she was seeing.

The driver gave her a quick glance before starting the engine. Dominique sank back onto the bench as the vehicle followed the ambulance.

She doubted it had been even two minutes since the first alarm. Where there had been controlled chaos, there was now silence. Just as unsettling was the realization that her daughter had been the one driving.

Until recently Dominique hadn't spent much time thinking about her daughter's day-to-day life. She knew

Chantal worked for the fire department, but had never considered what it was she did there. Seeing Chantal in real time wasn't comforting. There was no place for her in this world. She could never belong, never fit in. The sad truth was she was alone. She was also aware that she really had no one else to blame for that state.

Collecting her small Fendi bag, she walked out of the fire station. Justice was waiting by the limo.

"It was a fire or an accident," he told her. "An emergency. She had to go."

She gave him a smile. "You're being very kind." She glanced around. "I'm going to walk. Why don't you take the car back to the hotel."

He nodded and climbed back into the limo.

Chantal's station was in the middle of town. It was a Saturday morning and many people were enjoying the late-summer morning. She saw families together, mothers with daughters. A couple of teenage girls were laughing, each holding a Starbucks cup.

Growing up, Dominique had never had close friends. There was no time. She'd started dancing when she was three and hadn't stopped until she'd retired some forty years later. Her childhood had been spent studying dance. At sixteen, she'd joined her first ballet company. She'd soloed at seventeen, became a principal dancer at twenty. She toured the world, was a guest in the most prestigious ballet companies and starred in several television productions.

There had been no time for "normal" pursuits, nor had she been interested. She'd lived a life others could only dream of. She was wealthy, beautiful, remarkable. And lonely, she admitted to herself. Her recent health scare had shown her how isolated she'd become. There had been no one to call, no close friends to visit her in the hospital. No one she trusted to see her looking anything but her best.

She stopped in front of a bookstore. There was a display of mysteries by Liz Sutton. A sign declared her to be a local author. Dominique stepped inside to buy a copy of her latest release. Perhaps a novel would help pass the time until she decided what to do next.

She paid for her purchase, but before she could leave, two women approached. One was about her age, the other a decade or two older. The white-haired woman was dressed in a suit that seemed expensive.

"You must be Dominique Guérin," the older woman said with a friendly smile. She held out her hand. "I'm Marsha Tilson, the mayor of Fool's Gold. I've so wanted to meet you. How nice we could run into you today."

Dominique shook hands with her, pleased to have been recognized. "Mayor Tilson."

"Please, call me Marsha. This is my friend May Stryker." Marsha smiled at the dark-haired woman. "Or is it May Simpson?"

May laughed. "I haven't decided." She turned to Dominique. "I was recently married. While I love my husband, I must admit I've been a Stryker for so long, I can't imagine getting used to another name. Glen swears he doesn't care, so I'm still making up my mind."

Dominique listened with feigned interest. Something

she'd perfected as a child. People were forever telling her things about their lives that she didn't find the least bit compelling.

May seemed friendly enough, but her clothes! She wore jeans and a worn short-sleeved shirt. Her face had held up over time, but she had freckles and her arms were a little saggy.

"We were going to get a coffee," Marsha said. "Would you like to join us?"

"I, ah…" Dominique hesitated, not wanting to bother with the women. But she reminded herself that the only cure for loneliness was company. Better this than nothing. "That would be nice. Thank you."

They walked to the Starbucks on the corner and went inside. Once there, they stood in line and then ordered. Dominique was used to an assistant bringing her coffee. Things were different now, she reminded herself. She would have to get familiar with things like standing in line and ordering for herself.

Once they were seated, May smiled at her. "I know your daughter. Charlie keeps her horse at our ranch."

Dominique stared at her, not sure which was more horrifying. That May called Chantal *Charlie* or that her daughter had a horse.

"She rides?"

"Very well. You didn't know?"

"No."

"Oh. I'm sorry. I thought…" May shifted in the chair.

Marsha, who had much better posture than her friend, lightly touched May's arm. Dominique knew it was some kind of silent communication but couldn't figure out what was being said.

"I've come here to visit her," Dominique announced. "Chantal. That's her actual name. She seems less than thrilled to see me. We're not close."

"That must be difficult for you," Marsha said.

"It is. I know what you're thinking. That my life has been wonderful. But everyone forgets there's a price to fame and thousands of hours of hard work went into each performance. Then I lost my husband and Chantal left."

"Teenagers," Marsha said. "I know that story. I lost touch with my daughter, as well."

"Chantal could have stayed in touch with me," Dominique continued. "I'm the one who was traveling. I'm the one with the difficult schedule. But would she? Of course not. Do you know what she does for a living?"

"She's an engineer," May said.

"No, she's not. She drives a fire truck. My daughter. Astonishing."

Marsha and May exchanged a glance. Marsha leaned toward Dominique.

"Charlie, um, Chantal, drives the engine. You might know it better as the pumper truck. She is responsible for getting the engine to the emergency. She also operates the pump panels. They determine the amount of water flowing to the hoses. The captain is in charge and Charlie acts as a second in command."

"Thank you for the explanation," Dominique said, her voice more brittle than she would like. Although she appreciated the information, she hardly needed a stranger lecturing her on the details of her daughter's job.

May leaned toward her. "I know this is hard."

"How?" Dominique demanded. "How do you know that at all?"

"I have three boys of my own. Sometimes staying close is difficult. I'd love to help."

"I don't need help. I need a more obedient daughter." Dominique rose. "It was lovely to meet you both. If you'll excuse me."

She left her coffee on the table and walked out. As she stood on the sidewalk, she blinked against the bright sunlight. After slipping on her sunglasses, she told herself the burning in her eyes had nothing to do with the sharp pain in her heart. Nothing at all.

"Dominique?"

She turned and saw May had followed her. "Yes?"

May handed her a piece of paper. "My phone number. In case you want to talk."

"How kind," Dominique murmured, then walked away.

She passed a trash can and nearly tossed the number. But something made her fold up the paper and slip it into her handbag.

CHARLIE CHECKED THE street, then watched Michelle in the mirror. Her coworker waved her in. Charlie backed the engine into its spot in the bay.

The accident on the highway into town had been

bad. Both cars totaled. Fortunately everyone inside had been wearing seat belts and the air bags had done their thing. The passengers had walked away with only a few minor bruises. One of the cars had gone up in flames, but Charlie and her team had quickly taken care of that.

She got out of her gear and returned to the bay. The engine came first. Then she could clean up and get something to eat.

Michelle strolled over with two mugs of coffee. She handed one to Charlie and grinned. "You have a visitor."

Charlie held in a groan. "My mother?" Had Dominique waited?

"Not exactly." Michelle pointed.

Charlie turned and saw Clay leaning against the wall. When he caught her eye, he straightened and started toward her.

The man could move, she thought, watching his long strides. His body was perfection—a result of his career choice, she knew, but still impressive. The only thing better was his face. The lines and planes, the dark eyes. Her gaze drifted to his mouth and she wondered if he was going to kiss her again. Strangely, she found herself thinking she wouldn't mind. Well, except for the "in public" part.

"Hi," he said as he approached. "How was it?"

"Easy for us. Not so good for the people in the accident. Everyone is fine, but one of the cars caught fire. The other is totaled."

"Tourists?"

She nodded. "They get excited about their time away.

Sometimes they get distracted and sometimes it's just bad luck." She glanced around. "You didn't see my mother here, did you?"

"I don't know your mother."

"Some people have all the luck," she said with a sigh. "Petite." She held up her hand midway between her elbow and her shoulder. "Short, blond hair. Green eyes. Elegant."

"No. Haven't seen her."

"Good. She came by. I think she's decided to start haunting me early. You know, get in a few years of practice before she becomes a ghost."

"Sounds like a fun relationship."

Charlie's mouth twisted. "Oh, it's a thrill. I'm not sure why she's even here. Fool's Gold isn't her kind of place. She swears she wants to spend time with me, but that's just too strange to think about."

She paused, aware she was talking too much. A clear sign of nerves. It was being around him, she thought. Everything was different now. They'd kissed. They were going to have sex sooner or later. That was a point-of-view shifter.

There was also the fact that he'd promised a full-service seduction. She didn't know exactly what that meant. Even more confusing, she couldn't decide if she was more excited or more scared. The fact that she had any excitement at all was a real win for her. She told herself it was smarter to accept the progress than to question it but she wasn't that comfortable with the whole seduction idea.

"Stop," Clay said, holding up both his hands. "You're exhausting me."

"What are you talking about?"

"You're thinking too much. I can hear it. I knew you would be. That's why I came by. You need a schedule."

"Excuse me?"

He took her arm and drew her closer to the open garage door. "A schedule," he repeated, his voice quiet. "So you can know what to expect. And when. Then you won't worry so much."

She doubted her worry level was going to change significantly throughout the process, but she was willing to pretend so she didn't have to talk about it.

She folded her arms across her chest. "What did you have in mind? And while we're on the subject, how long is this going to take?"

He grinned. "The conversation or the full-service seduction?"

Heat burned on her cheeks. She knew she was blushing, damn him, and didn't know how to stop. "The, ah, doing it part."

He leaned close. "Seduction. Come on, Charlie. You can say it."

"I can also pick up a tire iron and beat the crap out of you."

"That's my girl. We'll take as long as you need. It's as much about the journey as the destination."

She glared at him. "Have you been taking yoga? Is this crazy yoga talk?"

"Trust me. You'll like it. All of it. That's the point.

To get you to where you can relax and enjoy. It's not going to happen in an afternoon."

Words to make her chest feel tight and maybe a little tingly.

She glanced behind her. No one was in the bay, but that didn't mean her friends weren't paying attention to Charlie and her visitor.

"We probably shouldn't discuss this here," she said.

"No problem. You're off tomorrow?"

She nodded.

"I'll come by in the morning. We can work on your schedule then."

She had a brief impression of notations on her calendar. September 3, 3:00 p.m. Clay gets to first base.

"Shift change is at seven." She thought about telling him that sometimes she stopped for coffee or breakfast and didn't get to her house until eight, but that seemed like too much information.

"See you tomorrow, then," he said.

He gave her a wave, then walked away. She allowed herself a couple of minutes to appreciate the view, taking in his very fine butt. She'd seen it plenty in pictures and in movies, but it was better in person. Just think, one day she would see it naked. Maybe even touch it. Having sex meant—

She came up against a mental wall and slammed right into it as reality took an unexpected turn. She and Clay were going to have sex. She'd asked him to do that with her. But what she hadn't considered was his part in all that. As in he would take his clothes off.

She was about to have the world's best-looking male model naked in her bed. What on earth had she been thinking? She wasn't beautiful or even pretty. She was too tall and too strong and not the least bit girlie. She didn't own any hair products or know how to do makeup. She'd never owned a curling iron. There were exactly two dresses in her closet and she would rather be gut-shot than wear a thong.

Talk about a disaster.

She couldn't do it, she realized. She couldn't go through with it. She needed a different type of man. One who was a few degrees closer to normal, and possibly desperate enough to be grateful. Now she was going to have to figure out how to tell Clay that he'd just been fired.

CLAY SAT ON Charlie's front porch steps and checked his watch. With shift change at seven, and Fool's Gold's nonexistent rush hour, she should be home any minute.

He'd stopped by Ambrosia's Bakery on his way over. He'd picked up an assortment of Danish, along with the coffee. He was comfortable bribing her with sugar as well as caffeine.

He'd been doing some reading on what rape victims went through as they recovered and the road to what Charlie would call normal wasn't always easy or straight. Partners were advised to be patient and pay attention to signals. He was willing to do both.

Right on time, her truck came into view. She drove into her small garage, then closed the door and stepped out the side door. She walked across the lawn and paused at the bottom of the steps.

She looked a little tired. He wondered if there had been a lot of calls in the night. Other than the dark circles, she was her usual slightly wary self. Her short hair stuck up at a couple of odd angles, as if she hadn't combed it since getting out of bed. Her face was bare, the skin smooth. She still wore her dark blue uniform and steel-toed boots.

But he saw past that to the feminine curves she hid behind shapeless clothes. He was sure she no longer thought about consciously being androgynous. That her style had evolved, first out of fear and then because it was what she did. Comfort mattered more than fashion to Charlie.

But beneath the baggy and shapeless attire was an impressively honed body. He'd seen her in shorts and a T-shirt during the volunteer workouts and he'd been impressed.

"You're here early," she said.

"I brought coffee." He held out the covered container. "And Danish."

She smiled. "Wanted to make sure I invited you in?"

"Something like that."

"Smart man." Her mouth twisted. "But I can't accept them."

"They're pastries, Charlie. Not an engagement ring."

Her shoulders squared and her chin came up. He recognized the body language. She was getting ready to do something unpleasant. He was a little surprised. He hadn't thought she'd get scared so fast.

"I can't do this," she told him.

"Have coffee and Danish?"

She drew in a breath. "No. The sex thing." She glanced to the side, then at the ground, before returning her gaze to his. "With you."

That was an unexpected kick in the gut. "Want to tell me why?"

"Because of who you are."

He checked the words for hidden meaning and couldn't find any. "I'm not a felon or married. What are you objecting to?"

"You." She waved at him. "This." Her hand moved up and down. "The total package."

He glanced down at himself. He had on worn jeans. He'd pulled a long-sleeved shirt over a white T-shirt, but hadn't bothered with the buttons. He had showered and shaved, so he knew he didn't smell.

He'd done his best to stay grounded in a business that had insisted on inflated egos with every level of success. Still, he'd looked in the mirror enough to know he'd been blessed with a great set of genes. Nothing he could take credit for, but he also wasn't going to ignore the obvious.

"At the risk of sounding like a jerk, you want someone better-looking?"

She made a strangled sound in the back of her throat. "No. I want someone closer to normal. Maybe even a guy who's a little desperate. You're so perfect. Physically. I can't—" She glanced around, then lowered her voice. "I can't be naked with you."

He relaxed. This was a problem he could handle. "Are you worried I won't be interested enough to get it up or that I'll be critical?"

She gulped air, then raced up the steps. "We're not talking about this."

He rose quickly and caught her before she could stick the key in the lock. He put his hand on her wrist. "We are. Which is it, Charlie. Tell me."

He was close enough to see the thousand shades of blue in her irises, the tiny lines at the corners of her eyes, the three freckles on her nose.

"Both," she admitted, her voice defiant. "Are you happy? It's both. I'm scared enough without dealing with having sex with some ass model."

"Ass model? That's dismissive. Slightly judgmental."

She pulled her hand free, then poked him in the stomach. "You have a six-pack."

"Most days, unless I eat Chinese. The salt is a killer."

"I'm not like other women."

"You have all the parts."

"They may not work."

He lightly touched her cheek. "They work. I know you're scared. We'll deal with that. Together. I'm willing, Charlie." He smiled. "Trust me, you don't have to worry about my mechanics."

"I've seen your mechanics. They're a little terrifying."

He leaned in. "Airbrushing."

Her eyes widened. "No way."

"Sorry to disappoint, but it's true. You know how they make models' legs longer in ads, or their teeth whiter?"

She nodded.

"They do the same thing for us. Make the bulge more impressive than it is. In person, I'm not all that."

The corner of her mouth twitched. "You're lying."

"You'll have to find out for yourself, won't you?"

The humor faded and she stared at him. "I am scared."

"I know."

"The message from my mother was to be feminine and men would like me. I tried and I got raped."

He touched her cheek again, enjoying how soft her skin was. "You don't have to change for me. I like you just the way you are."

She bit her lower lip, then nodded. "How many Danish?"

He laughed. "Three each."

"Then I guess you can come in."

She opened the front door. He collected the coffee and the bakery box and followed her inside to the kitchen. After grabbing a couple of paper towels, she motioned for him to join her at the table, in front of the window that opened out onto her backyard. She opened the pink box, then breathed in deeply.

"Heaven." She grabbed a cheese Danish and took a bite. Her eyes closed and she gave a low moan.

Clay stared at her, wondering if she knew how sexy

she was. There was nothing artificial about her. Just an in-your-face attitude. With Charlie, everything was on the table. He had a feeling that once she worked through her problems, she was going to be a guy magnet.

He took a cherry Danish and put it on the paper towel. "About the schedule," he said, pulling a pad of paper out of his shirt pocket. "What works for you?"

"Can't I finish my coffee before we talk about that?"

"Why not do both?"

"It's the morning. People don't have this conversation before breakfast."

"Sure they do. They have sex in the morning."

She chewed and swallowed. "You're just saying that to put me off my food. You think you can get an extra Danish."

He picked up his coffee and took a sip, then studied her over the container. "You don't think people make love in the morning?"

"No. Yuck. What about brushing your teeth?"

"You get up and go into the bathroom and brush your teeth. You can even pee if you want."

"That's romantic."

"It's better than wetting the bed."

She shuddered. "Can we change the subject?"

"Is it the idea of sex or bodily functions that bothers you?"

"I can deal with the peeing. I have medical training. I know how things work. It's just, really? Sex before lunch?"

"You're obsessed with meals."

"I like to eat." She stared at him. "This is all going to be normal, right? You're not one of those people who wants to wear fur handcuffs or anything, are you? Because that's not on my play list."

"You have a lot of rules."

"I like rules."

"I like breaking them." He stood and walked around the table, then held out his hand. "Come here."

Wariness darkened her eyes, but she put her hand in his and let him draw her to her feet. He walked to the sink and leaned against the cabinet, the small of his back braced against the counter. Then he pulled her in. She came to a stop about a foot away.

"Closer," he said quietly.

She took a single step.

He chuckled and put his hands on her waist. "All the way, little girl. We're going to have actual bodily contact. When we're done, you can have another Danish."

She pressed her lips together. "Can't you stand up so we're not touching there?" Her index finger pointed down to his crotch.

"Touching there is the point."

He felt her stiffen. He waited, hoping she wouldn't back up. Finally she inched forward another half step. He kept his hands on her waist, guiding her the rest of the way. Finally her hips settled against his.

He reminded himself this was a lesson and that reacting physically would be a bad idea. Still, she was warm and, despite her attempts to hide it, very much a woman.

They were at eye level with each other. He liked that.

He liked how she was strong and very much his equal. The combination of attitude and terror touched him in a way he hadn't expected.

"Hands here," he said, raising his arms and lightly tapping his shoulders.

She did as he requested.

"Breathe," he added.

"I'm breathing."

Barely, he noted. Shallow breaths would add to her anxiety, but his plan was to distract her. If it worked, she would forget to be afraid. If it didn't, she would probably give him a quick knee to the groin.

"Here's what's going to happen," he said softly. "I'm going to wrap my arms around you, but I won't pull you against me. You can break away anytime you want."

She listened intently, her eyes wide. He could hear the battle raging inside. Part of her wanted to get over her fear, but the rest of her wanted to bolt. This wasn't comfortable and Charlie didn't like being vulnerable.

He put his hands on her back, just below her bra. He splayed his fingers and pressed just firmly enough that she could feel him, but not so hard that she felt him urging her forward. If all went well, she would lean into him on her own.

"I'm going to kiss you," he continued. "You don't have to respond." He grinned. "It would be nice if you didn't slap me."

"I won't." She trembled slightly. "Okay. I'm ready."

He'd been hoping for a smile, but there was too much tension. His chest tightened with rage at the bastard who had done this and compassion for the woman he held. Then he closed his eyes and leaned in.

Her mouth was stiff as he brushed it with his, her body rigid. He moved slowly, gently, letting her get used to him kissing her. As he went back and forth, he felt something sticky. Icing, he thought and licked the spot.

Her breath caught and he felt her tense up even more. Fingers dug into his shoulders but not in a "take me, take me hard" kind of way. He drew back slightly, then pressed his mouth to her cheek.

From there, he kissed lightly, tenderly, moving to her jaw, then down her neck. He moved toward her ear and kissed the spot right behind it, lingering for a second. The fingers on his shoulders relaxed, as did her back. Her breathing deepened. He moved to her earlobe, brushing his mouth against it.

The return journey was just as slow. When he reached her cheek again he paused before touching his mouth to hers. He let the pressure linger and was pleased when she stayed relaxed.

He repeated the process on her other cheek, working his way down to her jaw, then along her neck. He was careful to stay high enough that she wasn't threatened. When he reached her earlobe, he lightly nibbled on the curve. He was rewarded with a soft gasp and her body eased a millimeter closer.

Slowly he moved his hands from her back to her face. He cupped her cheeks in his palms and stared into her eyes. Hers were wide with apprehension but less than they had been before. He also spied the first subtle signs of arousal. Flushed cheeks, parted lips, slightly dilated pupils.

"Charlie," he whispered, then touched his lips to hers.

For a second there was nothing. Then her mouth moved against his. Her arms eased around his neck and she leaned into him.

He held back, not wanting to startle her. He brushed his mouth back and forth, going slow. They stayed like that for several seconds, then she tilted her head a little and parted her mouth the tiniest bit.

He doubted she was aware of what she was doing, of the invitation. He would guess that back in high school, she'd had boyfriends and they'd made out. So kissing would be easier than anything else.

He dropped his hands to her hips. He wanted to ease around and put them on her butt, squeezing the curves. No, he thought, humorously. That wasn't what he wanted. He wanted to rip her shirt off her and feast on her breasts. Then he wanted her naked, sitting on the counter, so he could push into her with all he had.

The intense fantasy surprised and pleased him. His reaction was more than biological need. It was about wanting to be with a specific woman. Another sign of healing. Although he hadn't shared Charlie's concerns about his ability to perform, he was happy to be anticipating the journey…and the destination.

But that was a long way off. For now, it was enough to kiss her.

He brushed his tongue against her bottom lip. She

stayed where she was. He did it again, then slowly slipped inside her mouth. She hesitated a second before moving her tongue against his. Pleasure shot through him, followed by heat and wanting. He stayed in his head, knowing he couldn't get lost in passion. Not yet.

They circled each other, brushing tongues, deepening the kiss. She relaxed even more, her body leaning into his. He felt the pressure of her breasts against his chest. Her flat belly rested against his growing arousal.

She was still close, but they weren't touching. She rested her hands on his shoulders before sliding them down his chest to rest on his stomach. Her eyes were big and dark, her mouth swollen.

"Can I…" She paused. "Can I do what I want?"

The question sent a jolt of anticipation through him. "Does it involve knives?"

She laughed. "No."

"Then sure."

She leaned in and pressed her mouth to his. The kiss was light, barely there, then she straightened and looked at him. He watched her battle against her fear. He'd seen her work out, knew how strong she was. Charlie experienced life physically, rather than in her head. But she'd shut off the sensual side of herself for so long, he suspected she wasn't sure how to get it back.

He reached for her right hand. "Look at me," he said.

"I am."

"Trust me. Nothing is going to happen."

"What are you—"

Before she could complete the question, he took her

hand and pressed her palm against his erection. Her gaze followed the action and she stared at him. Immediately her body tensed and she took a step back. He let her pull back so she wasn't touching his penis anymore but didn't let go of her hand.

"The mechanics aren't going to be a problem." He kept his tone light as he spoke, rubbing her palm with his thumb. "In case you were wondering."

"Good to know."

"Charlie?" He waited until her gaze met his again. "Would you kiss me again? Please?"

She nodded once. A quick jerk of her head, then she stepped forward. Her arms went around his neck, her eyes closed then her mouth was on his. They stayed like that for several seconds before she relaxed against him. When her lips moved, he was still, letting her do all the work. He felt her tongue against his lip, but continued to not move. A sharp finger poked him in the ribs.

"Cooperate," she demanded.

He opened his eyes. "Did you want something from me?"

She gave him a smile. "I did. Now I've changed my mind."

He chuckled and wrapped both his arms around her. Without thinking, he hauled her against him and hung on tight. But instead of getting scared, she let her head rest on his shoulder.

Progress, he thought, ready to start the kissing again.

They were interrupted by the doorbell.

Charlie jumped, then leaped back. "I'm not expecting anyone," she said as she started for the living room.

He trailed after her only to find her looking through a window and shaking her head. The doorbell sounded again.

"You're not going to get that?" he asked.

She spun toward him and pressed her lips to her mouth. "Shh. It's my mother. If we're quiet, she might go away."

The sound of knocking followed the loud bell. A woman called, "Chantal? Are you in there?"

"Chantal?" he mouthed.

Charlie turned toward him and glared.

He grinned.

A minute or so later, the ruckus at the door stopped and Charlie sagged onto a sofa. "I really wish she hadn't come to town."

"You can't avoid her forever." He sat across from her, on the coffee table.

"I can try. I bet I'll be successful at it, too."

"So your name is really Chantal?"

Her gaze narrowed. "Don't even think about it."

"Fine. We'll talk about our sex schedule. I was going to say afternoon or evenings, but mornings seem to work for you."

She looked away, but not before he saw her blush. "My mother was just here. How can you even think about sex?"

"I'm a guy. I can think about sex nearly anytime. So what's your work schedule like?"

"I'm on the next two days. I traded shifts to help a friend."

"So the day after? Your place? We'll play escaped prisoner and the warden's wife?"

She laughed. "No, but we'll move forward with your plan."

"Good. I like my plan. Now about those remaining pastries. How many do I get?"

CHAPTER EIGHT

CHARLIE DROVE ONTO the Castle Ranch, parked her truck and climbed out. She'd spent the better part of an hour convincing herself it was okay to go ride her horse. Something she did nearly every day she was off. It was no big deal. Only it felt like a big deal. Because of the kissing.

Just a few hours before, Clay had stood in her kitchen and kissed her until she'd felt her world turn upside down. The things that man could do with his mouth, and she had a feeling he hadn't even been trying that hard.

Sure, she'd been nervous. Maybe even scared. But then she'd found herself relaxing and everything had been different. Better. Her lips still tingled and there was a sense of pressure low in her belly. That along with the thought of seeing him again kept her stomach churning. She was confused, but in a good way.

Which had made the decision to come ride Mason anything but easy. Because this was Clay's ranch, too. Or at least his mother's. And he was staying here. So the odds of running into him were decent. Once she saw him, she wasn't sure what to say or how to act. All circumstances the average fifteen-year-old would take for granted. She was definitely stunted on the man-woman front.

She climbed out of her truck and told herself that she was strong. If the situation got uncomfortable, she would simply hit someone. That would make her feel better.

She started for the corrals behind the stable. Shane usually let Mason out early so he could enjoy the late-summer weather. As she walked, she heard the rumble of a big engine and what she would swear was men yelling.

She doubled back and headed for the sound. As she came around the stables, she saw a massive flatbed delivery truck and a huge piece of farm equipment. Shane and Clay were literally climbing up and down the whatever-it-was, while another man shouted instructions.

"It's always like this."

Charlie turned and saw the delivery guy walking toward her. "Like what?"

He motioned to Clay and Shane. "This is nothing. I've seen lifelong friends go at each other over who was going to drive a Bobcat first. And this is a whole lot bigger than a Bobcat."

Charlie's knowledge of farm construction could fit in a teaspoon. She knew a whole lot more about how buildings came down than how they went up. She knew which beams were most likely to fall first in a fire and the safest way to cross a burning roof. But she knew nothing about the big-tired, drilling monster in front of her.

"What does it do?" she asked.

"Clears land. It'll dig up anything in its path. From what I heard, they're going to start farming some of the land. This'll get 'em ready in no time." The delivery guy grinned. "As soon as they stop fighting about who gets their turn first."

"Someone's going to teach them how, right?"

"That's his job." He motioned to the man shouting.

Charlie shook her head. "I guess an instruction manual is out of the question."

The delivery guy chuckled. "You got that right."

He headed back to his truck. Charlie watched Shane and Clay finally settle in the driver's seat and the one next to it. Clay was behind the wheel. The men shouted back and forth. She caught a word here and there, but knew this was something she couldn't understand. She drove her engine because it was her job. She enjoyed it but more for what it could do for the people in her town than because it was big and powerful.

Clay was such a guy, she thought indulgently as she walked back to the barn. A good guy who was taking extraordinary care of her. After their first session together, she was optimistic about her chances of getting to normal. Once that was accomplished, they could both get back to their lives. He would become a volunteer firefighter and start his Haycations, while she would figure out the best way to bring children into her world.

She hoped they would always stay friends. In a

town like Fool's Gold, they would run into each other often. He was going above and beyond with her and she wanted to make sure things were never awkward. *Something to remember,* she told herself as she went to collect her horse.

She smiled as she thought about how worried she'd been about seeing him. At least now she could enjoy her ride in peace. After all, she was merely a woman. There was no way she could compete against man nirvana— otherwise known as very big farm equipment.

CLAY MOVED THE résumés in front of him, switching which one was on the left, then discarding a couple. Two remained and he still didn't know what he was supposed to do.

He got up from the small desk in his bedroom at the ranch house and walked downstairs. Coffee wouldn't make the decision any easier, but getting a cup was a distraction.

He went into the kitchen and found Dante Jefferson standing by the window, staring out at the view. Dante was Rafe's business partner. A lawyer by trade and temperament, he hadn't been happy when Rafe had wanted to move the business from San Francisco to Fool's Gold.

Rafe had taken off on his delayed honeymoon about a week ago. Dante had driven in to take care of things in town while Rafe was gone.

"Settling in all right?" Clay asked as he collected a mug and moved to the always-full carafe.

"I brought one suitcase," Dante told him. "Unpacking didn't take long."

"What about the rest of your stuff?"

"I'm waiting."

"Refusing to pack in protest?"

Dante grinned. "Something like that." He looked out the window. "I miss the bay."

"It's warmer here than in San Francisco."

"It's warmer in hell, too. Doesn't mean I want to be there."

"You could have told Rafe you wouldn't agree to move the business."

Dante nodded. "I know, but he was so damned happy. All in love and beaming. It was disconcerting."

"Admitting to a moment of actual emotion?"

Dante turned and glared at him. "No. I'm a cold son-ofabitch and don't you forget it."

Dante was about Clay's height, with blond hair and dark blue eyes. He wore suits instead of jeans. Even now he had on a tie. Clay suspected it wouldn't be long until the town worked its magic and Dante fit in just like everyone else.

Clay poured his coffee, then turned back to Dante. "I have a business question."

"Need me to fly somewhere and file a brief? Because I'm happy to do it. New York? New York would be perfect."

Clay grinned. "Sorry, no." He thought about the résumés on his desk. "Rafe tell you about my Haycations idea?"

Dante nodded. "I did some research. There's a growing market for that kind of travel. Families like the chance to reconnect with each other and a simpler time. They can drive instead of fly to get here, which people like. What's the problem?"

"I need to hire a farm manager. I have plenty of theoretical learning, but not much in the way of practical experience. Based on that, I decided to get someone in for the first couple of years."

"Smart," Dante told him. "Hands-on education is best for a business like this."

Clay nodded, then drew in a breath. "I can't decide on the guy. I'm used to hiring a business manager or an accountant. This is different. I've narrowed it down to two guys."

"What are they like?"

"Nate is close to forty, experienced. He's worked on plenty of farms, has even helped one guy in Washington State start a vineyard. He knows how to get me where I want to go."

"And the other guy?"

"Ty is younger and less experienced." Clay hesitated. "I like Ty better. He seems more easygoing. But he's never done what I want to do and while he grew up on a farm, he has a lot less experience on his own."

"What does your gut say?"

"Ty," Clay admitted. "But my gut could be wrong. Nate makes the most sense. I don't know why I'm hesitating. He has good references. I checked them all and he gets positive reports from his previous employers."

The decision was important and Clay didn't want to make a mistake. He had something to prove. Ironically it wasn't to his brothers or even the town. This time he had something to prove to himself.

Dante shrugged. "You're going to have to pick one. If you make the wrong decision, you go back and correct it."

"Is that what you do?"

Dante chuckled. "I don't make mistakes. Didn't Rafe tell you?"

"No. He forgot to mention that."

"Sounds like him. Hogging all the glory." Dante walked over and patted Clay on the shoulder. "Trust your instincts. They're usually right."

He walked out of the kitchen. Clay watched him go, then stared out the window. The guys he'd hired to clear the land would be done by the first part of next week. He needed to make a decision by then.

He went back upstairs and stared at the résumés. Even though his gut said to go with Ty, he knew he needed the experience Nate had to offer. He picked up his cell, then dialed Nate's number.

DOMINIQUE STEPPED OUT of her car onto a very dusty driveway. She glanced down at her pale gray suede pumps and wondered if they would ever be the same.

"Beauty is a disposable asset," she murmured as she closed the car door and looked around.

She'd never been on a ranch before and hadn't known what to expect. There were horses in pens. She couldn't

see any cows, which was good. She wasn't one who enjoyed the presence of cows. Up on the hill was a large
open area with a—

She blinked, then stared. An elephant?

"Dominique?"

She turned and saw May Stryker standing on the
porch of the house.

"Is that an elephant?" she asked, pointing.

"Yes. Priscilla. We also have sheep and llamas. I
threatened my sons with a zebra a few months back,
but I was only kidding. How nice to see you. Why don't
you come inside?"

Dominique gave the elephant one more backward
glance before following the other woman into the house.

Yesterday, not knowing what else to do, she'd phoned
May Stryker and asked if they could meet. She had no
idea what to do about Chantal. Perhaps a woman with
several children would have some suggestions.

May led her into a shabby living room. The furniture should have been replaced years ago and the walls
were in need of fresh paint. Still, the room was a happy
place. There were family pictures everywhere, and fresh
flowers. Dominique always loved fresh-cut flowers.

"I made us tea," May said, taking a seat on the other
end of the sofa and motioning to the old-fashioned silver
tray she'd placed on the coffee table. "It seemed more
an afternoon beverage than coffee."

"Thank you," Dominique said, taking the delicate
cup and saucer May offered. She saw there were sliced

lemon wedges, a small pitcher of milk, along with sugar in a bowl. *Elegant,* she thought, relaxing a little.

May was probably her age, Dominique thought. Perhaps a little younger. Pretty enough, with dark hair and bright, intelligent eyes. She obviously hadn't tried to hold back time with injections or surgery. Dominique found that confusing, but perhaps ordinary people didn't have the same pressure to be perfect. What would it feel like to not worry about her appearance? To simply not care about every new line, every added pound? She couldn't imagine.

"How are you enjoying Fool's Gold?" May asked.

"I'm not sure. I haven't spent much time in small towns. The festival last weekend was interesting. I was surprised so many tourists came." She sipped her tea, not sure what else to say. She desperately wanted to talk about her daughter, but didn't know how to start.

A tall, handsome man walked into the room.

"Hey, Mom," he said as he crossed to May. "I'm heading over to Annabelle's." He leaned down and kissed her cheek. "Don't expect me before morning."

"I won't." May nodded at Dominique. "Shane, this is Charlie's mother."

Shane glanced at her, then smiled. "Nice to meet you, Mrs. Dixon."

"You, as well," Dominique said, startled by the name. No one had called her Mrs. Dixon in years. Not since Dan had passed. She had always been Dominique Guérin, the celebrated. Not Dominique Dixon, Dan's wife.

Shane murmured something in his mother's ear, then left. May watched him go. "He's engaged. My oldest, Rafe, was married a few weeks ago. Coming back to Fool's Gold has been so happy for all of us."

Dominique pressed her lips together, trying to hold in the words. But they had a life of their own and came out in a rush.

"Chantal hates me. She won't have anything to do with me. I've been to her house several times, but she doesn't answer the door. I tried to see her at the fire station, but there was an alarm and she left. I don't know what to do."

She stared at her tea, aware her eyes had that burning feeling again. Tears. She never gave in to tears. She'd danced with injuries that would have brought a linebacker to his knees and she'd never once let anyone suspect the pain. Why on earth would she cry now?

"How long have the two of you been estranged?" May asked quietly.

Estranged. What an odd word. "You're suggesting we were once close and something happened," Dominique said. "That's not true. We've never been close." She poured milk into her tea and stirred.

"Why not?"

"Many reasons. My work kept me traveling much of the time. I'm sure from the outside, the fame seems wonderful, but it's difficult. Draining. When I was home, I had rehearsals, press. And my husband. I wanted to spend every moment I could with Dan."

"Not your daughter?"

Dominique remembered what it had been like. "She had Dan. Chantal and her father were close." Too close, in Dominique's opinion. That man had worshipped his little girl. Sometimes she had wondered if he'd loved Chantal more than he'd loved her.

"That must have been a comfort to you," May said. "Knowing he was there to take care of your little girl."

"I was the star," Dominique snapped. "I'm the one who was important. But it was always Charlie this and Charlie that. He called her Charlie when I named her Chantal."

May smiled gently. "It must have been difficult to move between the stage and the regular world. To be a mother and a star. I would guess the lines blurred. But as I'm sure you know, it's important to let our children shine."

"Why? Chantal wasn't like me."

"But wasn't she special *to* you?"

Dominique knew the correct answer was yes. Of course. Her child was everything, her world, her reason for being. "I'm not that kind of mother."

"What kind?"

"The type who gives up everything. I wanted my life. My fans adored me. I danced for the president, for kings and queens. Was I supposed to give that up for a baby?"

"No. Not give it up. But Charlie is your daughter, not your staff. We have to be there for our children."

Dominique desperately wanted to leave. Nothing about this conversation was comfortable. Still, she needed things to change and she didn't know how.

"She's an adult. She doesn't need anything from me. She's made that very clear."

"Then you need to show her what you have to give."

"She should be taking care of me!"

May studied her. "Why?"

"What do you mean?"

"Why should Charlie do anything for you? Because you gave birth to her? Does she owe you for that?"

"It's what children do."

"And what do parents do?"

Dominique clutched the saucer in one hand and the cup in the other. She thought of all the movies where parents read to their children and played with them. Of Dan laughing with Chantal, tucking her in at night. She remembered Chantal bringing home a report card with a few A's on it and presenting it proudly. Dan had carried her on his shoulders and then put it on the refrigerator. Dominique had been busy with an interview.

She wanted to say that Chantal should care about her because of who she was. But the truth was the fans had all gone home a long time ago and when she'd been admitted to the hospital, the only people who had visited were those who worked for her.

She had nowhere to go and no one to truly care if she died tomorrow.

She put down her tea and faced May. "Pretend I'm from another planet and I've never seen parents and children together. Tell me what I need to do so that I can be Chantal's mother."

"CHAMPAGNE IS a classic for a reason," Clay said, pouring them each a glass.

Charlie eyed the liquid suspiciously. "You're trying to get me drunk?"

"If I wanted you drunk, I would have suggested tequila shooters. This is romantic."

Clay had shown up, as promised. This was their second lesson and she found herself even more nervous than she had been before.

Maybe it was the fact that they'd had an appointment. That had meant her thinking about what they might or might not do, which didn't make her burger from lunch sit very well at all. If she was tortured for three or four days, she might be willing to admit that some of her nerves came from anticipation. Because what had happened last time had been better than she'd expected. And every time she thought about them kissing, she got a little jolt. Or she had until he'd walked into her place.

Now she was just nauseous.

They sat on her sofa, in the living room. Although this was her place, she found herself uncomfortable. As if she didn't belong. She was all arms and legs, with nowhere to put them. Crap and double crap. She wanted to jump to her feet and tell him that she'd changed her mind. Only she hadn't and there was no way she was going to let fear win.

Holding in a sigh, she accepted the glass he offered and took a sip. The champagne was light and bubbly, without being too sweet. She didn't recognize the name on the label and wondered if it was expensive. Not that this was a date or anything, so there was no reason for him to spring for the good stuff.

She stared at him. "Should I reimburse you for that?" she asked, pointing to the champagne. "I didn't mean for you to have expenses."

One eyebrow rose. "No."

"But this is like a business deal."

"No."

She waited. "You're not going to say anything else?"

"On that subject? Unlikely."

"You're amazingly difficult."

He smiled. "Part of my charm. Drink up."

"Drink up? That's your idea of romance?"

He laughed and put his arm around her. "You're feisty. I like that."

She found herself leaning against him as he leaned against the sofa. He was warm and strong and the situation was less awkward than she would have thought.

"Feisty? That's what you call a spitting kitten. I'm a whole lot more dangerous than that."

"Not to me."

She glanced up at him, for once not the least bit concerned about how close he was. "I can be tough."

"You keep bragging, but I haven't seen any action."

"Excuse me?"

"You're all talk, Charlie. Admit it."

She started to sit up but the arm around her tightened, holding her in place.

"I'm willing to prove it," she grumbled. "When and where? I'll be there."

Instead of responding, he took the glass of champagne from her hand, set it on the table next to him, then lowered his head to hers and kissed her.

The movement was unexpected. One second she'd been ready to take him on and the next she was getting lost in the feel of his mouth on hers. The transition was seamless, shifting her from play to desire in a single heartbeat. There was no time for apprehension, no place for fear. The memory of their previous kisses had her relaxing into his embrace.

As he had before, he kept the kiss easy and light. He moved his lips back and forth, teasing, promising, allowing her to settle in to what they were doing. She shifted a little, angling toward him, then wrapping her arms around his neck.

She was aware of heat low in her belly. Of sensations growing, and a melting sort of fiery tingling. Her breasts began to ache. *Arousal,* she thought hazily. She sort of remembered this happening years before. Back in high school. Before the attack.

But while the memory of the rape was still floating around, it seemed less significant than it had. With Clay, she was safe. She knew that. So when his tongue lightly touched her bottom lip, she parted for him.

He slipped inside and she welcomed him with strokes and circles. She settled into the growing sense of need, welcoming the awakening of her body.

He continued to kiss her deeply. She was aware that he was holding himself slightly away from her, not touching his body to hers. Not letting his weight make her feel trapped.

She slipped her arms under his and rested her hands on his back. She traced the thick muscles, enjoying the way they rippled under her touch. He put his hand on her hip.

The casual act should have gone unnoticed. He'd done it last time. But in her present position—on her back, on the sofa, it was more intimate. She was aware of the light weight of his hand, of the heat from his fingers. At the same moment she was reminded of the growing ache in her breasts.

And then she knew. She wanted him to touch her breasts. She wanted to feel his hands and fingers touching her.

She believed in making a decision and accepting the consequences. But what worked in the rest of her life didn't seem to apply right now. Was it okay to move her hand? Should she wait for him to figure it out? How on earth did anyone get through all this without going crazy?

Clay raised his head. "Someone's lost interest."

"What?"

"You stopped kissing me back."

"Sorry. I was thinking."

"Big mistake." He moved his hand from her hip to her cheek. "Getting scared?"

"No. I'm fine."

His eyes were dark and filled with something she hoped was passion. There was an easy way to check, but in their current positions, she couldn't exactly look for an erection without being obvious.

"Then what?" he asked.

His voice was gentle. Concerned. Her gaze locked with his as the steady ache grew. She sucked in a breath, told herself she would survive whatever happened, then put her fingers on his wrist and slowly drew his hand down to her breast.

He continued to look in her eyes as he closed his hand over her breast. "I take it back," he murmured. "Think as much as you want."

His fingers moved lightly as he explored her. When he brushed across her nipple, she felt a jolt all the way down to her groin. Without thinking, she arched toward him and parted her legs. Before she could slam her knees back together, he was kissing her again, making it impossible to do anything but feel and kiss him back.

Sensation flooded her. He seemed to know exactly how to touch her so that her breath caught in her throat. Deep kisses competed with his hand touching every inch of her breast. He kept returning to her nipple, brushing it more firmly every time until he finally took it between his thumb and index finger and squeezed gently.

Another jolt had her holding in a moan. Images of him touching her without her T-shirt and bra filled her brain until she couldn't think about anything else. The wanting took on a desperate edge.

She broke free of the kiss and pushed him back long enough to pull off her shirt. She reached for her bra, only to stumble to a stop as reality intruded. What on earth was she doing?

Before indecision could take over, Clay was there, his hands reaching behind her to unfasten the hooks. Then he looked into her eyes.

"Hold it in place until you're ready," he told her.

He shifted on the sofa, angling toward her. He bent down and lightly kissed the side of her neck. Damp, hot kisses trailed from her left collarbone to her right, then back. Slipping lower and lower with each pass. She sagged back on the cushions and closed her eyes. The sense of safety returned, along with the desire.

Nice, she thought as his lips brushed her skin. Better than nice. She relaxed and tossed the bra to the side.

Seconds later his mouth settled on her breast. Warm, wet heat surrounded her tight nipple. He used his tongue to battle with the tip, then sucked deeply.

She was unprepared for the erotic ride. Desire flooded her as pleasure melted her bones. She couldn't breathe, couldn't speak, could only get lost in the delicious sensations washing through her body. She moaned and grabbed his shoulders. At the same time she arched her body toward his.

He moved to the other breast and caressed her the same way again. With each pull of his mouth, her body tensed. Need collected between her legs until she was ready to beg for relief.

He returned to kissing her mouth and used his hands on her breasts. She wrapped her arms around him, pulling him close, knowing she needed to crawl inside of him, or have him inside of her. Her blood was thick, her muscles trembled as every cell in her body awakened to the delight of this man.

"Clay," she breathed, an invitation in the word.

He sat up.

She sighed in relief, ready to rip off his clothes, her clothes, anyone's clothes.

But instead of undoing his shirt or reaching for his jeans, he bent down and collected her T-shirt, then carefully draped it over her. Then he stood.

She stared at him. "What are you doing?"

"Leaving."

She was amazed at how quickly passion could transform to anger. "What? You do that to me and then leave? We're not going to have sex?"

"You're not ready."

"You don't get to say what I am."

He leaned in and lightly kissed her. "I know that anticipation is better than fear. Trust me, Charlie. You're not the only one suffering."

As he straightened, she saw his erection straining at his jeans.

"Does it hurt?"

"Yes."

"Good." She pulled her T-shirt over her head and smoothed it into place. "Fine. Leave. Whatever. I don't care." She had more to say but noticed he wasn't looking at her face. Instead he seemed very focused on her braless chest.

He swallowed. "I want thirty seconds." His gaze

shifted to hers. "Just thirty seconds. Promise you won't get scared?"

She wasn't sure what he was asking, but nodded anyway.

He took a step toward her, then another. He reached for her and pulled her against him.

She went willingly. Unafraid, as he'd asked. They'd hugged before. What was the big deal? Then his arms tightened and his mouth settled on hers in a kiss unlike the others.

Where before he'd been gentle, this time he was a man on the edge. Passion radiated from him as he swept into her mouth, claiming, demanding. He was intense and hungry, his hands roaming over her body. He squeezed her rear, digging into the curves, before circling around to cup her breasts.

When he stepped back, they were both breathing hard.

"Are you okay?" he asked. "Did I—"

She put her fingers on his lips to silence him. There was nothing he could have said to make her understand. But the actions spoke volumes. In that moment, he'd been as vulnerable as she. Passion equalized.

"Thank you," she whispered.

He managed a shaky smile. "For what it's worth, it's going to be a long night."

He kissed her on the cheek, then walked out. She watched him go and knew that whatever happened, she would always be grateful. Clay had shown her that healing was possible and that being like everyone else wasn't just a wish.

CHAPTER NINE

"CHARLIE HAS DONE her usual excellent job of weeding out the candidates who aren't going to be able to handle the program," Olivia said. She turned to Charlie. "You make any of them cry?"

Charlie groaned. "I don't take pleasure in that. Why do you always act as if I do? I only want to make sure that everyone is prepared for the work involved and the physical requirements. It's not personal."

"That was a yes," another captain said with a grin.

"You make me sound like a monster," Charlie grumbled.

"No. You do your job." Olivia tapped the thin stack of applications. "We have more men this time. Always interesting integrating them into our department. Everyone ready?"

There was a murmur of consensus.

Olivia was weeks away from being promoted to Battalion Chief of Training for the department, so she was the one running the meeting. Charlie had been through the winnowing process enough times to know what was coming. Every applicant was discussed in detail. At least two firefighters would have interviewed the candidates and Charlie had taken them through three preliminary training sessions. It was rare for her assessment to conflict with the interview findings. In her experience, applicants had everyone's support or no one's. It made the process go more smoothly.

They worked through three potential volunteers, accepting one, dismissing two, before starting on Clay's paperwork.

Charlie went first, as she had on the others. "He's at the top of the class and by a wide margin," she began. "Physically, he's in excellent shape and he follows orders."

"He did well on my interview," Michelle said with a grin. "As much as I could concentrate on it."

"Did he offer to show you his ass?" another firefighter asked.

"No, which is too bad, because I'm sure I would have looked. Touching would have gotten me into trouble, but it might have been worth it."

Charlie didn't like the way the conversation was going. Not only because hearing them talk about Clay this way made her chest feel all tight, but because he deserved better.

"Could we be focused, people? Clay has everything we're looking for."

"And more," Olivia said with a wink. "But no from me."

Charlie stared at her. "What?"

Her captain shrugged. "Come on, Charlie. Be serious. Sure, he's physically fit and yes, he passed the interviews. I have no doubt he'd do fine on the psych exam, but so what? He's not someone we can depend on. We put a lot of money into training our volunteers. We need to know we can count on them. I'm not going to spend money on a butt model."

Charlie felt her temper rising slowly to the surface. "You're telling me you're not going to give him a chance because he's too attractive?"

"No. He's unreliable."

"What is that based on? He was on time to each of my classes and stayed to the end." She turned to Michelle. "Was he late to the interviews?"

"No, but…"

Charlie waited.

Michelle sighed. "He was on time."

Charlie turned back to Olivia. "So how is he any more or less dependable than the other candidates?"

"You know what he is," Olivia told her.

"No. I don't. What I know is he's interested and meets all our criteria. But that you don't want to give him a chance. Wow, this is kind of like saying if someone wears glasses he or she must be smart. Or if a girl is too pretty, she can't be intelligent, too. If he were a woman, we wouldn't be having this conversation. We would, in fact, be going out of our way to make sure we were fair to her. I'm shocked that this is the message we want to send to the department and the community."

Charlie stared at the other women at the table, genuinely surprised by the fact that they weren't giving Clay a fair chance.

Olivia shifted in her seat. "You're making this a big deal. Why do you care if he gets into the training program or not?"

"Because I do a lot of the training and he's the best one we have. It pisses me off that he's being dismissed because of how he looks. Probably because it's happened a lot to me, but for very different reasons."

Michelle drew in a breath. "She's right. He knew more than the others. Not just about firefighting in general, but how we do things here. He's put time into his research. Charlie has a point. Refusing to consider Clay because of how he looks or what he was doesn't speak very highly of us."

Olivia wasn't pleased. "Fine. We'll put him in the program, but if he screws up even once, he's out."

"No," Charlie told her boss. "I don't agree with that. We have very specific rules in place and consequences. If Clay breaks the rules, then the same consequences apply to him as they would to anyone else."

"Whatever." Olivia made a note on the list. "Who's next?"

"I WAS so angry," Charlie said at lunch. "They practically called him a piece of ass. It never would have happened if he were a woman. I don't get it. I've been dismissed because of how I look. I know how it feels. Most of them do, too. So why are they acting like this?"

Annabelle reached across the table and grabbed a French fry from Charlie's plate.

"Is that allowed?" Patience asked with a smile. "The fry, I mean. Not how the meeting went."

Charlie eyed the other two women's lunches, noting the big pile of greens in bowls. "If you don't want salad, why do you order salad?"

"Because I don't burn a million calories at my job and I'm as tall as a mushroom," Annabelle said, then popped the second half of the fry into her mouth.

"I like the pretense of eating healthy," Patience told her.

Charlie sighed and turned her plate so the fries were facing the other two, then motioned to Jo who stood by the bar.

Jo grinned. "They're stealing again?"

"It happens every time."

"I'll bring out more as soon as they're ready."

"Thanks."

Charlie picked up her burger. "What was I saying?"

"You were ranting," Patience told her. "It was a good rant. I admire your ability to say what you think. My daughter's good at it, too."

"Lillie is good at a lot of things," Annabelle said. "She's so fun when she comes to the library. But we were talking about Clay and the meeting."

"I've seen him around town," Patience said, then sighed. "Wow. He's seriously good-looking. It's like he's not really one of us. I admire you standing up for him."

Annabelle, who knew a little more of what was going on with Clay, looked amused and concerned at the same time. Charlie had a feeling she was going to get a talking-to fairly soon.

"Me, too," Annabelle told her. "And I'm surprised that it was an issue. I thought we were more evolved than that."

"They think he's going to be flaky. That he won't follow through. If he'd given them any reason for that, I would totally support their concern. But he hasn't. He's shown up when he's supposed to and done what he's told."

"An excellent quality in a man," Patience said, her eyes twinkling. "I like him already."

"Interested?" Annabelle asked causally, keeping her gaze on Charlie.

Charlie forced herself to take a big bite of her burger and chew as if she hadn't felt a single twinge of jealousy. That sharp pain in the region of her heart was just, um, preindigestion.

"Wish I could be, but no. My ex cured me of ever being willing to trust a man again." Patience's smile turned rueful. "Not as much for me as for Lillie. Ned wasn't interested in being a dad, so he signed away his rights to her. I'm not interested in breaking her heart a second time."

"Not all guys are jerks," Annabelle told her.

"I've heard the rumors. So far I don't believe they're true. Although your guy is pretty special."

"I know," Annabelle said with a sigh.

"Oh, the fries are ready." Patience got up and walked toward the bar.

Annabelle watched her go, then leaned forward. "Be careful," she said in a low voice. "About Clay."

"I wasn't reacting emotionally," Charlie whispered. "I defended him because it was the right thing to do."

"I agree, but I'm worried about you."

"We're just friends."

"You're having sex."

"Not yet, but soon." Anticipation sent an odd heat burning through to her thighs.

Her friend looked at her. "You're messing with forces you can't control."

"You sound like a sci-fi movie."

"Great truth can be found there. I'm serious, Charlie. I'm glad you're healing and it's great that Clay is helping, but things happen when a woman has sex. It's difficult not to get emotionally involved."

Charlie saw Patience was chatting with Jo. "I know," she said quietly. "He's helping me. Nothing more."

"You're trusting him with something intimate. What you do will affect you more than you think."

"I know myself. I'll be fine."

Patience returned with the fries. "Jo was saying all the hotel rooms in town are booked for the Fall Festival. That's one of my favorites."

"Mine, too," Charlie said. "I'm a sucker for candied apples."

Annabelle shook her head, as if accepting Charlie wouldn't listen, and joined the conversation.

Charlie appreciated her concern, but knew the truth. She wasn't at risk of falling for Clay. She knew exactly what she was doing and what was going to happen when they sealed the deal, so to speak. He was a way to get what she wanted—emotional healing that would allow her to be the best mother possible. She had no expectations for anything beyond his tutorial skills.

DOMINIQUE RANG THE bell and waited. She knew there was an excellent chance her daughter would leave her standing on the porch, but part of May's advice had been not to give up. Dominique planned to be as persistent as necessary.

She had several pages of notes from her afternoon at the other woman's house. None of it made sense to her, but she understood that she had to do something. The alternative was to give up and leave. An attitude that did not get one very far in life. Dominique was willing to admit she had flaws, but not being willing to do the hard work wasn't one of them.

She waited for several seconds, then pressed her finger on the bell again, this time not letting up until Chantal flung open the door and stood in front of her.

"I was coming," she said defensively. "I was in the back of the house."

"You were hoping I would go away. You've been avoiding me."

Her daughter's mouth twisted, perhaps in annoyance, perhaps in frustration. But instead of denying the obvious, she stepped back and motioned for Dominique to enter.

"No bodyguard?" Chantal asked.

"He's back in Los Angeles for a few weeks. He'll return soon enough."

Chantal led the way to a smallish living room. There was a worn sofa and a couple of chairs. The fireplace was nice—original, Dominique thought.

"This house has good bones," she said, settling on a sofa cushion. "But the wall color is drab and your fabric choices are plain. Whoever you hired as a decorator should be fired."

Charlie wore worn jeans and a T-shirt. Her feet were bare, as was her face. Her hair stood in unruly tufts, as if she'd been running her fingers through it.

Now she put her hands on her slim hips and sighed. "That's why you're here? To criticize my house?"

"No. Of course not." Dominique wanted to point out she'd simply been offering an opinion. She replayed the words and thought perhaps they had sounded critical, although that hadn't been her intent.

Chantal reluctantly sat in a chair, her arms crossed over her chest.

She looked so much like Dan, Dominique thought. The familiar ache, the pain of missing the only man she'd ever loved, returning to prod her heart. His eyes, his smile. Certainly his build.

He had loved her so much. She had been the center of his universe. And then Chantal had been born and he'd given much of that love to his daughter.

Dominique understood that it was good for a father to love his children, but she'd never understood his total devotion. She'd felt as if she'd lost the only thing that had ever mattered. Because being who she was and having all the accolades had never been as important as Dan's love.

"Are you all right?" Chantal asked.

"Yes. Of course. I was thinking about your father. He adored you."

Her daughter gave her a genuine smile. "He was great. I still miss him."

"I do, as well. He was such a wonderful man." Dominique put her hands in her lap and glanced around the room. "The windows are very nice."

"Thank you."

"You own the house?"

"Yes. I bought it shortly after I moved here."

"Why Fool's Gold?"

What she really wanted to ask was "What possessed you to choose this ridiculous little town when you could have lived in New York or Los Angeles" but felt that might sound slightly judgmental. May had told her to be accepting. To try to think about things from her daughter's point of view.

"I fit here," Chantal told her. "I'd been living in Portland when I came here on vacation."

"Maine?"

"Oregon."

"You lived in Oregon?"

Chantal smiled. "It's nice there."

"I doubt I'd like it. Too much rain. The weather is better here."

"They have seasons."

That established, they both looked around the room. Dominique was aware of the silence, of the awkwardness. How she didn't know what to say to her own child.

Chantal drew in a breath. "Mom, are you here for a reason?"

Dominique wasn't sure if she meant visiting at that moment or in Fool's Gold in general, but decided it was time to speak the truth.

"I was recently diagnosed with colon cancer."

Chantal stared at her. "That sounds bad. What do the doctors say? Are you going to be all right?"

The words were correct and there was a hint of concern in her voice, but Dominique was aware that her daughter didn't move toward her. There was no comforting hug offered. Until that moment, she hadn't realized a hug was exactly what she needed.

She shook off the weakness and squared her shoulders. "I'm fine. I had surgery and they got it all. But it was extremely unpleasant. Everyone talking about my bowels. A very undignified episode."

Her daughter's mouth twitched. "You're saying it would have been better if it had been a different body part?"

"Of course. But that's irrelevant. My time in the hospital reminded me of what's important. That's why I'm here. To spend time with you. We're family. We should be close."

One didn't need to be Chantal's mother to read the trapped expression in her blue eyes. "It's not something we can order off a take-out menu. Neither of us is very good at relationships."

Dominique wanted to protest. She was very good with people. She'd always handled the press extremely well. But she supposed Chantal meant personal relationships. Emotionally intimate ones.

"Your father was," she said instead. "Everyone loved being around him."

"I remember." Chantal smiled. "Whenever he came to school for a program, all my friends talked about him."

Dominique wanted to ask if they'd ever talked about her. After all, having a famous mother was certainly more interesting. But she held back the words, unexpectedly understanding this was not a moment about her.

With that insight came the uncomfortable realization that her constant need for attention wasn't about feeding an ego, but instead filling a void inside. Silencing the cruel voice that whispered she was one false step away from losing it all.

"Want to go get a cup of coffee?" her daughter asked unexpectedly. "Come on, Mother, we'll walk over to Starbucks. I'm buying."

"That sounds nice," Dominique murmured, thinking being outside might help. At least there would be more to talk about.

Five minutes later they were on the sidewalk and walking the few blocks to the center of town. Despite the fact that it was the middle of the day, there were plenty of people out, enjoying the perfect September weather.

Several of the women they passed either waved to Chantal or called out her name. A little girl of maybe six or seven ran over and motioned for Chantal to bend down. The girl whispered in her ear and then ran back to her mother.

Chantal laughed, then turned to Dominique. "Her grandmother has a cat who insists on climbing trees. He's on the chunky side and has trouble getting down, so I go out and rescue him."

"You climb a tree to rescue a cat?"

She nodded. "He's rarely grateful, but his owner is."

"You're risking your neck for a cat?"

"That's what I do. I take care of people here."

"If there's a fire."

"Not just fires. We show up at car accidents, or if a kid gets stuck somewhere."

Dominique didn't understand any part of her daughter's work. "Aren't there men who can do your job better?"

Chantal's eyes turned icy. "No. There aren't. I'm damned good at what I do. I work hard and I find the job rewarding."

Dominique sensed she'd made a misstep somewhere, but didn't know how it had happened. "I'm not saying you're not competent. It's just so dangerous. Wouldn't you rather do something safer?"

"Not really."

"I just don't understand."

"Hardly news."

They crossed the street. As they walked by a hair salon, a woman rushed out. She was in her twenties, with brown hair and brown eyes. *Not the least bit remarkable,* Dominique thought. It must be difficult to be ordinary.

Chantal stopped. "Patience, hi."

"Hi yourself." The other woman handed over a book. "I finished it and it's as wonderful as I thought. Very sexy. These days I have to get my thrills in romance novels. At least that guy always turns out to be one of the good ones."

Dominique saw a brightly colored cover and an author's name she didn't recognize. Chantal read romances? Dominique had always enjoyed them, as well. Something for them to talk about, she told herself.

"Patience, this is my mother. Dominique—"

"Dixon," Dominique said, interrupting. "Dominique Dixon."

"Nice to meet you," Patience said, shaking her hand. Her head tilted. "How strange. You remind me of someone. My daughter is crazy about ballet and she has several DVDs starring a beautiful ballerina who…" She paused and laughed. "I'm being silly. Never mind."

Chantal raised her eyebrows, as if waiting for Dominique to announce she was the beautiful star of those DVDs.

"I've always been a fan of ballet," Dominique said instead. "Discipline for the soul and the body. I hope she continues with it."

"Me, too. But she's nine. Who knows what will capture her attention tomorrow." She glanced back at the salon. "I've got to get back. Eddie Carberry is getting a perm and if I don't watch her every second, she starts messing with the curlers. Nice to meet you Mrs. Dixon."

"Call me Dominique."

Patience waved and ducked back into the building.

Chantal pointed to the Starbucks across the street. "When did you start going by Dixon?"

"I prefer it from time to time. There's no need for your friends to know who I am, so Dixon makes more sense while I'm here." Something she had just that second decided, but was pleased with her generosity.

"You're assuming I haven't told them who you are."

"Have you?"

"Not all of them."

They ordered their drinks, then took them outside to a free table. Dominique was careful to sit out of the sun. Laser treatments might erase unsightly age spots, but the damage never really went away.

"I remember when little girls would run up to me and beg for an autograph," Dominique said with a sigh. "It's been a long time since anyone recognized me."

"You're still beautiful, Mom."

Dominique picked up her coffee. "I'm old and don't fit anywhere. Fame is fleeting. I'd heard that, of course, but never believed it. You're much smarter than me. You have a place where you belong. It will still be here when you're my age." She managed a shaky smile. "Unless the big one comes and California falls into the ocean."

Chantal smiled back. "The tectonic plates are moving toward each other, rather than away. So we're not at any risk of disappearing under water. At least not from an earthquake."

"Good to know."

She put down her coffee and studied her daughter. Chantal had decent skin and nice bone structure. But her hair was a disaster, as were her clothes.

"Do you ever wear makeup?"

Chantal's expression tightened. "This was great, Mother, but I have to go."

Dominique realized how her question had been interpreted. "I wasn't being critical. I was just asking. I wondered if not wearing it is a personal choice or because you don't know how to apply it. You could be quite attractive."

"In the right light?"

"Lighting can be a woman's best friend. I could show you a few tricks. If you're interested."

"Maybe another time."

Dominique sensed she'd made another mistake, but wasn't sure where or how. Defeat weighed heavily on her shoulders.

"I'm sure you have things to do," she said at last. "We'll talk again later."

The relief in her daughter's eyes was as painful as her eager escape. Dominique sat with her coffee, grateful the bright sunshine made it reasonable to put on her sunglasses. The fake smile on her lips and the dark glass over her eyes hid the flood of tears she did her best to blink away.

CHAPTER TEN

"She makes me insane," Charlie ranted before digging her fork into Kung Pao Beef on her plate. "She shows up here, with no warning."

Clay sat across from her at her kitchen table and picked up his beer. The room was cozy, with only a couple of lights on and the curtains pulled.

"This morning, or are you talking about her being in Fool's Gold?" he asked.

"Either. Both. I'm not picky. But she is. She insulted my house, she practically clucked over my hair. Or maybe my clothes. Then she started talking about makeup. I don't wear makeup. I don't get it... I don't want to. I'm not like her. That's the real problem. She was hoping to give birth to a miniature version of herself. Instead she got me."

"Then she was lucky."

Charlie smiled at him. "Good line. You know, you're more than a pretty face."

"Thank you. I try."

"I wish she wasn't here."

"I got that."

Charlie took a bite, chewed and swallowed. "Even

saying that, I feel guilty. She was sick." She told him about the colon cancer. "But true to form, she complained about everyone talking about her bowels. I guess it wasn't an elegant enough disease for her."

Clay grabbed an egg roll. "You're torn. You don't want to have anything to do with her, and you're sorry she had cancer. But thinking about the cancer makes you worry about what she expects from you. It's a lot."

He was insightful, she thought. And not just for a guy. "I'm a horrible daughter because I would like her to simply go back to New York or London or wherever she came from and leave me alone."

"Is that likely?"

"I don't think so." She sighed. "Okay, I don't want to talk about her anymore. Let's talk about you."

"My favorite subject."

She laughed. "I happen to know that's not true, but we'll go with it. How's the Haycation plan coming?"

"I'm making progress."

She studied him. "The words sound good, but you're worried. What's wrong?"

"Self-doubt."

"It's a new venture. Of course you're concerned. Anything specific or just general nerves?"

"I'm a guy, Charlie. I don't have nerves."

"My mistake."

He shrugged. "I hired a farm manager. I had a choice of two and went with the guy who had more experience. Nate."

"But?"

"My gut wasn't happy."

"You should listen to your gut."

"This time it was wrong."

"If it was wrong, why aren't you happy with your decision?"

"I don't know."

She scooped more rice onto her plate, thinking he did know the answer, but didn't want to admit it. "So you have Nate and big farm equipment. That has to make you happy."

"I'll feel better when I get my crop in the ground."

She laughed. "Not a sentence you ever imagined yourself saying?"

"Not really, but it feels good."

"What is the magic crop?" she asked.

"Fall alfalfa."

"Which is different from spring or summer alfalfa?"

"It is."

"Would it make you feel all manly and powerful to explain the difference?"

"I believe it would."

They continued to talk over dinner.

"Ready to start serious training next week?" she asked.

"You don't scare me."

"I'm not sure I want to." She was more concerned about getting everyone to behave. "You tend to bring out the other men's spirit of competition."

"Sometimes. The guys in the group aren't a problem, but in other situations there can be assumptions."

"Someone wants to pick a fight simply because of who you are?"

"Sure."

"Which is why you have a black belt."

He grinned. "I had to protect the moneymakers."

She wondered which had been more lucrative. His face or the rest of him.

"What's that old saying?" she asked. "Men want to be you, women want to have you? Are the women easier to handle?"

"I tend to ignore the invitations. When I was first starting out in the business, I took advantage of the offers. That got old pretty quickly. I grew up, figured out what I wanted and was a lot more particular."

"Then you were married. Ever tempted to stray?"

He stared directly into her eyes. "Not even once. I don't have that itch. When I fell in love with Diane, I stayed in love with her. Even when we fought, I never thought about it." He reached across the table and touched her hand. "I'm not going to see anyone else while we're doing this."

His fingers were warm against her skin. She turned her hand so she could squeeze his back and smiled. "I wasn't hinting. I know we're in an unusual circumstance, as my mother would say."

"Either way. I'm with you until we see this through."

He flashed her a smile that had her clenching her insides.

He released her hand and rose. "Speaking about our

arrangement, I've been thinking about the lesson for tonight."

"Have you?"

She stood, aware that her skin seemed to be extra tingly. Anticipation hummed through her. She was ready for whatever he offered, especially if it involved more touching and kissing.

He reached for the hem of his T-shirt and pulled it off. "I decided we'd get you comfortable with the idea of being naked."

Charlie stared at Clay's bare chest. Of course she'd seen it before—on billboards, in magazines. But this was different. This was right in front of her—live and pretty damned close to perfect.

She tucked her hands behind her and stepped back. "I don't want to get naked in front of you. I just ate. My stomach will stick out and I don't look like those girls in the magazines."

He moved closer, cupped her face in his hands and kissed her. "Have I mentioned how much I like that you're honest?"

"No and you saying that doesn't solve the problem."

He stared into her eyes. "There's no problem."

"There is for me."

Unless today's lesson just involved him getting naked and she could keep her clothes on. Because she was good with that option.

He reached down and grabbed her hands, then put them on his chest. "Touch me."

A plea she couldn't ignore, she thought splaying her

fingers against his warm skin. Still looking into his eyes, she let herself explore the solid muscles of his chest and belly. She felt the individual ridges of his six-pack, the slight curve of his pecs. His shoulders were broad, his arms defined.

He was taller than her. Stronger. Masculine enough to make her feel feminine. Sort of. She circled behind him, still stroking him, liking the sense of being in control.

His jeans sat low on his hip. She traced the line of his waistband, then slid her palms up his back.

She stepped closer, pressing her front to his back. She rested her cheek against his back and wrapped her arms around his waist. He put his arms over hers, holding her in place. Then he reached for his belt and the button at the waistband of his jeans.

She felt his jeans hit the floor. He eased away enough for briefs to follow.

Charlie wondered how on earth she'd come to have Clay Stryker and his million-dollar ass naked in her kitchen.

She stood behind him, her arms at her side, not sure what to do or where to look. He started to turn around but she yelped and grabbed his arm.

"Don't do that."

"Don't do what?"

"Face me. I'm not ready."

"It's just a penis. You've seen them before."

"The last one attacked me."

"Mine is more well mannered." His voice sounded as if he were amused.

She glared at his back. "Are you laughing? This isn't funny."

"It's a little funny."

She tightened her grip on his arms. "I could leave a bruise, mister."

"You could, but you won't. You're going to have to look at me eventually."

"Not necessarily. We could do it in the dark."

"Where's the fun in that? I like looking. Did I ever tell you my ass was insured for five million dollars? It was for the vodka campaign."

The switch in topic had her stepping back and studying the body part in question. While she hadn't seen that many, she had to admit Clay's was by far the best. High, tight, muscled. He had dimples and long powerful legs.

"Would you get any of the money?" she asked. "If something had happened?"

"Nope. It would go to the company."

She put her hand on his hip. "You don't have any tattoos."

"I don't like needles. Hug me again, Charlie. I like how that feels."

She drew in a breath, then moved closer, again pressing her front to his back. As she was fully clothed, she couldn't feel his skin against hers, but knowing he was naked still seemed to change everything.

She placed her hands on his belly, one above the other and tried not to think about what was below. To distract herself, she lightly kissed him on his left shoulder blade. She liked how that felt, so she did it again.

"Nice," he murmured. "You could take your shirt off. Maybe your bra."

She considered the offer. She would like to feel her breasts pressing against him. "Okay, but you won't turn around."

"Not even if it kills me."

She pulled off her T-shirt and quickly unfastened her bra. She hung both over the back of the kitchen chair, then eased up behind him, sliding her hands around his body. Then she leaned close, her breasts nestling into his back.

She returned to kissing him as she had before, only this time she also moved her chest back and forth, dragging her nipples against his skin. The friction aroused her, making her breathing more shallow and igniting heat between her thighs. She added little nips to the kisses, biting gently, then soothing that spot with her tongue.

A shudder rippled through him. His muscles tensed then relaxed. Knowing she was playing with fire but unable to resist, she eased her hands to his hips and slid partway down.

When she stopped, Clay swore.

"Charlie."

Her name came out as a growl. Rather than frightening her, his need gave her courage. She moved her right hand toward his erection. She'd barely moved an inch when his fingers covered hers and he guided her into place.

She closed her hand around his penis. He was big and thick, plenty hard. She explored the length of him, circling her fingers over the tip, before sliding back to the base. Instead of fear or even apprehension, all she felt was desire. Wanting made her tremble and when she thought about him turning and pushing into her, her breath caught in her throat.

She straightened, prepared to turn him to face her, when his cell phone rang. The sharp high notes of his ringtone cut through the silence.

"Ignore it," Clay told her.

"Gladly."

She released him and stepped back, then put her hand on his arm. He shifted toward her. She kept her gaze on his face, determined to stay in the mood and not get scared. The passion in his eyes thrilled her. He might have taken her on as a project, but he was a man who was enjoying his work.

He held out his arms and she went into them eagerly. She raised her head, desperate for his kiss, his touch. Her phone rang.

Charlie drew in a breath. "Someone thinks it's important," she said and turned to grab her phone.

"Hello?"

"Charlie? It's Shane. Is Clay there?"

"He is. Just a second."

She handed over the phone. "Shane."

As Clay took the receiver, she retrieved her shirt

and pulled it on, then she leaned against the counter and waited, hoping nothing really awful had happened. There were only a handful of reasons Clay's brother would have chased him down and very few of them were good.

"You're sure?" Clay asked, after listening for about a minute. "It's not a mistake?"

He swore under his breath. "I'll be right there." He pushed the end button on her phone and handed it to her.

"Sorry. There's a problem at the ranch. I have to go." As he spoke, he pulled up his briefs and then slipped on his jeans.

She watched him dress, aware she was disappointed rather than relieved. A win for her, although she was sorry Clay had to deal with something difficult.

He gave her a quick kiss. "I'll call you," he promised as he jogged to the front door.

Then he was gone.

She stood alone in the kitchen, aware the "I'll call you" statement hadn't been part of their deal. She assured herself it was an automatic response. It wasn't as if she and Clay were involved on an emotional level. Still, she found herself glancing at the phone and wondering when that call would occur.

THE NEXT MORNING the news wasn't any better. Clay stood by the side of what should have been his alfalfa field, unable to grasp what had happened.

In an effort to get the land cleared ahead of schedule, Nate had gone out to put in a couple of hours after dinner. The days were still long and the weather was good. He'd been doing his thing, minding his own business, when the metal teeth had pulled up something that shouldn't be there. Human bone.

Annabelle squeezed his arm. "I'm so sorry," she told Clay.

"Me, too."

"I might be wrong."

"Not likely."

"You don't know that."

"I'm pretty sure."

The area he'd wanted for his alfalfa field was smack over a Máa-zib burial site.

Shane had called Annabelle right after he called Clay. She had a minor in Máa-zib studies. She'd taken one look at the partially uncovered grave and had given him the bad news. Sure enough, just walking over the area had been enough for them to see at least two other graves.

Clay wasn't sure exactly how these things worked, but he knew the bottom line was he would lose at least a couple of acres to the city, maybe the state. Worse was the time that was lost and the nagging sense that the graves were an omen of more to come.

"We have company," Annabelle said.

He turned and saw several older women walking toward him. He recognized the mayor and a few of the city-council members. Despite wearing a suit and low heels, the mayor still looked completely comfortable as she walked over tilled soil.

"I understand we have an important discovery," the mayor said as she approached. "Very exciting."

Clay shook her hand. "You'll excuse me if I don't share your enthusiasm."

"Of course. You see this as a setback. I suppose in the short-term it is. But not to worry, Clay. I have every confidence in what you're going to accomplish."

Clay wished he could say the same about himself. Having doubts had been bad enough, but this was a serious problem.

Mayor Marsha turned to Annabelle. "Thank you for recognizing the find. This is going to be so interesting for the experts." She smiled. "They'll start complaining about how we keep calling them back. Last year for the gold find and earlier this summer for the cave paintings."

Annabelle's gaze shifted away at the mention of the cave paintings. "Yes, well, these seem to be very genuine graves," she said. "While I feel badly for Clay, the importance of the find is extraordinary." She briefly leaned against him. "I know this messes up the planting for now, but just think. We could have a small museum, maybe a working site with archeologists that tourists could observe. That would be fun for your Haycation people."

"I'm sure it will be," Clay said.

The mayor studied him. "Do you have enough land still? I can speak with the owner of the outlying area and see if he will sell you a few more acres. The price would be fair."

"Thank you," Clay said. "I appreciate the offer. I'm good for now. We're going to have to clear more land to plant. We still have the equipment, so it's not a big problem. If the weather holds, the fall alfalfa will still be planted."

There was more polite chitchat. When the mayor and Annabelle started talking access roads, Clay excused himself. He walked toward the main house. Nate was waiting for him.

"How bad is it, boss?" the other man asked.

"Bad enough. We're going to have to clear two more acres to make up for this one."

"That's going to put us behind."

"Tell me about it."

CHARLIE ARRIVED HOME from her shift to find Clay waiting on her front porch. Once again he had coffee and a box of Danish. While the caffeine and sugar rush were appealing, she was willing to admit she was just a little more interested in the man himself.

She climbed out of her truck, aware this wasn't one of their scheduled times. Still, she went all tingly anyway and had to consciously keep from running up the walkway.

"Morning," he called when he saw her. "Is it okay I stopped by?"

"Of course."

He rose as she approached. She expected him to step out of her way. Instead he leaned in and kissed her.

The contact was brief. More greeting than seduction.

But she liked the way he was so matter-of-fact about it. As if they'd reached the place where they kissed easily and without thought.

She took the coffee he offered and led him inside the house.

"Any more news on the burial site?" she asked. He'd called her at the station the previous day to tell her what had happened. She'd had to hang up to go on a run.

"The experts will be arriving today. Nate and I have figured out where we're going to plow next. Time is ticking for my crop."

He smiled at the words, but she could see worry and self-doubt in his eyes. When he set the Danish on the table, she crossed to him and put her hands on his shoulders. A seemingly casual act. Fortunately Clay couldn't feel her pounding heart or know there was nothing casual about it for her. Touching a man was still strange. But she was determined to follow the "fake it until you make it" philosophy of getting by when it came to Clay.

"You'll be fine," she said, staring into his dark eyes. "This is a setback, but one you can manage."

"I know. Mayor Marsha came by. She said if I needed to buy more land, she knows a guy." The smile briefly returned. "Okay, she didn't say it like that."

"Good. Because I don't like thinking of the mayor as someone who knows a guy." She dropped her hands. "You'll get your fall alfalfa planted and all will be well."

"I'm telling myself that."

"You don't sound convinced."

"I'm still questioning myself on picking Nate. Maybe

that was a mistake. Even Dante said to listen to my gut and I didn't."

"Are you unhappy with Nate's work?"

"No."

She tilted her head. "Then what's the problem?"

"Rafe's always been in charge. He was running the family when he was ten. Shane managed one of the biggest Thoroughbred breeding programs in the country. I'm a former underwear model."

Self-doubt she understood. She took his hands in hers. Again, a conscious and slightly uncomfortable action, but it seemed appropriate.

"You're a smart guy. You have the education and a vision. Drive matters more than experience. If you need help, ask. Until then, don't assume you've made a mistake until the evidence is in. If you do screw up, then fix it."

"Advice I've heard before."

"Then why aren't you listening?"

He leaned in and kissed her again, more slowly this time. His mouth lingered, which caused her thighs to heat up and her breasts to start that achy thing they were so good at.

When he straightened, she found herself wanting to protest.

"Sorry," he said. "I shouldn't be bothering you with this. You're in it for the sex and this is not me at my most appealing."

She squeezed his hands and stared at him. "Hey, we're friends. Whatever else is going on, that won't change. As for you not being sexy, you couldn't be more wrong."

"Into the vulnerable thing? I don't think so."

"You're wrong. You being real is much more appealing than any guy on a calendar. I didn't pick you because of how you look. If you'll remember, that actually freaked me out a little. I picked you because I trusted you. I still do."

He pulled one of his hands free and stroked the side of her face. "Thank you," he whispered. "I think of us as friends, too." He kissed her mouth. "Good friends."

She felt the exact moment his intentions shifted from conversation to something more. They weren't touching anywhere except her hand in his and his fingers on her cheek, yet she knew she was right.

If asked a few days ago, she would have honestly claimed to be more interested in coffee and a Danish than anything a man could offer her. This morning, she was far more intrigued by Clay moving closer and pressing his lips to hers.

She parted her lips before being asked and met his tongue stroke for stroke. As the kiss deepened, she wrapped her arms around his neck, needing to get as close as possible.

He put his hands on her waist and quickly moved them higher. When he cupped her breast, she felt the contact all the way down to her toes.

She'd changed out of her uniform before leaving the station. Now she wore her usual jeans and a T-shirt. He explored her breasts through the fabric, pausing to run his fingers across her tight nipples. She shivered with delight.

He reached for the hem of her T-shirt. She helped him pull it off. Her bra went flying. Then his mouth was on her right breast with his hand on her left. He licked and sucked, drawing her into his mouth.

Desire turned liquid. She trembled, hanging on to him, wanting him to never stop. The heat inside intensified. With each pull, she felt an answering tug between her legs. She needed this, needed more.

Her breathing ragged, she ran her hands up and down his back, then tugged at his shirt. He stopped and jerked it over his head before tossing it away. Then they were kissing again, her bare breasts nestling against his perfect chest.

"Not like this," he murmured against her mouth. "Not in the kitchen. But Charlie…" He swore. "I just have to—"

His hands dropped to the waistband of her jeans. He undid the button and then the zipper.

She drew back from their kiss, her breathing still fast. Apprehension battled with need. She saw the passion in his eyes and knew he was as aroused as she was. He gave her a gentle smile.

"Turn around."

"What?"

The smile turned into a grin. "Turn around. That way you can run if you need to."

Aware she was topless, she did as he requested. He drew her close and put his left hand on one breast then the other. At the same time, he kissed the side of her neck. The combination of sensations chased away lingering doubt. His body was warm against her. Almost protection. This was Clay, she reminded herself. She trusted him.

He put his right hand on her belly, his fingers pointing down. He didn't move them, even as he continued to stroke her breasts and tease her aching nipples. The tension returned and with it a need she hadn't experienced before.

She knew about the whole concept of orgasms. After the rape, she'd done her best to avoid any sexual feelings. She ran from them, figuratively, most of the time. Occasionally literally. Now she found herself curious about what really happened. Was her body capable of surrendering that much? Would it be as great as everyone claimed?

Minutes passed. While his fingers worked their magic, his mouth nipped and kissed and licked her neck until she was having trouble catching her breath. She leaned more of her weight against him. Her hands fluttered at her side until she finally slipped them behind her to cup his narrow hips. She felt his erection against her rear and wondered what would happen if she turned and told him she was ready.

Before she could gather the courage, the hand on her belly moved. Clay eased his way under her plain cotton bikini panties. She felt the individual fingers, the pressure of his palm. She knew where he was going, although not what he would do when he got there. She froze, unclear on how she would react.

He slipped lower and lower, before sliding his fingers against her swollen flesh. He moved in a slow circle, passing over a spot that made her gasp.

It was like electricity, but not. Hotter, more intense, but just as jolting. Without meaning to, she parted her legs. No, that wasn't right. She needed—

He circled again and again.

She shuddered, lost in the moment, unable to think about anything but what he was doing to her. She could feel her insides tightening, her legs trembling. He dropped his left arm to her waist and held on, as if supporting her. None of it mattered. Only what he did when he touched her.

He moved a little faster, pressed a little harder. She put her hands on his arm, hanging on. She pushed down, wanting more. Needing.

He withdrew his hand, which made her whimper. Then he grabbed her wrist and pulled.

She stumbled after him aware they were heading down the short hallway and toward her bedroom. When they reached it, he guided her to the bed.

"Shoes," he said.

She kicked off the boots she'd worn that morning. Figuring it was too late to play hard to get now, she pushed down her jeans, taking her underwear with them, then stepped out of her clothes.

He looked her over, swore, then urged her onto the bed.

She was aware of him still wearing his jeans, although nothing else, as he joined her. Then he was kissing her and his hand was back between her legs and she really didn't care what he had on.

Lying on her back, she was able to part her legs more. She rocked her hips in time with his steady movements. He shifted from kissing her mouth to kissing her breasts and the sensations flooded her. She grabbed the bedspread with both hands and moaned.

He moved faster and faster. She couldn't keep up. She couldn't think she could only—

She'd heard it was like falling, she thought as the first contraction rippled through her. They were wrong. It was like flying. Her body shook and trembled as waves and waves of pleasure washed through her. There was more and more until it eased and waned and she was able to find her way back to her house, and her bedroom. She resurfaced and stared into Clay's very satisfied face.

He'd propped his head up on his other hand and was still stroking her. Lightly, barely touching. A last little ripple shook her. With their eyes locked, he eased a little lower, then pushed one finger into her.

She supposed she should have gotten scared and tense but right now she couldn't summon the energy. Plus, having him inside of her felt really good.

"Okay?" he asked, watching her intently.

"Oh, yes."

"Good."

He withdrew his hand, then leaned over and kissed her. "Like I said before, morning is your time."

"If it always feels like that, anytime is my time."

He pulled her close. She went into his arms and held on, listening to the steady beat of his heart.

"Thank you," she whispered against his bare shoulder.

"You're welcome." He kissed the top of her head. "Come on. There's a cup of coffee waiting for you. And I get first dibs on the Danish."

"Didn't you want to…" She motioned vaguely. "You should, you know."

He smiled at her. "Next time. You've done well. Let's not screw things up."

She was torn, wanting to give him what he'd given her, but afraid of what would happen when they tried actual lovemaking.

He sat up. "I mean it. I'm fine."

"I don't believe you. Can't we do to you what we did to me? Or is that not satisfying?"

For a second fiery passion flashed into his eyes, then he blinked and it was gone.

"Do *you* want to?" she asked, pouncing on the information.

"I don't want to frighten you."

She reached for the button of his jeans. "Come on. Let's see what all the fuss is about."

He put his hand over hers. "You're sure?"

"Yes. I believe in playing fair."

"An excellent quality."

He pushed her fingers aside and quickly unfastened his jeans. He pushed them off, then his briefs, leaving him naked to her gaze.

She stared at his whole body before settling her attention on his erect penis.

He was big and thick, but not scary. She did a quick internal inventory and found only eager expectation. She knelt between his legs and drew in a breath.

"Show me."

"Always direct," he said with a grin. "Give me your hand."

She put her hand in his and let him guide her until she was holding on to his erection. He positioned her fingers, then moved her up and down in a steady rhythm.

"You sure you're all right with this?" he asked.

"Please be quiet. I'm trying to give you an orgasm here."

He chuckled and his eyes drifted closed. "It's not going to take long."

She continued to move the way he'd shown her. Up and down, running her fingers across the tip before slipping down the shaft. A sense of happy power filled her. She was able to please him, to touch him.

His breathing increased. She watched the rise and fall of his chest, then let her gaze drift over the rest of him. All the while she went up and down, up and down.

Without warning, he raised his head and looked at her. "Charlie," he breathed, then his eyes closed and he came.

She stroked him until he laughingly told her stop.

Then they cleaned up together and picked up the various pieces of their clothing.

By the time they were dressed and back in the kitchen, the coffee was long cold. She made it fresh and they sat together at the table, eating Danish and talking.

While they argued about cheese versus cherry pastries and shared what was going on in town, she was aware of a newfound sense of connection. Of wholeness. She wasn't all the way back, but she'd made an excellent start on the journey.

"Thank you," she told him.

He smiled and winked at her. "Anytime."

CHAPTER ELEVEN

"I'M NOT COMPLAINING," Patience said with a grin as she flopped down on the grass. She was flushed and her breath came in short gasps. "I heard that was the kiss of death in your class."

Her long brown hair spread out around her. Her eyes were bright with amusement, even as she struggled to catch her breath.

"You make it sound like I beat them," Charlie grumbled, keeping an eye on the recruits who were in the middle of their three-mile run around the track. With thirty-pound packs on their backs.

Although her focus was training the volunteers for the CPAT test, the town had a standing invitation to join in any outside exercises. There were usually one or two who came along to the stair training. This morning Patience had joined them for the first half of the three-mile run. She'd turned down Charlie's offer that she, too, wear the thirty-pound pack.

"You're tough because you have to be," Patience said, sitting up, her breathing more regular. "Speaking as someone who might need the services of the fire department someday, I appreciate that."

"Thank you."

Charlie watched the runners, her expert gaze looking for signs of distress. She made sure her attention didn't linger on Clay, which took a lot of self-control. Not only was he pretty to look at, every time she caught sight of him, her entire body sighed in appreciation for what he'd done to her and for her. Tiny, interior cells were busy sending thank-you notes and begging for a repeat performance.

"Maybe if you told them you had to work hard to get where you are," Patience said. "Women have a lot less natural upper body strength. I've seen you in the gym. You bust your butt, so to speak. I can't seem to get past the pink weights."

Charlie laughed. The "girl" weights, plastic and in a delicate shade of pink, only went up to ten pounds each. Charlie worked with the standard set of free weights. They were black, rather than pink, and a whole lot heavier.

"I could show you a few things," Charlie offered.

"I'd like that," Patience told her, then glanced at her watch. "But not today. I have to get home. Lillie and I have our afternoon planned. Ice-cream sundaes followed by a movie. I know one day she'll be a teenager and rather eat glass than be seen with me, but for now, I'm one of her favorite people."

"Lucky you."

"I think so."

Patience scrambled to her feet, waved and headed toward her car. Charlie watched her go, wondering if she would have had as much courage as her friend. She supposed having courage wasn't the actual point. Patience had handled what life had offered.

Although she'd been married, her husband had ducked out after an affair. Which left Patience raising her daughter by herself. Added to that, Patience's mother, Ava, had MS. There were good days and bad days.

Patience could have turned angry and bitter. Instead she was upbeat, optimistic and kind. Ava was the same and together they were raising Lillie.

Patience stopped to talk to a couple of older ladies who were walking along the outside of the track. Charlie recognized Eddie Carberry from her brightly colored tracksuit. The seventy-something whistled and pointed to Clay. He gave her a brief wave and kept on jogging.

Charlie wanted to complain but she, too, admired the view. He was a fine-looking man. Better than fine, she thought absently, wondering when they would have their next "lesson." She was more than ready. She had a feeling the next time they were together, they would, um, complete the process. Imagining him inside of her made her squirm a little. She'd seen him naked, had touched him and been touched. She wanted the rest of it. She wanted to know what it was like to be with him.

Of course once he considered her "healed," their lessons would end. Not something she wanted to think about. She supposed that her hunger for Clay meant she was ready for a real relationship. That she should look around and find a man to fall in love with. The thing was, she didn't want to be with anyone but him.

The realization surprised her and made her uncomfortable. They weren't involved. He was helping her. She wasn't falling for him, was she?

As Clay led the pack in their final lap, she turned the concept over in her mind. No, she told herself as she walked over to the post she'd marked as the finish line. She was smarter than that. She knew Clay and liked him. He was safe and familiar. That was why he was her first choice for a sexual partner. She'd spent the past decade ignoring her sexual side and assuming being with a man was impossible. Of course it would take her a while to warm up to the idea. But she would get there. Her feelings weren't about Clay.

The volunteers crossed the line one by one. Most of them tugged off their packs, let the weighted bag fall to the grass, then flopped down next to it, panting and exhausted. Clay stayed upright. He was breathing hard and sweaty, but not done in by the task.

"What else you got?" he asked with a wink.

"You're saying I haven't beaten you yet?"

"Not even close."

She finished the workout with a stretching session and instructions for everyone to spend at least an hour a day on a stair-climber.

"Next week we hit the drill tower," she reminded them. "It's seven stories of stairs."

One of the women raised up on an elbow. "Let me guess. We do it in full gear, with a hose on our back."

Charlie grinned. "Not the first time."

AN HOUR LATER, Charlie and Clay were settling onto a big blanket in the park for a late lunch. Neither of them had bothered showering so dining in a restaurant wasn't the best choice. They'd settled on take-out sandwiches and a picnic.

Clay still wore the clothes he'd worked out in. A T-shirt and shorts. Despite the sweat stains on his shirt and the fact that he hadn't shaved that morning, he looked good.

"Let me guess," he said, sitting across from her. "You always have a blanket in your car."

"Of course."

"Along with a first-aid kit."

She passed him one of the large sandwiches. He shoved straws into the drink containers.

"I'm not going to apologize for being prepared," she told him. "Emergencies happen. I have training and if I'm first on the scene, I'm not going to be hampered by a lack of equipment. Before you ask, yes, there's a fire extinguisher in my truck, as well."

"Impressive."

"Hardly. Everyone should carry one. It could save a life."

His dark gaze settled on her face. "You're earnest."

"I'm also capable of beating the crap out of you."

"You threaten me a lot."

"I like threatening you."

One corner of his mouth turned up. "There's a famous philosopher who said that violence was the refuge of the unintelligent."

"I'm guessing he also spent most of his school days with a wedgie."

Clay laughed. "I like that you're tough."

"You say that because we're practically having sex," she said as she unwrapped her roast-beef sandwich. "But the truth is you like those little petite women with dainty feet and mouse sneezes."

He took a bite of his sandwich and frowned. "Mouse sneezes?" he asked when he'd chewed and swallowed.

"Sure. They make this tiny noise that's so delicate you have to ask if they sneezed. It's annoying."

"I don't like mouse sneezers."

"You say that now, but I know the truth."

He shook his head. "Is this your idea of flirting? Telling me why I shouldn't like you?"

"I'm not flirting. And you should like me. I'm great."

"It *is* your modesty that first drew me to you."

Charlie opened her bag of potato chips. "I'd throw one of these at you, but it would be a waste of junk food. A sin I never commit."

They were in the town's main park, close to the lake. Trees provided shade from the warm midday sun. There were people everywhere. Families, young couples, but Charlie felt that despite the crowd, she and Clay were alone.

She liked the way they laughed together, how they could tease each other. Being with him was easy. He was smart enough to be interesting but not so intelligent that he got on her nerves. He was funny and charming, but also kind. It seemed the older she got, the more she appreciated kindness in people.

She supposed if she were in a less mellow mood, she might have a crossing thought about them being seen together. One of the other volunteers could hint Clay was trying to get Charlie to take it easy on him. But she wasn't overly concerned. Clay was the best in the group. Even with a good-size table tied to his back, he would still be the best at all the physical challenges. Well, assuming she wasn't competing.

"Heard from Rafe and Heidi?" she asked.

"Mom said Heidi called to say they'd arrived and that Paris was beautiful. Otherwise, it's been radio silence."

"It's their honeymoon. I guess that makes sense."

Clay finished up his sandwich, then dropped the wrappings back into the paper bag. "Construction is finishing up on Mom and Glen's new house."

"That's fast."

"They paid for speedy service. I think they want to be on their own."

"Is it strange having your mother fall in love?"

"Kind of," he admitted, stretching out on the blanket and reaching for one of the cookies they'd bought. "I was pretty young when my dad died, so I don't remember him much. Rafe's the one who missed him the most. Shane has memories, but Rafe was hit the hardest."

"Your sister has a different dad, right?" Charlie didn't know much about the lone Stryker sister. She was a dancer of some kind and was estranged from her mother. Something Charlie could relate to. The estrangement, not the dancing.

"Right." Clay bit into the cookie. "A one-night stand with consequences. We didn't know very much about the guy. Nine months later, Evie arrived." He stared up at the sky, then back at her. "She never fit in. That must have been tough for her. Mom was busy working and stuff. Rafe did his best to take care of the family, so Shane and I looked after her. We were only a few years older, so it's not like we were qualified."

He glanced at her. "I don't think Mom ever dated much. It's been years. I told her no one expected her to live like a nun." He chuckled. "Something Rafe didn't appreciate when she moved here and fell in love with Glen."

"It worked out. Now they're going to have their own place."

He nodded. "Shane's house is nearly done, too. He'll be moving in with Annabelle. She's making him crazy. She wants to wait to get married and he wants that ring on her finger."

"Typical guy. It's all about possession."

"He's kind of in love with her."

"Annabelle is great. But Shane isn't going to win the argument. She's tough."

"Despite being a mouse sneezer?"

Charlie thought about her petite friend and laughed. "I can't remember hearing Annabelle sneeze. I'll have to get back to you."

"Hello, Chantal."

Charlie wanted to issue a sternly worded letter to the universe. Wasn't she supposed to have some kind of sixth sense that warned her when danger approached? Shouldn't clouds have appeared to block the sun? Or maybe birds could have suddenly taken flight. Anything to give her a half second to prepare before her mother appeared.

She looked up to find Dominique was indeed standing next to their blanket. Even more startling was the fact that her suit-wearing mother was dressed in jeans. Jeans with a silk blouse, but still.

"Hello, Mother."

Clay scrambled to his feet and wiped his hands on the side of his T-shirt. "Mrs. Dixon," he said, holding out his hand.

Dominique looked him up and down very thoroughly. "Who are you?"

"Clay Stryker."

They shook hands, then Dominique sank gracefully onto the blanket and looked at her daughter. "You're still avoiding me."

Charlie held in a groan. "I have no idea what you're talking about."

"Of course you do." She returned her attention to Clay, who had settled next to her. "My daughter does not appreciate my sudden return to her life."

"Why were you gone?"

"I wasn't gone. Chantal left."

"Children tend to do that. It's a cycle-of-life thing."

Dominique dismissed that with a wave of her delicately formed hand. "I had a career and those who needed to see me."

Charlie found the conversation fascinating. She had the sense that Clay and Dominique were equally matched. Gifted with a kind of perfection that those stuck in the normal world could only experience vicariously.

"Now you need Charlie?"

Dominique's gaze narrowed. "Who are you and why are you here?"

"I'm Clay."

"I'm aware of your name. You've already mentioned it once. You're avoiding my question." She turned her sharp gaze on her daughter. "Who is this person?"

A question Charlie didn't know how to answer. The truth was impossible. She would rather cut off an arm or a leg than give her mother that kind of power.

"I'm the man your daughter is seeing," Clay said quietly.

Dominique's expression shifted to pure confusion. "Excuse me?"

"We're involved."

Clay spoke with a certainty that made Charlie want to offer him a kidney. Not that he was telling the truth, but still. It was nice. Like she'd thought before. Kind.

Dominique glanced between them, then tossed her head back and started to laugh. The high sound cut through the afternoon and reminded Charlie of all her uncomfortable days in high school when she'd been too tall, with large feet. Awkwardness had followed her like a stray dog she couldn't shake.

Clay finished his cookie and reached for his soda. "What's so funny?"

"You and Chantal? Why would someone like you be interested in her?"

Charlie felt heat on her cheeks. Had the speaker been anyone but her mother it would have been a toss-up between a verbal evisceration and a hard punch to the jaw. As it was, she could only wish to be struck by a meteor.

"You really don't know your daughter, do you?" Clay asked. He leaned across the blanket and lightly touched Charlie's knee, then turned his attention back to Dominique. "There's the usual. Smart and funny. She's a part of this town, which I admire. She's brave, which speaks to her character. She doesn't take crap from me, and I like that a lot. She's the kind of woman who gets under your skin."

Charlie knew he was protecting her, which she appreciated. The words had just enough truth that Dominique might believe them, without going over the top. Had he gone on and on about her beauty, they all would have known he was lying. But this was different.

Dominique glanced between them. "How interesting," she said, her chin coming up. "If what you say is true, I must be in the way. If you'll excuse me?"

She rose with a fluid grace that spoke to her years of dance, then glided away without looking back. Charlie felt the first whispers of guilt, but quieted them.

"You didn't have to do that," she said when they were alone.

"I wanted to." He reached for another cookie. "You really do take after your dad."

"Mostly. Although she was the tough one, so I get that from her."

"She's lonely."

"Don't say that."

"Why not? It's true."

"Because I don't want to have to feel bad for her. She bugs me. Ever since I was a little kid, the whole world had to rotate around her. My birthday parties were scheduled around her performances. If she was tired, we had to be quiet. When I was seven, she told me to stop growing. That if I got too big, I would never find a man. She resented my dad for caring about me and when I told her about the rape, she didn't believe me. She said I was wrong to lead a boy on and she hoped I'd learned my lesson."

Clay shifted so he was sitting across from her. He took both her hands in his. She tried to pull away, but he wouldn't let her.

"Look at me," he commanded.

She did, her gaze locked with his.

"You're not that girl," he told her. "You're strong. You can take care of yourself. So it's okay to trust people again, Charlie. You have the experience to recognize a jerk now. You didn't before, but you've grown up. You have friends and a community. You're not alone. You made those choices—no one else. Be proud of yourself."

"I am," she murmured. "Mostly."

"Your mom really is lonely."

She winced. "Don't make me feel sorry for her. I like it better when I'm slightly annoyed and she's four thousand miles away."

"She's family."

"Want to trade?"

"She came here for a reason."

"Yes. She wants to be worshipped. She's getting older and the legions of fans have lessened."

Charlie remembered what her mother had said about the colon cancer. How she'd been in the hospital on her own, wondering if she would die.

"Okay," she admitted. "Maybe there's a little more to it than that."

"I'm not saying you have to be best friends."

"I wouldn't listen if you were."

"I'm saying, she's your mother. There's no escape. So try to figure out a way to make it better for you."

"Aside from buying her a plane ticket to Beijing? I hear it's lovely this time of year."

"My Charlie doesn't run from her troubles."

My Charlie?

Her heart gave a little stutter. He didn't mean that, she told herself. Not in any way that wasn't friendship based. They were buddies. Buddies who had seen each other naked. She wasn't looking for love; she was look-ing for sex and the healing that would follow.

"I'm not running," she told him. "I'm complaining. There's a difference."

"There is no way in hell."

Dante stared at the sign by the door. The office space Rafe had rented was on the bottom floor of an older building, with more businesses upstairs. Clay followed the other man's gaze, read the sign and did his best not to laugh.

Dante swung toward him. "Did you know about this?"

"No."

Dante swore. "Was this the only place in town? I don't think so. Rafe did this on purpose. While he's off in Paris on his honeymoon, I'm supposed to get our office set up here? I'm going to kill him. I'm a lawyer. I can keep myself out of jail."

Clay grinned. Rafe and Dante's company's temporary location was right under The Fool's Gold School of Dance.

"Maybe it won't be so bad," he offered.

Dante glared at him. "Not bad? Children dancing above my head? Those wood shoe dances and tap and God knows what? The music playing the same damn song over and over again?" He turned his attention back to the building. "This place was built in the forties. I doubt they'd even heard of soundproofing back then. Did I say I was going to kill him, because I am."

Clay slapped him on the back. "Come on. I'll buy you a cup of coffee while you plot your revenge."

Dante swore again, then followed Clay to the Starbucks.

After they had their coffees, they sat outside. Dante scowled at the people passing by.

"Have you noticed how damn happy everyone is here?" he asked. "It's not natural."

"It's small-town America," Clay reminded him. "What's not to like?"

"Everything. I miss the city."

"You don't want anyone to know your name?"

"Exactly. The woman who cleans my room at the hotel was telling me about her kid playing football. She invited me to the game."

Dante sounded outraged, as if the woman had suggested he violate laws of nature.

"You don't like football?" Clay asked.

"Sure. But pro games. Or college. Why would I go to a high-school game?"

"For fun."

Dante's confusion made Clay laugh.

"This is Fool's Gold," Clay told him. "Embrace it. It's the parade capital of California."

"I'm not a parade kind of guy."

"You will be."

"When hell freezes over."

"Famous last words."

CHAPTER TWELVE

BEING AWARE THAT she was reacting out of guilt didn't change the facts, Charlie thought as she stirred the simmering pot of pasta sauce. In a moment of weakness, she'd invited her mother over for dinner. Now, as the moment of Dominique's arrival neared, Charlie kept looking longingly at the back door. Was it wrong to want to bolt? Surely she could find a good job somewhere in Nebraska. Or Costa Rica.

Precisely at five, her doorbell rang. Charlie wiped her hands on a dish towel and walked to the front of the house. She pulled open the front door and forced herself to smile.

"Hello, Mother," she said, stepping wide to allow the other woman in.

"Chantal."

Dominique had dressed for the occasion. She wore a simple wrap dress in a subdued pattern. Her green eyes were enhanced by makeup. Pearl and diamond earrings glinted from her earlobes and a pearl necklace hung around her neck.

Charlie was aware that despite putting on dark-wash jeans and a blouse rather than a T-shirt, she was still nowhere in her mother's league. She wasn't wearing makeup or jewelry and her lone concession to fancy was a pair of rhinestone covered flip-flops she'd been given as a gift by someone who obviously didn't know her.

Dominique followed her into the house, then passed over a bottle of red French wine. "A Bordeaux," the other woman said. "It goes with nearly everything."

"Thanks. I made pasta."

"That sounds lovely."

Dominique followed her into the kitchen. Charlie had set the small table with place mats and the brightly colored stoneware dishes she favored. She collected two wineglasses, then easily opened the bottle. After pouring them each a glass, she handed one to her mother.

They stood looking at each other. Dominique cleared her throat, raised her glass without saying anything and took a sip. Charlie did the same.

"Nice," she murmured as the wine slipped smoothly down her throat. She was off tomorrow. Getting drunk was completely fine and perhaps the best way to get through the evening.

Silence filled the kitchen. It was too early to start the pasta or serve salad. Charlie studied the floor, then the far window. Finally she sighed. "We could, ah, go into the living room."

"Of course."

Unfortunately the quiet followed them. Charlie sat uneasily on the sofa, searching for a topic of conversation.

"How are you enjoying Fool's Gold?" she asked.

"The town is very nice. Small and quiet, but the people are pleasant enough." Dominique took another drink. "I met May Stryker. She lives on the ranch where you board your horse."

Charlie nodded. "May's nice."

"Yes. She is. Nice."

Charlie sucked in a breath and tried again. "I'm friends with May's new daughter-in-law. Heidi married May's oldest son last month. They're in Paris right now."

"Paris," Dominique said with a sigh. "I do love Paris."

"When was the last time you were there?"

"Two years ago. There was a celebration for one of the theaters where I danced."

She mentioned the name, which was meaningless to Charlie.

"It was wonderful to see everyone after so long. Time is not always our friend, but at least we're still alive. One night we stayed up late drinking too much wine. Dmitry tried to recreate his solo in *Swan Lake*. A disaster, of course. He nearly broke a hip and we had to rush him to the hospital." She gave a soft laugh. "So many good memories."

She smiled at Charlie. "The dance world is inescapable. I was taking a flight to New York the other day and lo and behold, there was Johanna Howard. Remember her? She used to come to the house when you were a baby. She was so beautiful. Well, time has not been kind. She made a fortune, so why she doesn't have a little surgery done, I'll never know. Muriel got fat. And Elizabeth..."

Her voice trailed off. "You probably don't remember any of these people."

"Not really, but it's nice to hear you talk about them."

Dominique raised her eyebrows. "Nice again? Is it really that bad between us, Chantal? We're mother and daughter."

"Biology doesn't guarantee communication."

"Obviously."

Charlie thought longingly of a ten-mile run. At the end, she would have accomplished something and be assured a good night's sleep. Unfortunately this dinner didn't promise anything close to either.

Dominique looked at her. "Why a firefighter? It's not a traditionally feminine occupation."

"I wanted to be able to help people. I enjoy the intense work environment and the friendships."

"Like a dance company."

"Yes. A little. We share experiences that the rest of the world can't always relate to. We work hard and have a common goal."

"I remember a choreographer wanting to modernize *Giselle*. I'm in favor of updating the classics as much as anyone, but his ideas were ridiculous. We banded together and told the producers we would not destroy something beautiful in the name of change." She pressed her lips together.

Charlie could see she was trying. She wasn't sure why, but Dominique had made it clear she wanted to have a relationship. As they were the only family each of them had, Charlie knew she should make the same effort.

"You must miss your friends," she said.

Her mother nodded. "I do. The travel, as well. In the last few years, I was exhausted all the time, but when I stepped onstage, it was still magic."

"You brought beauty to people's lives. For a few hours, they could forget everything but the dance. They were transported. That's a gift."

"Thank you."

"I remember Dad taking me to see you dance. Even though I knew it was you on the stage, sometimes it seemed like you weren't real. More fairy princess than mother."

"It's the stage makeup."

Charlie laughed. "I suspect it's about your brilliance more than stage makeup. You had a gift. Not just the talent, but the willingness to do the incredible work. I admired that."

"I wanted you to have the same."

"I know. It didn't happen."

"That was obvious from an early age." Dominique sipped her wine. "It's possible I pushed you a little too hard when you were young. I hoped you would grow into someone more…"

"Graceful?" Charlie offered.

"Perhaps."

"I wasn't going to grow smaller, Mom. I wanted to be like you. I just didn't know how."

"You turned out very well."

An unexpected compliment. Charlie told herself to accept it and not look for anything more. This was a start.

"At the risk of shattering the mood," she said carefully, "I'd, uh, really appreciate it if you could not call me Chantal."

Dominique's eyes widened. "It's a beautiful name."

"It is and nothing about me fits it."

Her mother wrinkled her petite, perfect nose. "You want to be called Charlie?"

"Yes."

"But it's so ungainly." Dominique nodded. "All right. I'll try. It may take some doing."

"I appreciate any effort."

For the first time since her mother's arrival, Charlie felt herself starting to relax. Maybe she'd been too quick to assume the worst. Dominique would always be the star, but everyone could grow and change. Even in small ways. She'd been without family for so long that it would take some retraining to get used to having a mother around, but that was okay. They only had each other. Dad would want them to get along.

"Are you really dating that man? Clay?"

Charlie's good mood vanished. Her muscles tightened as she automatically braced herself for attack. "Clay and I have been seeing each other," she said, avoiding the actual *D* word. Because they weren't dating. They were having sex.

"How did you meet?"

"He's been staying on the ranch for the past few weeks. He's moved back to town and wants to open a business. He's also interested in being a volunteer firefighter."

Dominique put her wine on the coffee table and leaned forward. "You need to be careful. I looked him up on the internet."

"I know he was an underwear model," Charlie said, not happy with the turn in conversation. She thought about bouncing up to start the pasta, but knew her mother would only follow her into the kitchen. Better to get it out now.

"More than that." Dominique studied her. "He's very handsome and from all accounts, quite charming. Chantal, I'm concerned."

So much for the name thing getting through, Charlie thought, aware that was the least of her problems. "Meaning, what? He's too good for me? A man like him would never be interested in a woman like me?"

"You're not his type."

The blunt words shouldn't have been a surprise. Under any other circumstances, Charlie would have agreed with them. "You're saying I'm not pretty enough, right? Or glamorous or special?"

"I'm saying you could get hurt."

"Because I'll fall for him, but he'll never fall for me."

Truth, Charlie thought. She would be the one in danger. Except their relationship wasn't about her heart.

"You don't understand men like him." Dominique's

voice was gentle. "You live in a small town. You don't have the experience."

That was more true than her mother knew, Charlie thought, trying to find the humor in the situation. "I'll be fine."

"I'm only trying to help."

"By telling me I'm not good enough?"

"By being honest. Chantal, really. Look in the mirror. You could do something with yourself, but you don't. Those clothes, your haircut. Clay has been with some of the most beautiful women in the world. I'm sure he can't walk into a store or a restaurant without stunning girls begging him to sleep with them. Everywhere he goes, women want him."

The question hung in the room then turned slowly and slapped Charlie across the face. In that second, she had what could only be described as an out-of-body experience. She could see herself clearly from the outside. She was aware of being too tall, too big-boned, too muscled. Her mother was right—she wore no makeup and had been known to take scissors to her own hair if it started to bug her.

She dressed for comfort and had always told herself that if people didn't like her appearance then they were shallow. That beauty was meaningless.

Only Clay had spent his adult life surrounded by beauty. The world's obsession with it had rewarded him handsomely. He was the kind of man who turned heads and made hearts beat faster.

Under normal circumstances, he would never have

seen her, let alone wanted her. She was part of the invisible ordinary. The only reason they had any contact was because she had gone to him and asked him to help her.

Humiliation blended with shame as she grasped what she had done. What must he be thinking of her, of what they were doing?

"Oh, God," Charlie whispered.

Dominique nodded. "Better to face it now, while you can still get out. I'm sure you can find someone else. Someone with whom you have more in common." She paused. "I don't say this to be cruel. You're my daughter and I care about you. But we both know that Clay would never be interested…."

She didn't finish the sentence, but then she didn't have to. Charlie rose. "That's your motherly advice? Get out because he would never want someone like me? Are you even human?"

Dominique flinched. "Why are you angry? I'm simply telling you the truth."

"Right. Like you did after the rape. I believe that time your great advice was to not lead on men. That there would be consequences. A guy like him had expectations."

Anger joined shame as Charlie remembered how the hits had kept on coming. First the police hadn't believed her, then her own mother had chided her for not playing fair.

"I'd been raped. Do you get that? Do you understand anything that doesn't involve you?"

Dominique stood. "You don't need to yell at me. I'm

trying to help. Reality can be unpleasant but is best faced head-on."

"Okay, Mom. Here's your reality check. I don't want you here. You and I have nothing in common, which I could live with, but there's more. You're a selfish bitch who has only ever been disappointed in me. You don't want to be a parent—you want to be the lead dancer in a production. Well, that time is over. Take your AARP discount and get the hell out of here."

Charlie felt her eyes burning. Dammit, she hated to cry.

"You're throwing me out?" Dominique seemed to shrink. "But why? I'm only trying to help."

"I don't want your help and I sure as hell don't need a mother like you."

Dominique remained in place for another couple of seconds, then nodded once. She crossed to the table by the door, collected her purse and let herself out. Charlie walked into the kitchen and turned off the pot of simmering sauce, then she sank onto the floor and dropped her head onto her knees.

Determined not to cry, she ignored the burning in her eyes and the moisture trailing down her cheeks. She was strong, she reminded herself. Tough. She'd been through worse and she would get through this.

The problem seemed to be, she wasn't exactly sure what "this" was.

CLAY STARED AT the drill tower. Today it was benign enough—a seven-story frame of metal and brick. Openings where windows would normally be. Stairs led to the roof. During actual training, recruits would have to find their way through smoke, with victims on different landings and tucked into corners. Fire would add to the heat and chaos.

But that was for later. Today he simply had to climb seven stories of stairs, first on his own, then carrying a hose.

The other volunteers stood in small groups. They eyed the building, probably trying to gauge how bad it would be. Clay knew he was more than capable of completing the task. Being physically fit wasn't the issue. Right now he was more concerned about Charlie.

He hadn't seen her in a couple of days. Although they hadn't had an appointment, he would almost swear she was avoiding him. When he'd arrived at the drill tower, she'd been busy unloading hoses. In front of others, she was usually all-business. Still, he couldn't escape the sense that something was wrong.

"Line up, people," Charlie called. When everyone was in front of her, she pointed to the skeleton structure. "This is the drill tower. Today you're only going to have to climb it. Twice. If you are selected for actual training, you will spend hours in it, learning every brick. You will grow to love it and hate it." She grinned. "At the same time."

It was mid-September. The heat of summer had eased a little, but it was still going to be close to eighty. Which meant it was already in the seventies. The first trip wasn't going to be too bad, Clay thought. The second one would be a bitch.

"You will have five minutes to climb seven stories," she continued. "Once you've completed that, you'll put on the gear, pick up a hose and go again. The second climb must be completed in ten minutes. Any questions?"

Someone asked about a water break. Clay was impressed that Charlie didn't bite the guy's head off. He knew the times given were generous. When there was a fire, no one could afford to wait ten minutes for someone to saunter up seven stories. He planned to take the stairs at a run.

An hour later, the volunteers were dripping sweat. They'd all passed easily. Charlie warned them not to get cocky. When they faced the drill tower again, the times would be more realistic and challenging.

Clay helped load the equipment into Charlie's truck. When they were finished, she turned to him.

"Would you please stay a second?" she asked.

"Sure."

They waited until everyone else had driven away. Charlie stood by her truck, her shoulders tense, her eyes not meeting his. As he'd suspected, something was wrong. But Charlie wasn't the type to play games. She would tell him and they would discuss it. Work together on whatever it was. He liked that about her.

She drew in a breath. "I really appreciate all you've done," she began. "Helping me and everything."

He grinned. "My pleasure, and I mean that."

She didn't smile. If anything, her expression tightened and her eyes darkened. "Yes, well, I'm fine now. We don't have to do that anymore." She motioned between them. "Be together."

He leaned against the truck and considered her words. "Why the change of heart?"

"I shouldn't have asked you to begin with. It's ridiculous and inappropriate."

"I'm not complaining."

He didn't understand. Seducing Charlie had been something he looked forward to. They were good together. They had chemistry and enjoyed each other's company. They trusted each other. He knew how rare that could be. Sure, it wasn't love—there hadn't been a lightning bolt—but it was more than he'd felt in a long time. Being with Charlie wasn't anything he was willing to lose.

"You've been great and I want to say thank you," she continued.

"What happened?" he demanded. "Who said something?"

Her head came up and for the first time, she looked at him. "No one."

"You're a bad liar."

"I'm not lying."

There were only a handful of people she would let get to her. Charlie had good friends. None of them would hurt her or make her feel small. Which left the clueless Dominique Guérin.

"It was your mother."

Charlie opened her mouth then closed it. "I have no idea what you're talking about. I don't want to do this anymore. What about that isn't clear?"

"Nothing," he told her. "Nothing at all."

It wasn't in his nature to walk away from a challenge, but this was different. Charlie wasn't like everyone else. He needed a strategy for getting to the truth. Which meant he needed time.

He walked to his truck without looking back, knowing it wasn't over. He hoped she figured that out, too.

CHARLIE ALTERNATED BETWEEN trying not to cry and being pissed. Anger was a much easier emotion for her to deal with. She didn't like being sad or feeling stupid and she loathed crying. It was such an expression of weakness. She prided herself on being tough. Toughness and tears didn't go together.

She hadn't seen Clay in two days. She refused to regret what she'd done. She'd made a sensible choice. Asking him to help her had been beyond ridiculous. She'd been smart to end their agreement.

Only she didn't feel smart. She felt lonely and lost. Even her house, the one place she enjoyed being more than any other place except the fire station, had ceased to be a refuge. She found herself wandering from room to room, not sure what to do with her day off. She had plenty of chores, but they weren't appealing. She could call one of her friends and go to lunch, but doubted she would be good company. She alternated between knowing she was a fool to let her mother win and wondering if Clay was thinking of her half as much as she was thinking of him.

Missing him was an unexpected development. The man was good company. He got her, which she appreciated. She liked to think she got him, too. That while there wasn't a romantic connection, they'd become friends. She liked him. More important, she trusted him.

Why did he have to be so damned pretty?

That was the real problem, she told herself. His looks. If he was just a regular guy, she wouldn't be having this dilemma. She would have been able to handle her doubts. But all kinds of wishing wasn't going to change that.

Someone knocked on her door. She had the feeling it could be her mother and wouldn't that be a nightmare. She hesitated and the knocking came again.

"Open up, Charlie."

She froze in the center of her living room. Clay? What was he doing here?

She crossed to the door and pulled it open.

If she had to come up with a plan, it would probably be to tell him to go away. That she'd told him what she wanted and he wasn't listening. Except the second she saw him, she couldn't speak.

He looked good. Not perfect, model-good, but the guy who made her bones melt kind of good. He was all sexy in jeans and a T-shirt. His expression of determination didn't hurt, either.

His gaze narrowed as he stared at her. "Done being

stupid?" he asked as he stepped into her house and closed the door behind himself.

"What?"

"You let your mother get inside your head. You know better. I'm here because I want to be here. No other reason. I'm not that altruistic."

She blinked. "How did you know it was my mother?"

"It wasn't hard to figure out. Plus I've caught her glaring at me a couple of times at the grocery store. What's the deal? She doesn't think I'm good enough for you?"

Charlie managed a strangled laugh. "Right."

He crossed to her and cupped her face in his hands. "Don't doubt yourself. Not you. You're the strongest person I know. I admire you." One corner of his mouth turned up. "You're also sexy as hell and right now all I can think about is how much I want to get you in bed."

Fifteen minutes ago, she would have sworn there was no way he could talk himself back into her life. That she was determined to be smart about what was going on. That she wasn't like other women, seduced by a man's words...and touch.

But she would have been wrong.

The first second his mouth touched hers, she was lost. She found herself clinging to him, holding on as if she would never let go. He was strong and solid, warm and familiar. She knew his scent and the sound of his laugh.

When his lips brushed against hers, she parted for him, then stroked his tongue with hers. Wanting turned liquid. Need burned through her. In less than a heart-beat, she was hungry for all that he did to her.

He drew back and stared into her eyes. "Tell me you want me," he murmured. "I mean it, Charlie. I need to hear the words."

Perhaps to be sure this was what she wanted, too. Perhaps because he knew she needed to say them.

She stared into his dark eyes, seeing the passion there. The acceptance and maybe even affection.

"I want you."

Her voice was a whisper, but it must have been enough because he gave a low groan and kissed her again. Harder. His touch more insistent. She felt the passion in him and it fed her own. His mouth claimed hers before moving lower. He kissed along her jaw, moving toward her ear. When he reached the sensitive lobe, he nibbled until her breath caught.

She rested her hands on his shoulders, feeling the broad, thick muscles, then moved her fingers down his chest. Each defined rise and dip excited her. When she reached the waistband of his jeans, she pulled his T-shirt free and put her hands on his bare belly.

Clay sucked in a breath. "Okay, we're doing this right," he said, stepping back and taking her hand.

He led her down the hall to her bedroom. Once there, he kicked off his shoes, then pulled a box of condoms from his front pocket and tossed them on the nightstand.

Charlie stared at the small box, waiting for the first wave of panic. After all, she knew what they meant.

What would happen next. She waited, braced for the need to run. But there was only anticipation.

She was ready. Ready to be touched and taken. Ready to have him inside of her. What had happened to her before had nothing to do with this man. This moment. Clay had truly set her free.

She turned her attention back to him and smiled. "Let's see what you've got."

He chuckled and tugged off his shirt. The rest of his clothes quickly followed, then he was naked in front of her.

He was already hard, his erection jutting toward her. She reached for him, taking his arousal in her hands, stroking the length of him. His breath hissed.

Before she could settle into a steady rhythm, he was pulling off her T-shirt. Her bra quickly followed, then his mouth was on her breast and she was the one caught up in the magic he created.

He sucked deeply, pulling her tight nipples into his mouth. He flicked the tip with his tongue before gently pressing his teeth into her skin. His hands roamed her back before settling on her rear and squeezing. She let her fingers trail down the small of his back to his famous ass.

He shifted to her other breast, putting his hand on the one he'd abandoned. Fingers and tongue worked in tandem. She shuddered, her chest tight, clenching her muscles in anticipation.

When he straightened, she unfastened the waistband of her jeans. His hands joined hers and together they pushed off her jeans and bikini panties. Then he was easing her onto the bed.

She slid over to make room for him, wondering if the bad memories would return now. If she would once again be caught up in the past. But there was only desire for the man settling next to her. When he opened his arms, she went willingly.

He kissed her deeply, his tongue dancing with hers. They touched each other, stroking, exploring. She ran her fingers along his side, down his hip and over his thigh. He shifted her onto her back and moved over her.

When he drew back, she opened her eyes and stared into his.

"Doing okay?" he asked.

She nodded.

He bent down and kissed her and then moved back to her nipples. Her insides tightened. Between her legs she felt both tension and swelling. When he knelt between her thighs, she parted her legs willingly. She remembered what had happened the last time he touched her there and she was ready for a repeat performance.

But instead of settling his fingers against her core, he kissed his way down her belly. Lower and lower, his mouth moving against her bare skin. Goose bumps erupted. He circled her belly button, then went lower still.

He reached for her, parting her gently, then kissed the very heart of her.

She was unprepared for the sensation of his tongue against her clitoris. Unprepared for the shudder, the hunger, the need. Tremors rocked her as her knees bent and her heels dug into the mattress.

He licked her again. Slowly. Softly, with just enough pressure to make her breath catch in her throat. *Exquisite,* she thought hazily. *Divine, maybe.* He raised his head and she nearly whimpered.

"Give me your hands," he told her.

He took her fingers and showed her how to spread herself for him. When she was completely exposed to him, he settled his mouth against her center and proceeded to love every inch of her.

He worked slowly, licking all of her, darting his tongue inside then withdrawing. He blew on her damp flesh and chuckled when she shivered. Finally he returned to that one swollen spot and danced across it. Once, then twice. A third time. Then over and over again, back and forth, around and across. A steady rhythm that trapped her in his control.

She tried to regulate her breathing, but couldn't. Tried not to cry out, but the sound escaped. Closer and closer, her muscles squeezing, her hips pulsing. And still he touched her, keeping her on the edge.

She'd never felt sensations like this. Every cell tasted pleasure. Every inch of skin, every ounce of bone, vibrated with need. She was beyond hungry and completely in his control.

Her orgasm ripped through her without warning. She cried out and pushed against him, desperate for all he had to give her. The crest of her climax carried her on and on, pleasure shuddering through her.

He slowed but didn't stop. The last tremor stilled and she was able to breathe again.

Clay kissed the top of her thigh, then sat back on his heels and grinned at her. "How was it?"

She waved a hand, which took more effort than she would have guessed. "Good."

He chuckled. "Good? Not great?"

"Life changing."

His eyes were bright with passion and he was still very much aroused, but he seemed content to enjoy his moment of glory. She was fine with that. The man deserved praise. A sonnet or two, or maybe a sports stadium named after him. While the shaking had stopped, she wasn't sure how long it was going to be until she could gather the strength to move.

But at least for now, lying in bed with Clay seemed like an excellent way to spend the rest of the day.

"Your turn," she said, reaching for the condoms.

He took the box, but didn't open it. "You sure?"

Two simple words that asked a whole lot of questions. Was she ready? Was she scared? Did she want to postpone the actual deed?

"Very," she told him, locking her gaze with his. "I stopped being afraid a long time ago."

Which was about him, she knew. About how he'd been so careful to earn her trust and make her laugh at the same time.

"I can wait," he told her.

"I can't."

He opened the box and pulled out the condom. It was

only when he went to slip it over his erection that she realized his hands were shaking.

At first she didn't understand. Why would Clay be nervous? But then she saw what she'd missed before. The tension in his muscles. The tightness in his jaw. He wasn't nervous—he was aroused. He wanted to be with her as much as she'd wanted to be with him.

The knowledge added to her confidence. When he knelt over her, she instinctively reached between them to guide him.

He pushed in slowly, inch by inch. Probably to give her time to adjust to him, but it had the added benefit of increasing her anticipation. He stretched her as he sank in deeper. The sensation of fullness excited her and she pulsed a little, wanting all of him.

Then it was done and he was inside her. He stayed still for several seconds.

"Still okay?" he asked, his teeth clenched as he spoke.

She smiled up at him, aware of their intimacy, loving all of it and wanting to complete what they'd begun.

"Show me what you've got, cowboy."

He gave a strangled laugh, then slowly withdrew. When he pushed in again, she arched her hips forward, taking him deeper. His breath came out in a hiss. His arms started to shake.

She sensed he was holding back, trying to be gentle. She touched his shoulders. "I'm not scared. It's okay. Just do what you want to."

He shook his head.

She squeezed his tense muscles. "I mean it. I'm perfectly okay. Do you really want me to have to report back to the town that your performance was disappointing?"

That earned her another laugh, then he nodded. "Okay. I'll go for it, but if you get uncomfortable, tell me and I'll stop."

He would, too, she thought, closing her eyes to better enjoy the sensations. He would stop and start as many times as she wanted. He would suffer so she would feel safe. Pretty irresistible.

There were probably more nice things she could think but he started moving and she was too distracted by sensations to do anything but feel.

He did as she requested, moving more quickly, pushing in and pulling out. He went faster, then faster still until he tensed and groaned. She wrapped her legs around his hips, pulling him in all the way, savoring his release.

Even at the end, he was careful. He didn't rest his weight on her, probably so she wouldn't feel trapped. Next time, she promised herself, running her hands up and down his back.

He rolled onto his side, bringing her with him. They faced each other.

"Not bad for a rookie," he told her.

She stared at him, then started to laugh. With the sound came a warm sensation deep inside. That cold, angry wound had finally healed.

CHAPTER THIRTEEN

Dominique passed over the half cup of brown sugar, then watched as May stirred it into the contents of the bowl.

"I don't understand," she said. "I thought the visit was going well. I was only trying to help. To save her."

May cracked an egg into the batter and picked up the wooden spoon. "By telling her Clay is too good for her? I'm his mother and even I'm offended by that."

Dominique paced the length of the small, old-fashioned kitchen. The farmhouse needed a major renovation. The furniture in the living room was beyond appalling. Still, she found the place oddly homey. It looked nothing like her beautifully decorated residences, but there was something here that went beyond appearances.

"I wanted to help," Dominique insisted, not sure why her position was so difficult for everyone to understand. She'd spoken the truth. Why was she the villain?

"Trying to help isn't an excuse for bad behavior," May said bluntly. "You hurt Charlie's feelings. You were mean and thoughtless."

Dominique flinched. "How can you say that?"

"I'm only trying to help."

Dominique opened her mouth, then closed it. "Not a very subtle lesson."

"I wasn't trying to be subtle. When it comes to interpersonal relationships, you tend to miss subtle cues." Her expression softened. "Think about how your words sounded to her. She didn't hear the concern. All she understood was criticism. You're her mother. You're supposed to be on her side. Yet there you were, telling her she wasn't pretty enough or special enough. I like Charlie very much. As far as I'm concerned, Clay would be a lucky man to have her in his life."

"But she's so odd with her short hair. She won't wear makeup and I think she would rather die than put on a dress."

May laughed. "So? She's loyal and caring. She risks her life every day on her job. If she'll do that for strangers, imagine how much she would give to her husband or her children. Why wouldn't I want that kind of devotion for my son and grandchildren?"

Character over appearance? Dominique considered the concept. "You're saying you don't mind she's not beautiful."

May reached for the measuring cup filled with peanut butter. "I'm saying Charlie is beautiful in ways that matter to me."

"My way is easier," Dominique told her.

May laughed. "I'm sure that's true, but it's not helping your relationship with your daughter."

That was true enough. Dominique thought about the angry words Chantal had yelled at her. About the rape.

The accusations made her uncomfortable, as if she'd been in the wrong. But at the time, the college boy had been so clear. He'd said Chantal had been following him around campus, as if she had a crush. That had made so much more sense than the alternative. But if she'd been mistaken, she'd abandoned her daughter when she'd been needed most.

"There's an old saying in medicine that I think applies in life," May told her. "First, do no harm. That might be a good place for you to start."

"Don't hurt her feelings?" Dominique asked, already knowing the answer to the question. "I can try. What else?"

May pointed to the bowl. "I don't like peanut-butter cookies. But Shane and Clay do. So I make them. Because it's a way for me to show my boys how much I love them. If you want Charlie in your life, you need to offer her something. A relationship with a person that is positive to her. We all want to be around people who make us feel good about ourselves. I'm sure you're always the most interesting person in the room, but children aren't always looking for witty conversation. Sometimes simply being accepted is enough."

"But shouldn't she be doing that for me? I'm her mother."

"You're the one who wants to connect."

Dominique wanted to point out that was hardly fair, but suspected May wouldn't be impressed by the argument.

She glanced out the window and saw a white van

driving onto the property. The vehicle didn't stop at the house.

"Who are they?" she asked, pointing.

May glanced up. "Archeologists. We have an old Máa-zib burial site on the property. It's quite the find."

Old bones weren't that interesting to Dominique. She had more contemporary problems.

"I don't know how to do it," she admitted. "I've only ever cared about myself. And Dan. I did love him." But he'd always been the one to take care of her. She wasn't sure what it meant to give.

"I suspect it will take less effort than you think."

CHARLIE MONITORED THE obstacle course she'd set up. While it wasn't part of the CPAT testing, it increased agility and endurance—both of which the potential trainees would need. She held a stopwatch in one hand and yelled for the next person to go.

Normally she enjoyed the obstacle course. She could set it up different ways, presenting different challenges. Everyone could score themselves on accuracy versus time and it was fun. But today she couldn't seem to concentrate. Not with Clay around.

This was the first time she'd seen him since they'd made love. She was hyperaware of him and worse, afraid every person within a ten-mile radius knew what they'd done.

Telling herself she was imagining things didn't seem to be helping. Logically she knew that Clay was acting exactly the same and that even if she was the one being weird, the potential volunteers were more worried about getting it right than any ticks or sidelong glances on her part.

Still, she couldn't figure out what to do. Should she look at him? Not look at him? Even standing there, blowing the whistle, made her feel self-conscious.

"Next up," she yelled. "Get ready."

Clay waited by the start line. He wore shorts and a cropped T-shirt—one that exposed his sculptured abs. Charlie knew exactly how that part of his body would feel against her fingers. She also knew the sensation of him filling her with every deep, passionate stroke of his—

"Charlie?"

"Huh? Oh. Right." She blew the whistle and Clay took off. Damn.

She managed to start the stopwatch and then glanced at his progress. Before she could decide if she should watch him or not, her cell rang. She pulled it from her pocket and glanced at the screen.

Her mother.

Dominique had been calling every day. Charlie had been avoiding the calls. This time was no different as she pushed the ignore button and started to slide her cell back into her pocket. It rang again.

"Give me a break," she muttered, looking down at the screen. Only it wasn't her mother's New York number. Instead it was the 911 dispatch operator.

"What?" Charlie barked, knowing she wouldn't be contacted unless there was a problem.

"Brushfire by the campgrounds at the north end of town." She detailed the location. "Equipment is in place. Can you get there?"

Charlie thought about how long it would take her to get to the station for her gear and then to head to the campgrounds. "Twenty-five minutes," she said, waving her volunteers in.

"There's a fire," she said. "I have to go. If you want to come, you may, but only if you abide by my rules. Number one, stay the hell out of the way." She listed the rest of them quickly, heading to her truck as she spoke. "If anyone breaks a single rule, you'll be out."

She got into her truck and had already left the parking lot before any of the others even had their keys out. As she drove, she thought about calling Clay. Telling him this was a time to stay in the background. But her promise to help had only extended to giving him a fair shot at proving himself. She wasn't going to do more than that. Not unless she was willing to do the same for everyone else.

What surprised Clay most about the fire was the sound. He'd expected the heat and smoke, but not the volume. There was the crack of trees heating, the roar of the flames themselves. The rush and hiss of water, the calls of the firefighters. Pumps rumbled, nozzles clinked. Controlled chaos reigned in a hell storm of noise.

He and the other trainees gathered together behind the three engines. As ordered, they observed without getting in the way. Clay had been doing his homework and was able to place each firefighter with his or her station by the numbers. Despite the gear they wore, he recognized a few of them. Charlie was easy to spot. She was tall and commanding as she barked out orders.

He returned his attention to the fire, aware of how the smoke had changed from black to gray, indicating the firefighters were gaining control. When the front line shifted, the volunteers moved, as well, careful to stay out of the way.

Captain Fargo yelled for a two-inch hose. Clay was by the rig. He quickly grabbed it and handed it to the woman who came running to take it, then he stepped back.

The afternoon was clear and warm, the sky blue around the billowing smoke. To the left, a tree exploded sending sparks flying. Grass by a picnic table ignited.

"Shovels," Clay yelled, grabbing two in each hand and passing them out. "This way."

He hurried toward the burning grass and started piling dirt on the flames. The others followed, doing the same. In less than a minute, the fire was out.

"Look around," he told them. "Check for other hot spots, but stay out of the way."

The other two guys glanced at each other, then shrugged. The rest of them simply did as he instructed. They checked in a widening circle and put out a pile of smoldering leaves. When they were sure the rest of the area was secure he collected all the shovels and returned them to the rig.

Captain Fargo came up to him and grabbed his arm. "What the hell do you think you're doing?" she asked.

"There was a grass fire." He pointed to the shattered trunk of the once-tall tree and explained what had happened. "We went out twenty yards and checked for hot spots. We found smoldering leaves and covered them with dirt. Now I'm putting the shovels back so they'll be ready when you need them."

The captain stared at him, her eyes boring into his. "Good work," she said at last. "Now stay out of the way."

"Yes, ma'am."

The captain's eyebrows rose, then she shook her head and she walked away.

AT THE STATION, Charlie walked around the engine and confirmed that everything was back in place. Michelle Banfield walked up.

"You know this isn't your shift."

"It's still my rig."

"Not when you aren't working."

"Details."

Olivia Fargo strolled up. "That was exciting. The preliminary investigation suggests idiots caused the fire."

Michelle groaned. "Let me guess. They walked away from their fire without making sure it was out."

Olivia shrugged. "It looks like it. We'll know more in a few days. Thanks for coming in. We needed the help." She turned to Charlie. "You brought the volunteers."

"I was working with them. I thought it would be a

good chance for them to observe. I was clear on the rules."

She braced herself for what was to follow. She'd already heard about Clay organizing the others to fight a small grass fire. Although accounts said he'd done exactly the right thing and then had returned the equipment, she wasn't sure the captain would see it the same way. Everyone knew the most important rule was to stay out of danger. A case could be made that Clay hadn't.

"You know about the grass fire?" the captain asked.

Charlie nodded.

"I already told Clay he did a good job. He stayed calm…. He took control of the situation. He made sure his people were safe and then he put the equipment back where it belongs." She smiled. "I was wrong, Charlie. You said to give him a chance and that was the right thing to do."

"Thank you." Charlie was careful to keep her expression neutral. No one needed to know that on the inside, she was doing quite the dance.

"I expect him to be one of our best," Olivia continued.

Michelle turned. "There it is. The high sign. Clay's heading to the showers. I want to enjoy the show."

Charlie's stomach twisted. But before she could react, the captain stepped in front of Michelle. She drew her eyebrows together and glowered.

"I must have misunderstood you, Michelle. Because I know how you would cause a stink to high heaven if a man wanted to spy on you in the shower. Clay Stryker is one of us now. You will show him the same respect you'd show anyone you worked with. Or anyone in the community, for that matter. Do I make myself clear?"

Michelle flushed and ducked her head. "Yes, ma'am."

Olivia sighed. "I'm going to make sure no one else has your bright idea."

Charlie exhaled slowly.

Michelle waited until the captain had left to put her hands on her hips. "I just wanted to *look,*" she grumbled.

"I believe that's illegal in all fifty states."

"But he's perfect."

Charlie thought about him touching her, kissing her, then taking her to the stars. "He really is."

CLAY FOUND THE drive back to the ranch anticlimactic. Okay, maybe he didn't qualify for superhero status and a cape that made him fly, but he deserved something pretty damned close.

It had been a great day. Watching the firefighters work the line had been a rush and a half. Actually being able to do something was even better. But the best part had been the captain saying he'd done a good job.

He was used to being complimented. But all the accolades were about how he looked—something he had very little control over. Sure he worked out, but he knew that his appearance was simply the luck of the draw. He'd been gifted when it came to certain genes, nothing else. But putting out that grass fire, taking charge and getting it right was about who he was inside.

He drove onto the ranch and parked. As he climbed out of the cab, he saw Nate slipping into the barn. While there was nothing unusual in that, he didn't like the way the other man glanced over his shoulder, as if hiding something.

Clay walked into the barn. It took his eyes a second to adjust. When they did, he wished they hadn't.

Nate stood by a girl, his hand at her waist, her arms around his neck. Clay didn't care if his farm manager was making friends. What he did object to was the age of the friend. His use of the word *girl* had not been idle. She didn't look old enough to drive.

"Afternoon," he said into the silence.

The couple jumped apart. Nate turned and swallowed. "Boss. You're back."

"I am." He crossed to them. "I'm Clay Stryker."

The girl—a pretty blonde with big blue eyes, smiled shyly. "Hi. I'm Candee." She held up two fingers. "With two *e*'s."

"Nice to meet you, Candee. I need to talk to Nate for a minute. If you'll excuse us?"

Candee giggled her agreement. Clay grabbed Nate by the arm and dragged him to the other side of the barn.

"I won't even get into the fact that you're supposed to be working," he growled. "What the hell are you doing with a girl her age?"

Nate bristled. "She's over eighteen."

"You sure?"

"She swore she was."

"Did you bother to confirm that?"

Nate shook free of Clay's grasp. "This is my personal life we're talking about. I run your farm. Whom I date is my business."

"Not when it's on my time." He paused to remind himself that getting pissed wouldn't help the situation. "This is a small town, Nate. You're new here. If you expect to avoid getting attacked by a crowd of angry mothers with pitchforks or worse, you need to be sensible. Find someone closer to your age. Or at least out of high school."

Clay glanced back at the girl. "If she's under eighteen, you're fired."

Nate went pale. "No, boss. Don't say that. She's not. I know she's not. I really need this job."

"Maybe you should act like it."

Nate nodded. "You're right. I won't see her again."

"Fair enough." Clay returned to Candee's side. "I need to see your driver's license."

Candee blinked at him. "Why? I'm not trying to get a drink."

"Humor me, please."

She opened her small handbag and held out her wallet. He leaned in to check the date.

God was smiling at him, for sure. Candee had turned eighteen the previous month. He straightened.

"It was nice to meet you, Candee."

"You, too." She rocked forward and back on her feet. "Are you who they say? That model?"

"Not anymore."

She glanced at Nate, then back at him and lowered her voice. "You want my number?"

"I'm seeing someone."

"Is she prettier than me?"

The easiest question of the day. He thought of Charlie in her gear, shouting instructions and taking on a fire, then nodded. "She's spectacular."

"If you change your mind, I work part-time at the bakery."

"Good to know."

Then, feeling decades older than his thirty-one years, he walked away. When he was outside, he turned back to the barn and wondered if the decision to hire Nate was going to come back and bite him in the ass. Or maybe *if* was the wrong word entirely.

CHAPTER FOURTEEN

DOMINIQUE WRESTLED THE empty suitcases onto the bed. Justice, her bodyguard, had left for a few weeks. In truth, she'd let him go because they both knew there was nothing for him to do here. He would return after his assignment and then she would be forced to face the truth about her career. That she was no longer famous. There were no fans and anyone who remembered her was probably an octogenarian and not really much of a threat.

Tears filled her eyes. She brushed them away angrily. She'd cried more in the past few months than she had in the past decade and it was time for the unseemly display of weakness to end. She had survived cancer and she would survive being rejected by her daughter. People might think that ballet dancers were delicate creatures, but Dominique knew the truth. There was steel behind successful dancers and she had been the best.

She would return to her life and find a way to make it less lonely. Maybe she could volunteer or read to orphans. Take a lover. Although in truth, she didn't really want any man. Dan had been her one true love and when he'd died her heart had died, too.

Friends then, she told herself as she carried the contents of the drawers to her suitcases. Even a monkey had friends. Somehow she would learn how to have one, too. She had to. Otherwise she would truly die alone.

Someone knocked on the suite door.

Dominique crossed the living room and opened the door only to find the mayor and another woman standing in the hallway.

"Hello," Marsha Tilson said, stepping into the suite. "Dominique, this is Denise Hendrix. She lives here in Fool's Gold."

"Nice to meet you," Denise said with a warm smile.

Dominique nodded. Denise was in her fifties. Pretty enough, in a natural way. Her clothing was casual— jeans and a long-sleeved blouse—but the simple styling suited her.

"How can I help you?" she asked, wondering why they'd stopped by and how long they would be staying. She had packing to get to and then a long limo ride to the Sacramento airport. From there she would fly to New York and lick her wounds.

"I heard you were planning on leaving," Marsha said, taking Dominique's hand and leading her to the sofa.

Dominique sat and stared at the white-haired woman. "How could you know that? I barely decided myself a few hours ago."

"I have a sense about people. I know things have been difficult with Charlie."

Denise took a chair and watched them without speaking. Dominique had no idea why the mayor had brought her along, but decided to simply go along with things until she could get the two women to leave.

"More than difficult," she said. "Impossible. That's why I'm leaving."

Since their fight, her daughter had been ignoring her calls. Dominique had gone by her house twice. Even though Chantal's truck had been parked out front, her daughter had refused to come to the door.

Dominique had been forced to retreat. Now she knew that she'd abandoned their relationship too long. They had nothing in common. While she didn't completely understand all that May had told her, she did believe she was at least partially responsible for the chasm between herself and her daughter. She also knew she'd been wrong about the rape. When Chantal had needed love and support, Dominique had offered criticism.

"I had a daughter," Marsha said. "A sweet girl I drove away through unreasonable discipline and too-strict rules. Her teenage years were difficult, to say the least. It got so bad, she ran away and refused to see me ever again. I lost her because I was a fool."

Dominique stared at the older woman. "How is that possible? You're not like that."

"It was a long time ago," Marsha admitted with a sad smile. "I let her go and by the time I realized I'd lost her, she didn't want anything to do with me. She died young and I never got that second chance." She looked away and drew in a breath, then turned back to Dominique. "You still have Charlie. You're here. Don't give up. Because you never know what life is going to send your way."

Dominique thought about the cancer she'd beaten and how afraid she'd been. She knew the prognosis could have easily gone the other way. Chantal had a dangerous job. What if something happened to her?

Denise leaned toward Dominique. "I realize you don't know me from a rock." She smiled. "But I have a feeling Mayor Marsha wanted me here because I have six kids. If you'd come by when they were younger, I might have begged you to take a few. At least for the weekend."

Dominique blinked. "Six children? On purpose?"

Denise laughed. "Not exactly. The last one turned out to be triplets. Unexpected, to say the least. But wonderful."

Six? She couldn't begin to imagine what that must have been like. There wouldn't have been a moment of quiet. Although Dominique had to admit her days recently had too much silence in them.

"Chantal doesn't like me," she said flatly, knowing there was no point in avoiding an obvious truth. "She thinks I'm selfish and cruel."

"Are you?" Marsha asked quietly.

Dominique stiffened. She was about to protest the question when she realized there was no point. She was already leaving. Why would she care what these people thought of her?

"Perhaps a little," she admitted softly. "Certainly

selfish. I'm an artist. My career was important. Of course it's gone now."

"You could start by calling her Charlie," Denise told her. "It's what she calls herself."

"She did mention it. Charlie is a horrible name."

"She would argue the same about Chantal."

Dominique pressed her lips together. This Denise person was overstepping her bounds.

Denise drew in a breath. "The thing I can tell you about having children is you get back so much more than you give. I know things are difficult with Charlie right now, but she's a wonderful, giving woman with a big heart. I don't think it's going to take very much to change her mind. Tell her that you were wrong and that you're sorry. Ask for a second chance. If you mean it, if you're sincere, she'll give it to you."

Dominique wanted to point out that Chantal also needed to apologize to her. After all, Chantal had been the one to walk away. But she'd tried that argument before and no one seemed to care about the wrongs done against her.

She thought about what May had said. Her advice had been to care about Chantal. It was what Denise was telling her, as well. Her years of training had taught her that if more than one person made the same criticism, she should listen and correct what she'd been doing. Perhaps that lesson applied to this situation.

Marsha touched her hand. "What have you got to lose, Dominique?"

She thought about the silence and realized there was only one answer. "Nothing."

"You HAVE the better horse," Clay said.

Charlie laughed. "I'm the better rider. Face it, pretty boy. You're not the best at everything."

"I never said I was."

"It's implied. You have a swagger when you walk."

He grinned. "You like my swagger."

The normally competent, in-charge Charlie Dixon turned away, but not before he saw her blush. Clay held in a chuckle. He got to her. She might not admit it, but he knew it and she knew it. The best part was she got to him, too.

He guided his horse next to hers, along the trail that followed the fence line of the ranch. The day was warm, with a few white clouds passing across the blue sky. Up on the mountains, the first leaves were starting to turn. Fall was rapidly approaching.

"We're getting the fall alfalfa into the ground this week," he said.

She glanced at him. "Your first crop."

"It's going to be a good one. The forecasts are for a late frost, so even with having to replow fields, we should have time. The plants need six weeks of growth before the first frost to survive."

"Someone's been doing research."

"I want to know what I'm doing. Nate is the pro, but I make the decisions."

His farm manager wasn't a topic he wanted to get

into. The situation with Candee still pissed him off. But Nate had sworn he wouldn't play around with anyone's teenager again. Clay had agreed to give him another chance and he would abide by that decision. He just wished it sat better in his gut.

"You'll soon be the Fool's Gold alfalfa king," she teased. "You won't have time to be a volunteer firefighter."

"I'll make time. I'm serious about my commitment, Charlie."

Her smile faded. "I know. I wasn't saying you weren't. You were good at the fire, Clay. Everyone noticed. You followed directions, you took charge when necessary and then you backed off."

Her praise pleased him. "I listened."

"A rare quality in a man."

They continued on another half mile or so, then Charlie reined in. "Want to take a break?"

"Sure."

They dismounted and put their horses in the shade, then settled by the tree. Clay sat across from her, wanting to be able to see her while they talked.

Her short hair fluttered in the slight breeze. He could see a couple of freckles on her cheeks and amusement in her blue eyes. She wasn't traditionally beautiful, but the more time he spent with her, the more attractive he found her. The sexier she was to him.

"You're staring at me," she said.

"I like the view."

She reached out and punched him in the arm. The blow was hard enough to get his attention.

"Stop it," she told him. "You're acting like an idiot."

"You can't take it when I treat you like a girl instead of one of the guys."

"Maybe."

Her admission surprised him.

"Leftovers from the rape?" he asked.

"No. I was having trouble being girlie back when I was fourteen."

"There's a difference between girlie and feminine."

"Not much of one."

"You're strong, Charlie. You don't need to always be protecting yourself. It's okay to let the other sides of you show once in a while."

She plucked a blade of grass and tossed it at him. "I'm not wearing a dress."

"No one's asking you to. I'd prefer you to wear nothing at all." He grabbed her wrist and pulled her toward him.

He'd thought she might resist, but she shifted easily, leaning toward him. He tugged a little more until she was off balance, then eased back onto the grass, bringing her with him.

She was stretched out, half on top of him, her gaze locked with his. Everything about her tempted him, but he wasn't going to be the one initiating this time. He was going to let her do all the work.

"You can kiss me," he told her.

She raised her eyebrows. "Can I?"

"Sure." He stretched out his arms, then tucked his hands behind his head. "I'll be right here."

"I could also beat the crap out of you."

He smiled. "In your dreams. Or naked. Naked would work."

"You're a strange man."

"No. Most guys think about women naked. Especially the woman they want to have sex with." He needed to touch her, but held back. "At the fire?"

She glared at him. "You did not think about me naked."

"Sure I did. You looked great, by the way."

She muttered something he couldn't hear, then sighed. "You make me crazy."

"Good. Now shut up and kiss me."

She surprised him by doing just that. Leaning in and pressing her mouth to his.

Her lips were warm and yielding. She moved slowly, as if finding her way. Until then, he'd always been the one to take charge, to make the moves. But he knew that being able to be the aggressor would chase away any lingering ghosts.

So he stayed as he was, even as his fingers itched for the feel of her body. He wanted to run his hands up and down her back, to find the more interesting places and linger. Instead he forced himself to relax, to let her lead the way.

She kept the kisses light, then drifted across his jaw to his neck. She unbuttoned the front of his shirt and explored his chest with her lips and tongue. The feel of her teeth on his nipple sent electric jolts through his body. The blood already heading for his groin quickened its pace.

She pulled his shirt free of his jeans, then sat back on her heels and studied him.

"You're just going to lie there?" she asked.

"Uh-huh."

She tilted her head and then rested her hand on his erection. "I can do anything I want?"

"Even if it kills me."

She chuckled. "I don't want you dead."

"What do you want?"

Color stained her cheeks, but she didn't look away. "Were you smart enough to bring condoms?"

"Oh, yeah. Front pocket."

She reached into his pocket and pulled out two condoms. "You're ambitious."

"I'm a guy with a hopeful attitude."

She glanced around. "We're outside. Anyone could see."

"No one's around. Besides, you'll like it."

She returned her attention to him. "And you're really not going to do anything?"

"I'm going to come inside of you, Charlie. With you on top."

He figured his words could send the afternoon in one of two directions. If she was still fighting demons, his verbal image might scare her into backing off. But the woman he knew and liked was tough. She had a sexual side she'd kept locked away for a decade. He was counting on her body winning over her mind. If he was right, he was in for a hell of a ride.

She stared at him for several very long seconds, then shrugged. "Okay."

With that, she pulled her shirt over her head and un-fastened her bra. Before he could blink, she'd pulled off her boots. Jeans and panties quickly followed. She stood next to him, naked and beautiful, sunlight dappling her body. His dick throbbed out a drumbeat of need.

He swore but didn't move. Rules were rules and this was all about her.

She knelt next to him and reached for his belt. When it was undone, she went to work on the button at his waistband. He watched her work, eager to feel her hands on his body. Then she shifted direction and pulled off his boots.

"You're going to have to help a little," she told him as she started tugging on the hem of his jeans.

Rules were meant to be broken, he told himself as he shoved down his jeans and briefs and kicked them away. Then he lay back on the grass and put his hands behind his head again.

She stared at his erection. "Nice. How does it work? Me being on top. Do I climb on or what?"

"You straddle me and we take it from there."

He was aware that they were both naked. That her breasts were well within reach and that he could have his fingers between her legs in a heartbeat. He remem-bered the taste of her and how she'd given herself to him. His arousal flexed as blood pulsed. Need pushed at the base of his groin.

He wanted her to touch him. To rub and stroke and suck and lick. He wanted the release, but first he wanted to hear her scream in pleasure. He swallowed against the pressure in his throat and knew that if this killed him, it would be a hell of a way to go.

Charlie knelt next to him. "So it's all up to me?"

"Uh-huh."

Her blue eyes danced with amusement. "You have to do what I say?"

"You're letting this go to your head, aren't you?"

"It's not my head I'm worried about."

She leaned in. For a second, he thought she was going to kiss him, but at the last second she changed direction and gave the tip of his cock a quick swipe with her tongue.

He swore.

She sat back and smiled. "I'm feeling the power."

"No surprise there."

"I'm not sure what to do first."

"You don't have to do it all at once. I can promise you a repeat performance."

Her eyebrows rose. "With me on top and in charge?"

"Yup." As many times as she wanted, he thought as his body began to beg. "Don't you get it? I want you, Charlie. Isn't that clear?"

Her gaze slid to his erection. "There's obvious evidence."

"Then be a good girl and put both of us out of our misery. We can do it all again later."

"Sort of like getting a to-go box at a restaurant?"

He gave a strangled laugh. "Sure."

"I like that."

This time she did bend over and kiss him. He gave in to the need and wrapped his arms around her, drawing her against him.

Skin on skin felt exactly right, he thought as he pushed his tongue into her mouth. She met him, stroking and circling, their lips moving against each other's.

He moved his hands up and down her back. What he really wanted to do was flip her over and push into her. Again he reminded himself of the rules. That they would serve a purpose and that having Charlie riding him would be worth the wait, not to mention the pain of blood pumping with each heartbeat.

She drew back slightly. "Okay," she whispered. "Let's see how this is going to work."

He reached for the condom and slipped it on. She knelt over him, slightly forward of his groin, and braced herself on her hands and knees. He settled his hands at her waist.

"You're in control," he reminded her, staring into her eyes. "You tell me what you want."

She nodded, her expression both expectant and slightly apprehensive. He guided her back.

They both caught their breath when they connected. The very tip of him nestling against her warm, swollen heat. The need to push, to fill, to pump, screamed in his head. He held on to control with all that he had and waited.

Her blue eyes crinkled with good humor. "You're a little tense."

"Yes, I am."

"Because you want to be inside?"

"I want to be a lot of things."

She tilted her hips a little, drawing him in maybe an inch. Then she stopped. "How's that?"

He stroked her cheek. "Do your worst. I'll be fine."

The amusement faded and something far more caring took its place. "I do trust you, Clay."

"I know. You trust me enough to play. It's a great compliment. It's killing me, but it's a great compliment."

Her gaze locked with his, she reached for his hands and guided them to her breasts. He went willingly, wanting to feel the smooth, soft skin.

He cupped her in his palms, then used his fingers against her nipples. He rolled the tight tips, causing her eyes to sink closed and her breath to quicken. In one unstudied movement, she sank back, taking all of him inside.

He froze, not sure if she'd meant to do that, or if she'd scared herself. But this was Charlie. Her sensual nature might have been dormant, but it sure hadn't been irrevocably damaged. She settled more firmly over him, sending him deeper. He felt her body tighten around him.

She shifted her weight a little, rocking forward so she could move back and forth easily. Her eyes opened and she stared at him.

"I'm ready," she whispered and began to move.

He kept his hands on her breasts, as much because he liked touching her as to give himself a distraction. Because what was happening to the rest of his body was nearly irresistible.

She set up a steady, relentless rhythm, sliding back and forth, enclosing him in liquid heat. With each stroke, she sucked him in deeper, pushed him along further, until he knew he was seconds from losing it.

Alfalfa, he thought frantically, aware of her breath, of her whispering his name, of the building pressure at the base of his groin. There were different types. He needed to do more research on different kinds he could plant. The goats could help. Maybe pull a cart with Priscilla and alfalfa. He'd have to rent some kind of trailer to get them all there. He could find one on the inter—

She sat up, pulling him back into the moment. Her gaze still locked with his, she pushed up and down, frantic and frenzied as she got closer and closer. Her breath came in gasps, her breasts bounced, her skin was flushed. She was as beautiful as a pagan goddess, all light and sensation.

His climax threatened, but he held back, determined to make this as good for her as possible. He slid his right hand up her thigh, then reached his thumb between their bodies. When he found her swollen, wet clit, he rubbed it, pushing deep into her body, right to the root of it. He circled around it and on the second pass, she screamed.

She continued to move up and down, so fast she was nearly a blur. Her body shook and trembled. Deep inside, the shock waves began, squeezing him until he had no choice but to give in to her invitation. He pushed up with his hips, shoving into her even more and losing himself in the explosion of his release.

After what felt like a lifetime, she slowed. Her gaze refocused and she stared at him. The color on her cheeks deepened and he knew they had reached the critical moment of their relationship.

"Don't," he said, sitting up and wrapping his arms around her. "Don't you dare. Dammit, Charlie, that was incredible. You leave me weak. Never doubt that."

She bit her lower lip. "I'm afraid I'm too much."

He chuckled. "Right. Because every guy wants to walk around saying, 'Yeah, I'm dating this girl. She's not really enough for me in bed. I like that.'"

"I don't want to scare you."

"Do I look scared?"

"No, but…"

He kissed her. "No buts. Just promise me we can do that again. Soon."

She nodded and swallowed. "Why do I want to cry? I never want to cry."

"I could bullshit you into believing it's about the sympathetic nervous system and emotional release, but the truth is, I'm so damned good-looking, you're weeping with gratitude."

She leaned back her head and started to laugh. He joined in, then he rolled her onto her side and started kissing again. In the shade of a nearby tree, the two

horses looked at each other and sighed. Apparently they
were going to be here for a while.

"THANK YOU for joining us, Mr. Stryker," Mayor Marsha said from her place behind her impressive desk in
her office at City Hall.

"Clay, please."

"That's what I want to be saying," Gladys mumbled.
The other woman sat in the chair next to his.

The mayor sighed. "If we could focus on the business at hand," she said, then pointed at Gladys. "Nothing from you. Do you hear me?"

Gladys held up her hands. "I'll behave. I promise."

Clay winked at her, in too good a mood to take of-
fense.

His afternoon with Charlie had been the stuff of leg-
ends. They'd stayed another hour, making use of the
second condom. This time he'd participated more, but
she'd still been in charge. It was a role she was born to,
he thought happily. He couldn't wait to see what happened next.

"Clay," the mayor said. "We've asked you here today
because the city council has been approached by several businesses in town. People have heard about your
Haycation idea and they're intrigued."

She handed out folders. Clay flipped his open and
saw a list of restaurants, stores and recreational facili-
ties.

"There's some interest in product placement, cou-
pons and theme nights," she continued. "For example,

every Thursday there could be square dancing. An instructor would teach guests, but locals could also pay a small fee and attend. Two or three of the restaurants could cater the event. The craft store in town wants to offer quilting classes. The class would be free and anyone attending would get a ten-percent off coupon at the store. That kind of thing."

"This works with what I've been planning," he said. "I like it. The more we can offer our guests, the more they'll enjoy themselves. I want repeat business and plenty of word-of-mouth. Fool's Gold is a unique tourist destination."

"Exactly." The mayor smiled at him. "We can each grow our success."

"I'd like to see—"

"Gladys," the mayor warned.

"Sorry."

"I wanted to check with you, Clay," the mayor continued, "before setting up a meeting with the Chamber of Commerce and our Business Development Council. If you're willing, I'll send out an email and suggest a few dates."

"That works for me."

"If there's anything we can do to help, let us know."

He wondered if any of the old ladies could scare some sense into Nate and keep him away from the teenagers in town. So far his farm manager had been behaving. But Clay didn't know if that was because of a change of heart or if Nate was simply being more careful.

"I'm good for now," he said.

Mayor Marsha glared at Gladys, then stood. "Excellent. I'll be in touch."

He shook hands with her, waved at Gladys, then left. On his way to his truck, he held on to the folder. The businesses in town believed in him. There was no way he was going to let any of them down. Fool's Gold was his home now. He wanted to be a part of things. His Haycations were going to be a success—no matter what it took.

CHAPTER FIFTEEN

CHARLIE STOOD UNEASILY in her mother's hotel suite. Her attempts to avoid Dominique had come to an end when her mother had left a message, saying she would be buying a sleeping bag and camping out in the fire station until Charlie agreed to speak to her. Or her daughter could show up at the hotel the next day and they could talk it out.

Charlie had chosen the conversation.

Now, looking at the woman who had given birth to her, she had to admit to a small amount of grudging respect for Dominique's tactics. She would have assumed that in a test of wills, she would have been the winner. But her mother was also determined. Maybe a trait they shared.

Dominique perched on the edge of her suite's living-room sofa and laced her fingers together.

"I want to apologize," her mother began.

Charlie waited. With Dominique one could never take an opening statement at face value. The follow-up phrase could be anything from "for visiting in the first place" or "for thinking you deserved my attention." She wasn't going to assume.

Her mother swallowed, then looked at her. "I should have been more supportive when you were attacked back in college." Her chin came up. "No. You weren't attacked. That's me avoiding ugliness. You were raped and I didn't believe you."

Tears filled her eyes and her mouth trembled. "I never thought..." She drew in a shaky breath. "I assumed..." She cleared her throat. "He seemed like such a nice boy. So handsome and charming. I met him in the campus police station. He introduced himself to me and said he was sorry you'd had second thoughts. But he wanted me to know he hadn't hurt you or done anything you hadn't wanted."

Charlie felt her body tense. Anger grew into rage and she wanted to hunt down the shithead who'd attacked her so callously, then lied about it to everyone. She'd done everything right, she thought grimly. Reported the crime, subjected herself to the humiliation of the rape kit. But it hadn't mattered. In the end, he'd been the one believed. Because rape was a "he said, she said" crime. And he was popular and handsome. A good student who'd never been in trouble. She was the awkward nobody.

"I was wrong," Dominique told her quietly. "So very wrong. You're my daughter and I should have been on your side, no matter what. I should have trusted you. I'm sorry."

Charlie let the words wash over her. They were too little, too late, and she wasn't completely sure she believed them, but even hearing them helped.

"Thank you."

"No," her mother said forcefully. "It's not enough to be sorry. I see that now. Except I want us to be friends. Is that too much to ask? Is it too late? Have I lost you like Mayor Marsha lost her daughter? Are you going to move away and die so we never have a chance?"

Charlie had heard bits and pieces about the mayor's past so she sort of had an idea about the tragedy in her family. "It's a big leap from what we're dealing with to my early demise."

"I know, but if you're dead, I'll be all alone."

Charlie wasn't sure if she should laugh or scream. "Because it's all about you?"

"I'd miss you very much."

"And you'd be alone."

Tears filled Dominique's eyes. "Yes. That, too."

Her mother was who she had always been. She might make small changes and try to act differently, but in her heart she would be the prima ballerina she'd been in her youth. Known throughout the world, a woman to be envied. A star who had danced for queens and presidents and prime ministers.

Charlie knew she could dredge up a thousand horrible memories. Times when her mother had dismissed her or ignored her. She could remember Dominique telling Dan that sending their only child to boarding school wouldn't be such a bad thing. But she also recalled men coming to the door and begging for a crumb of attention. Dominique always told them that her heart belonged to one man. And it always had.

"I love you," Dominique whispered.

The words caught Charlie off guard. She tried to steel herself against them, to say they didn't matter, but the simple phrase seemed to slip through her defenses and settle into her bruised and hungry heart.

Unexpected longing made her shift in her seat. Despite everything, she couldn't dismiss her mother or what she'd said. She couldn't say she was finished and that Dominique should go back to wherever she'd come from.

"I can do better," Dominique continued, her gaze pleading. "I can change."

"I'm not sure I believe that," Charlie admitted. "But I'll accept that you...care." *Love,* she thought. She wasn't ready to go there. But caring was a little easier.

"I do. I want this to work. We can be there for each other."

"Oh, joy."

Dominique either didn't get or easily ignored the sarcasm. "Did you know there's a dance school here in Fool's Gold?"

"Yes, but what does that have to do with anything?" Horror swept through her. "No," she said quickly, holding up both hands. "No way. You can't."

Her mother beamed at her. "I already did. I bought it."

"When?"

"I made the offer this morning. It's very generous, so I'm sure she'll agree. The owner will stay on as the director, but we're changing the name to the Dominique Guérin Academy of Dance. I'll offer creative direction."

Charlie stifled a groan. "From, ah, New York?"

Her mother smiled. "That wouldn't be very practical, would it? No, I'll live here part-time. I'll keep the house in New York and London but sell the one in Los Angeles. This will be my West Coast residence."

"Fool's Gold?" Charlie was impressed she could speak what with her chest so tight.

"Yes. It will be wonderful. I won't be teaching. Can you imagine me with a class full of beginning students? I would intimidate them too much. Perhaps I can give the older students a lecture or two. The ones that have promise. I could help them."

"Just knowing you're around will be an inspiration," Charlie said, almost meaning what she was saying. She was sure that for some little kid all excited about dance, Dominique was a big deal.

"I hope so. While I'm in town, we can spend time together. I meant what I said, Charlie. I want us to get to know each other. We're the only family each of us has left."

There was a sense of inevitability in the situation, Charlie thought. Her mother's use of her preferred version of her name was a huge concession. Perhaps she should stop fighting and simply accept. Dominique would never be warm and fuzzy, but someone who doted too much would drive Charlie crazy. Dan had loved them both and they had both loved Dan. That was a place for them to start.

Charlie stood and motioned for her mother to do the same. Dominique did as she requested. For a second they looked at each other, then Charlie held out her arms. Her tiny, perfect mother flung herself at her daughter and hung on tight. Charlie did the same. In that moment, it seemed like they might never let go.

CLAY STARED AT the tidy rows that would grow into his alfalfa crop. The planting was done and now there was just the waiting.

"I'd say it's like having a baby," Shane told him. "But I'm thinking this is cleaner."

Clay chuckled. "And no one's screaming."

His brother winced. "Don't even joke about that. Not with Annabelle pregnant."

"She'll be fine."

"I don't want to think about her in pain."

It was a part of birth, Clay thought. The cycle of life and all that, but he didn't think his brother was in a mood to be philosophical.

"She's not in pain now," Clay said.

"Good point. I heard from Rafe this morning."

"Me, too. I don't think he and Heidi are ever coming home." So far the newlyweds had put off their return twice.

"Heidi will eventually start to miss her goats," Shane said. "Sooner would be better for me. Athena is getting a wild look in her eye. I think she's planning a breakout."

Heidi's small herd was mostly well behaved. But every now and then Athena organized a field trip.

"As long as she doesn't let Priscilla out," Clay said. "I don't think Fool's Gold is ready for a free-roaming elephant."

The two men turned from the field and headed toward the truck.

"How's the house coming?" Clay asked.

"Nearly finished. It will be done by mid-October." Shane shook his head. "Annabelle is willing to move in with me, but she's still insisting on waiting until next year to marry me." He muttered something under his breathing that sounded like "damn fool woman" but was smart enough not to say it too loud.

"You love her," Clay said, opening the driver's side of the truck and getting in.

Shane climbed in on the passenger's side. "I know, but why does she have to be so stubborn? Why would anyone care that she's pregnant? Okay, sure, it's unconventional, but so what? We love each other. We're spending the rest of our lives together. But can we start that now? Nope. We have to wait so she can be the perfect bride."

"She wants to have the right kind of memories."

"She wants to drive me crazy."

"That's a bonus. Accept it, bro. From now on, she's going to run your life."

Shane grinned. "I wouldn't have it any other way."

"You're a lucky man."

"Yes, I am."

Clay started the engine and headed back for the main

house. "Annabelle's not the only one's who's stubborn," he said. "Charlie insisted on replacing her dishwasher herself, even though it was clearly a two-person job. By the time I got there to help, she was wedged between the counter and the dishwasher." He glanced at his brother. "It's not just you."

"I don't really find that knowledge comforting."

Clay grinned as he turned down the dirt road. They bounced along in comfortable silence. His thoughts once again returned to Charlie. Because he liked and respected her. She was fun, interesting and one of the sexiest women he knew. A lethal combination.

He knew it wasn't love. Love was dramatic. It was meeting someone's eyes for the first time and knowing that you wanted to be with her forever. But what he felt for Charlie was still significant. She was the first woman to interest him in years. The first one he wanted to spend time with. They were friends and lovers. It wasn't being in love, but it was still good. Something he wanted to hold on to.

"What are you going to do when Rafe and Heidi finally come home?" Shane asked.

Clay grinned. "You hinting I won't want to live with the newlyweds?"

"It's up to you."

"I'll figure something out. Mom and Glen are moving into their place next week. So I'll stay in the main house until Rafe and Heidi get back. Maybe rent a house in town." He wondered what Charlie would say to having a roommate.

CHARLIE LIFTED THE boy up so he could run his chubby fingers along the side of the hose.

"Pretty cool, huh?"

The four-year-old's eyes widened as he nodded.

She laughed and set him back on the ground. "Thinking you want to be a fireman when you grow up?"

Another nod.

"Thanks," his mom said. "I'm sorry he's so shy now. This morning all he talked about was seeing the big red fire engine."

"Don't worry about it. I love having big strong boys like him come by." She winked at the kid. "I'm here all day. Come back and see me."

Charlie waved as they walked away. Getting kids excited about the fire department was all part of the job. Traditionally, the Fall Festival was one of the times when the equipment was set up in town for everyone to admire and learn about. Although she considered herself a somewhat crabby person, she liked the public meet-and-greets. Especially with the little kids who were so wide-eyed and intrigued.

"Here you go."

Clay walked up and handed her a large lemonade from the stand by the park. Charlie took it.

"Thanks. I love these and I don't care that they use real sugar."

Clay held up his own drink. "I tried mine on the way back and I agree. The best ever."

As he wasn't with the fire department in any capacity yet, his presence was strictly as a civilian, but she was willing to admit, she liked having him around. He was good company. *Too good,* she thought, aware she wasn't as immune to him as she would like.

In truth, their deal should be over. Based on what happened the other day while they were out riding, she was plenty healed. The captain's actions after the fire proved that he was being given a fair shot. They'd both gotten what they wanted. She needed to cut him loose. Even if she didn't want to.

"What's next?" he asked.

Charlie stared at him, wondering how he'd figured out what she was thinking. Then she saw him pointing to the schedule posted by the rig.

"I have a fire-safety talk at eleven," she said. "Seven- to twelve-year-olds, so it's more entertainment with a few facts hidden in fun demonstrations than lecture."

"Get 'em while they're young," he said.

"Exactly. The holidays will be here before we know it and that's a prime time for house fires. People can be so stupid."

Clay grinned. "Ah, my delicate flower. You have to learn to open up and share your feelings."

"Shut up."

"Whoa! You didn't threaten me. I must be getting to you." He winked and lowered his voice. "As a reward, I have an idea about something we could do later."

Her chest suddenly got tight as heat burned a path to the center of her body. Wanting followed, leaving her weak at the knees. The man knew how to get to her, she thought, unable to summon any regret for the fact.

Two college-age women walked past. They caught sight of Clay and did a comical doubletake. One of them nudged the other and said something Charlie was glad she couldn't hear.

It happened all the time. Everywhere he went, women noticed. She would guess that he was offered phone numbers and sexual invitations on a nearly daily basis. Was he tempted or did it get old? She was almost afraid to ask.

As far as she could tell, he'd never been unfaithful to Diane. Personality-wise, Clay didn't seem interested in screwing around. Maybe he'd gotten it out of his system while he'd been younger. He had mentioned his dog days, before he'd met Diane.

"You got serious," he said. "What happened?"

She jerked her head toward the girls. "You have fans."

He didn't bother looking. "It doesn't mean anything."

"You don't get bored and think 'what the hell'?"

"No."

"As simple as that?"

"I've got what I want. Why would I go looking?"

Meaning her? She didn't think he was saying that, exactly. They weren't involved. Not in the traditional sense.

"I've suspected that being you isn't as easy as it seems," she admitted. "Now I'm starting to learn that being with you isn't that easy, either."

"I'm worth it," he said with a grin.

She thought about how she felt when she was with

him. Not just sexually, but how she enjoyed his company. With Clay there weren't any games. Just a sense of connection.

He was worth it, she realized. He was someone she wanted to be with. Which was going to make saying goodbye more difficult than she would like.

BY FOUR O'CLOCK, Charlie had lost her glow. She was tired, her feet hurt and the endless parade of small children asking the same question over and over again had ceased to be charming. She reminded herself it was her own damn fault for signing up for a double shift at the festival. Michelle would be on to relieve her any second. Then Charlie was going to go home, open a bottle of wine and sink into a bath. She might never come out.

Fifteen minutes later she'd handed over the reins, so to speak, and was about to head to her house. Clay appeared at her side.

"Hey," he said. "Finally done?"

They were across the street from the fire engine, standing next to the seating for the band that would start in a couple of hours. The sidewalks were crowded, the attendees loud and the late-afternoon warm. Around her were perfectly normal men, some of whom were even good-looking. Life would have been so much easier if she'd just been attracted to one of them.

"Charlie?"

She grabbed his hand and drew him away from the streaming pedestrians and over to the side of the stage.

It seemed to be the quietest, least crowded place in the festival.

She had to tell him the truth. Honor dictated she come clean and release him. It would be wrong to take advantage of him. Temptation was strong, of course. Need. Tingles. All reasons to keep things going. But she'd always prided herself on her character. She might have flaws but not being honest wasn't one of them.

"We need to talk," she told him, allowing herself to get lost in his dark eyes.

One corner of his perfect mouth turned up. "You know guys hate hearing that, right?"

"Maybe, but it's true. I'll make this easy on you. I'll talk and you listen and then we'll call it a day. How's that?"

"It depends on what you have to say."

"A cautious man."

"I've been married. I know there are hidden pitfalls."

She wanted to laugh, or at least smile. But right now it was hard enough to keep breathing. In a very short period of time, Clay had become important to her. Not in-love important—she wasn't a complete idiot. But he was someone she liked having around. She would miss him. A whole lot more than she would have thought possible.

She supposed the good news was that with her healing came the prospect of a regular relationship. Sadly, she wasn't interested in anyone else. Which made her the star in a bad teen movie.

She reminded herself that doing the right thing might

hurt in the moment, but it always felt better in the long run. She sucked in a breath and plunged ahead.

"I want to thank you," she said. "For helping me. For being patient and funny and godlike."

She expected him to smile at that, but his gaze remained serious. "I know where this is headed."

"Maybe so, but I'm still the one doing the talking. Remember?"

"Go ahead."

She tucked her hands behind her, then dropped them to her side. "You were great. Better than you had to be. The bottom line is you're going to get fair treatment at the department and I'm healed. So, technically, we're done."

She stared into his face, trying to figure out what he was thinking. There was no obvious sign of relief, for which she was grateful. A loud "Thank God!" would have been humiliating.

"No more deal," he confirmed.

She nodded.

"No obligation."

"Right."

"Good to know. Now we can start dating." He put his hands on her waist and drew her closer.

She stared at him. "What?"

"Dating. You know, going out. Seeing each other." He leaned in close and pressed his mouth to her ear. "Hot monkey sex whenever we want."

She shivered in anticipation, but still had to pull away and stare at him. "You're saying you want us to go out?"

"No, I'm saying I want us to be a couple. Exclusive. I don't like casual relationships. It's too confusing."

"Dating?"

"Yup."

She felt bubbly inside. Almost girlie. But she wanted to make sure she understood. "We'll exclusively date each other for an undetermined period of time."

He gave her a slow, sexy smile, then took her hand in his and laced their fingers together. "Uh-huh. What do you say, Charlie?"

"I say yes."

CHAPTER SIXTEEN

"IT'S A BAR," Dominique said as she glanced at the name on the door. "Are you sure?"

"That it's a bar or that we should be here?"

"Both."

"Mom, you gotta trust me. I eat here all the time. You're going to love it."

Dominique glanced from the sign proclaiming they were about to enter Jo's Bar back to her daughter. "Very well."

This was their first outing together. Dominique had offered lunch and Charlie had agreed. It sounded shorter than dinner, but offered more time together than coffee. Not that Charlie was looking for more time. Still, it was a good compromise.

They stepped into the bar and Dominique paused as she looked around. Charlie tried to see it from her mother's worldly and elegant perspective.

The walls were a pretty mauve, the lighting bright enough to keep the place from being creepy, but still flattering. Dominique had always been a sucker for good light. The big televisions were turned to what looked like a fashion show and shopping and the clientele were all women.

"Very nice," she said, at last. "I like it."

"I'm glad." Charlie motioned to a booth on the side. "Want to sit here?"

"Yes. Thank you."

"Hey, Charlie."

She glanced toward the bar and waved to her friend. "Hi, Jo."

"Great burgers," Charlie told her mother when they were seated. "I hear the salads are terrific."

Dominique glanced at her daughter. "Ah, to be young and physical again and not have to worry about my weight."

"Mom, you look great. Seriously. You're practically bony. Give herself a break and have a burger."

"Is the meat organic and grass-fed?"

Charlie rolled her eyes.

"I'll take that as a no," Dominique murmured.

Jo walked over with a couple of menus. "Ladies," she said. "We're running a special on the barbecue chicken salad. I can also make it into a wrap. And in honor of the fact that it's nearly fall, we have sweet-potato fries today."

Charlie moaned. "I love those."

Jo grinned.

"Jo, this is my mom. Dominique—"

"Dixon," Dominique said, interrupting her. "Dominique Dixon." She held out her hand.

"Jo Trellis. Nice to meet you."

"Likewise."

"You have a mother," Jo said, raising her eyebrows.

"I didn't just hatch," Charlie told her. "I'll have a diet."

"A glass of Chardonnay for me," Dominique said. "No. On second thought, I'll have a Corona with a lime."

Both women stared at her. She stared back.

"Beer?" Charlie asked when Jo had left. Before this moment, she would have assumed her mother didn't even know what beer was.

"It will go better with my nonorganic burger. And sweet-potato fries."

"Impressive."

"I can be fun," Dominique said with a sniff.

"Apparently."

Annabelle and Patience walked into the bar. When they saw Charlie they waved but didn't approach. Instead they joined a table that included Nevada Janack and Liz Hendrix.

"Friends of yours?" Dominique asked.

"Yes. Annabelle works at the library. She's engaged to Shane." Speaking of Clay's brother reminded her of a conversation she needed to have with her mother, but she would get through the who's who list first.

"Patience works at one of the local salons. Divorced. Her husband was a real jerk, but she's got a great kid. Lillie. Nevada—" Charlie pointed "—is one of three triplets."

Dominique glanced at her. "I've met her mother. Denise. She's very nice."

"I'm glad you think so. Liz is married to the oldest Hendrix son, Ethan. She's a mystery writer."

"I've seen her books in the bookstore. What a wonderful place. I know we're all going to be getting books directly implanted into our brains soon enough, but I still enjoy a good old-fashioned book in my hands."

"Paper over electronics?" Charlie asked.

"Yes."

Jo returned with their drinks. As Charlie watched, her mother expertly squeezed lime into the chilled glass, then poured in the bottle of Corona.

"You've done this before," she said, not sure if she should be admiring or shocked.

"More than once." Dominique took a sip, then smiled at Jo. "I'll have the burger. Medium, with the sweet-potato fries."

"You got it." She glanced at Charlie and raised her eyebrows. "Same for you?"

Charlie nodded.

When Jo had left, she took a drink of her diet soda, then squared her shoulders. "Mom?"

Dominique sighed. "I know that tone. You're about to tell me something I won't like."

Good call, she thought. "I'm about to tell you that Clay and I are dating."

Her mother tilted her head. "I already knew that."

Big oops. "Um, we're exclusive," she said quickly, knowing that she would take the truth to her grave. No way was she discussing her long-term sexual dysfunction with Dominique.

"It was his idea," she added, both proud and defensive.

Dominique picked up the napkin and blotted her lips. Then she nodded slowly. "I think that's wonderful. If you're getting serious, I should probably get to know him. Isn't that the traditional next step?"

Charlie felt her mouth drop open. She consciously closed it. "You want to spend some time with Clay?"

"Yes. Don't worry. I'm not going to ask any embarrassing questions. I just want to get to know him. He's your boyfriend and an important part of your life."

Charlie hadn't thought in terms of the *b* word. She found it a little startling to think about. "Okay," she mumbled, knowing she would do her best to put off the meeting for as long as possible.

"Good." Dominique took another drink of her beer. "I hope it works out for the two of you. Falling in love is so wonderful."

Had Charlie been drinking, she would have choked. "No one's in love."

"You don't start out that way, of course, but who knows what could happen. Love is a miracle. I still remember when I fell in love with your father. He swept into my life without warning and changed everything."

She smiled fondly. "It was freezing outside. I remember how he brought the cold in with him. I was about to complain, but then he smiled and I couldn't speak. He was wearing a ridiculous plaid coat. I hated it. He let it fall to the ground and he had a plaid shirt on underneath. I hate plaid. But it looked so good on him.

As I looked at him all I could think was that I wanted those strong arms around me and that I never wanted him to let go."

Dominique paused, then glanced down at the table. "Sorry. I got carried away."

"No. Don't apologize. It's nice to hear you talk about Dad. I know you loved him."

"I did. He was everything. In a world where I could never be sure of anyone, he was my rock." She looked at Charlie. "I would have given it all up for him."

"He wouldn't have wanted that. He knew how your career made you happy."

"He made me happy. I was so lucky to have him, even for those few short years. I will love him forever." She reached across the table and touched Charlie's hand. "I hope you find that kind of love. With Clay or someone else. I hope you know what it's like to be with the one person who truly loves and respects you."

Charlie felt the sincerity of her words. "Thanks, Mom. I'd like that, too."

"Your father saw me for who I really was and he loved me anyway. So few people were interested in me as a person. They wanted to be with the star, the dancer. He loved the woman, flaws and all. That was very powerful."

Dominique drew back and stared at her drink.

Her sadness was tangible. Charlie missed her father, but had a feeling her pain was on a different plane. Dominique had been shattered. It was unfortunate that the two of them hadn't been able to connect over the loss and find solace in each other. Maybe they could change that now. Reconnect with each other. Charlie wasn't looking for a sitcom mother who baked and giggled about boys. But she wouldn't mind having someone she could think of as family.

ANNABELLE STRETCHED OUT on one of the lounge chairs in Charlie's backyard. She had a sun hat pulled low and her feet up. "Don't for a moment think I'm leaving without getting an answer. You two have been seen all over town, making out like teenagers. I consider myself a close personal friend, so I want the truth."

Annabelle raised her hat and narrowed her eyes. "Do you doubt my determination?"

Charlie laughed. "Not for a second."

"Good. Now start at the beginning. Last I heard, you were using Clay for sex. I totally respect that, by the way."

"I know. It's why we're friends."

"And?"

Charlie was glad Annabelle worried about her delicate complexion. That meant she was more concerned with keeping her face covered than watching Charlie's expression. As Charlie was currently grinning like an idiot, she didn't have to be embarrassed. She could revel in her happiness and still be considered one of the cool kids.

"Clay and I have been sleeping together," she began. "It's been going well."

"I should hope so. I'm going to marry into the family.

I would hate to have to be embarrassed by my brother-in-law's bedroom skills."

"You can rest easy. He's spectacular."

Annabelle groaned. "TMI."

"Sorry. Anyway, I was thinking that I was, you know, healed, so I told him."

Annabelle pulled off the hat. "Just like that?"

"I thought I had to."

"You are principled, young lady. Then what happened?"

"Clay listened and agreed. We were done with our deal." She did her best not to beam. "Then he said he wanted us to keep seeing each other. Exclusively. So we're dating."

Annabelle laughed. "You have a boyfriend."

"Something like that."

"Patience said you were holding hands when you went to the movies. It's very sweet."

"Don't make me hurt you."

"Come on, let us have fun with this. You've got this amazing guy. The little people should be able to find happiness where they can."

"Fine. Mock me all you want."

"I will." Her eyes widened. "I know. Marry Clay and then we can be sisters."

Charlie was surprised by the jolt of longing that shot through her. "Calm down. No one's getting married."

"I knew you'd say that." She replaced her hat and sighed. "I like this. We're all in love. Except for Patience. We need to fix her up with someone. Know any single guys?"

Charlie considered who was in town. "There's the new guy."

Annabelle removed her hat again. "What new guy?"

"Gideon. Gabriel. Something like that."

"What? Why don't I know about this? Who is he?"

"He bought the local radio station. Mayor Marsha told me a few weeks ago. It's all very mysterious."

"Have you seen him? Is he good-looking?"

"I haven't seen him and I don't care what he looks like. I only have eyes for Clay."

"As you should." Annabelle paused and re-covered her face. "I was going to ask more questions about the radio guy, but you've distracted me. About Clay... Should I worry?"

"Like I said, I'm not in love with him."

The hat moved again and Charlie saw one green eye staring at her. She shook her head. "No. I'm not."

"Are you sure?" Annabelle asked. "Love is sneaky."

"Clay says it's an at-first-sight kind of thing."

"Maybe it was for him, but it wasn't for me. Of course I had a sucky childhood. His was better."

Charlie had never been in love. She'd felt loved by her father, but that had been different. She believed Dominique felt a form of love, although they were still working their way through that.

"How is loving Shane different from the relationship you had with your first husband?" Charlie asked.

Annabelle pushed off her hat again. "I'm different,"

she admitted. "Stronger and more sure. With Lewis, I was so desperate for someone to care about me, I didn't look past what he said to judge his actions. With Shane, I see love in both his words and deeds." She wrinkled her nose. "I know that sounds old-fashioned but both are important. I need to hear the words, but what he does makes me feel special."

"Like the fact that he doesn't want to wait to get married? That he built his house to suit you?"

"Something like that." Annabelle grinned. "He gives with his whole heart. I've never had that before. Loving him makes me a better person. Being loved by him makes me feel safe. We each want to be the one who gives more."

That, Charlie could relate to. Clay didn't take her for granted, or dislike the parts of her she liked best. She felt the same about him. She knew his flaws and was okay with them.

"Clay's a good guy, too," she said.

"He is."

Charlie waited, but Annabelle didn't seem to have any more to say. "Are you going to warn me to be careful?" she asked.

Annabelle sat up and faced her. "I don't think so."

"But I haven't been with a man in a decade. Clay's basically my first adult relationship. It would be easy for me to fall for him. He's been married. He's loved and lost and he's not looking for anything else. That puts me at a disadvantage. I could get hurt."

Annabelle leaned forward and patted her arm. "My little girl is growing up so fast. I'm just so proud."

Charlie swatted away her arm. "Shut up."

Annabelle's smile faded. "You don't need me to tell you the potential pitfalls. You already know. Besides, I think Clay's at just as much risk as you are."

"I am pretty great," Charlie said, stretching out on her lounge chair.

"Exactly."

Charlie wondered if Annabelle knew the words were just cheap talk. When it came to Clay, she found herself both hopeful and terrified. Being around him was amazing. From what she could tell, he was everything she wanted. But he was also a man who had already had one great love and wasn't looking for another. Clay had said love was a lightning bolt and so far there hadn't been a single flash in the sky.

She planned to enjoy everything about her experience with him, all the while protecting her heart as best she could. If she got hurt, she would recover. She would move on. Whatever the cost, it was worth it. He'd made her whole and no matter what happened, she was better for having known him.

CLAY LED KHATAR out of the corral. The white Arabian stallion playfully nuzzled Clay's neck.

"I'm not Annabelle," Clay grumbled, pushing him away. "She'll be by later. In the meantime, behave."

The majestic animal snorted, as if amused. Despite his massive size and the strength that went with it, he was one of the gentlest horses Shane owned. *Good news for his brother,* Clay thought. Shane had gotten the million-dollar horse for a discount due to his difficult and potentially killer nature. Which had turned out to be the result of bad training and some abuse.

Since arriving in Fool's Gold, the once-mean-tempered horse had turned into an equine kitten. Last week Khatar had escaped from the corral to join one of Shane's riding classes. He'd decided that next to Annabelle, he adored a little girl named Kalinda best. She had suffered life-threatening burns the previous summer and was still going through various surgeries as she healed. She'd started riding a small pony but Khatar had made it clear that when she was ready for a horse, he planned to be the guy.

While the class circled the ring, Khatar had kept pace with Kalinda and her pony. He'd stayed close when she'd dismounted, stepping between her and the other horses.

"You're kind of a sap, you know that?" Clay patted the horse. "Ready for a good long ride?"

Khatar's ears perked up at the mention of riding. When Shane had mentioned he'd had to spend the afternoon signing the final paperwork on his house, Clay had offered to exercise the horses. With his alfalfa crop in the ground and no firefighter training scheduled, he had the time.

He'd just finished saddling Khatar when an unfamiliar Taurus pulled in next to the house. Clay watched a guy climb out. He was in his mid-to-late thirties and had on a shirt that said "Gil" and the name of the local hardware store.

Clay made sure Khatar was secure and went to greet the man.

"Can I help you?" he asked.

"I'm looking for Nate."

Gil was an average kind of guy. Not too tall, with more paunch than muscles. But there was rage in his light brown eyes. Seconds later a teenage girl climbed out of the passenger seat. Her eyes were red and her mouth trembled.

"Daddy, no," she cried.

It didn't take Clay long to figure out what this was about. His stomach tightened as he realized his farm manager had continued to play the game Clay had warned him against.

"Your daughter?" he asked, motioning to the sobbing girl.

Gil jerked his head in agreement. "Do you know where he is?"

Clay reached for his phone and pushed a button. "Nate, would you come out by the house, please?"

"Sure, boss."

Gil's gaze settled on Clay. "You brought him here?"

"Yes. I'm sorry."

"Like that's gonna help."

Nate appeared at the doorway to the barn and surveyed the situation. Clay watched the indecision cloud his gaze.

"Don't make it worse by running," Clay told him. "Come face what you've done."

Nate nodded slowly and approached.

Clay was willing to let this play out. If Gil wanted a piece of Nate, Clay didn't have a problem with that. If the girl was under eighteen, Clay would be the first one to call the police. He hadn't decided if he was going to beat the shit out of Nate or not. He supposed that was up to Gil.

Nate closed about half the distance and then raised both hands, palms out.

"It's not what you think," he began, his weasel eyes darting left and right. "She's over eighteen."

"She's seventeen," Gil said with a growl. "And she's my baby girl. What the hell were you thinking?"

Clay felt the other man's rage and knew he couldn't begin to imagine what this father must be feeling. He thought of Charlie and what had happened to her, then knew he couldn't touch Nate. Once he started, he wouldn't stop.

"Daddy, no!" The girl grabbed her father's arm, tears pouring down her cheeks. "Nothing happened. I've told you and told you."

"Get in the car," Gil told her, starting toward Nate.

"Daddy, stop! Daddy, we didn't—" She sucked in a breath. "Daddy, I'm still a virgin. We never did that."

Gil stopped. He glanced back at his daughter who was bright red and still crying. "You swear?"

"We can go see Dr. Galloway if you want. I wouldn't do that. Not with him."

Gil glanced between them. "All right, then."

Clay stepped toward him and lowered his voice. "I'm still sorry, sir. Nate worked for me and that makes what happened my responsibility."

"Worked?" Gil's gaze was steady.

Clay nodded.

"I'll leave you to it, then."

He motioned for his daughter to get in the car. He got in, as well, and they drove away. Clay watched Khatar work his way free and stroll over. The big horse ignored Nate and walked to Clay, as if showing where his loyalties lay.

Nate shuffled his feet then stuck his hands in his back pockets. "I didn't do anything to her."

"You took her out."

"That's my business."

"It is. But I've got no use for you here. This is a small town. You don't respect that or me. I'm going to write you a check for the pay I owe you, plus two weeks. If I see you around here again, I'll escort you out of town myself. Am I clear?"

Nate nodded and took a step toward the barn. "I'll go get my things."

"You do that."

Getting rid of Nate only solved one problem, Clay realized. It wasn't that he had chosen the wrong man that bothered him so much. It was the fact that he hadn't listened to his gut when he should have. He knew better. Now he had to figure out what other mistakes he'd made and how he was going to fix them.

CHAPTER SEVENTEEN

CHARLIE TUCKED HER feet under her as she sat on her sofa. "You're taking this too much to heart."

Clay, normally easygoing and optimistic, stared past her. His mouth was tight, his expression troubled. "I screwed up. I'm the one who hired Nate. I know about two girls. Who knows how many others there were."

Charlie wanted to point out the young women in question had at least been over sixteen, but didn't think that information would help. Nate had been a dog when it came to dating habits. The girls might have been plenty willing, but they were far too young.

"I talked to the police chief," he said. "She assured me Nate is gone. Last she saw, he was heading over the mountains."

"Good riddance."

"It's not enough. Dammit, Charlie, why did I choose him?"

"Because you thought you were doing the right thing. Because he had experience and when you ran a background check, he was clean."

"He's still clean," Clay muttered. "He didn't break the law and it's not illegal to be a jerk."

"Too bad." She reached out and put her hand on his. "You made a mistake. Now you learn from it."

"That's it? I'd feel better if you'd at least yell at me."

"Sorry. I'm not in the mood to yell. Everyone screws up. You found out the truth about Nate and fired him. That's the right thing. You'll do better next time."

"I should have listened to my gut. But I went with experience because I didn't trust myself. Which means there were two mistakes."

"We can come up with a whole list of them, if you want. Does that help?"

He managed a faint smile. "Using logic against me? That's kind of low."

"I get in my hits where I can."

He laced his fingers between hers. "Thanks for listening. And kicking me when I'm down. It keeps things in perspective." He drew in a breath. "Maybe I can't do this."

"You can."

She leaned in and kissed him. Despite everything going on, his mouth was willing. Warm and ready to claim hers. A quality she found she liked in a man. She raised her arms and put them on his shoulders.

"I can think of a few things that will make you feel better," she said, resting her forehead against his.

"Yeah? Like what?"

"I could take all your clothes off and—"

Someone knocked on her front door.

Charlie glanced up and swore. "If that's my mother,

I'm sending her back to New York. Seriously, I'll pay for overnight delivery."

Clay chuckled.

Charlie stood and walked to the door. But when she pulled it open she found an unfamiliar man standing there. He was dressed in a work shirt and jeans, but carried a briefcase.

"I'm Miles Tessler," he said. "I'm looking for Clay Stryker. His brother said I could find him here."

Clay appeared at her side. "I'm Clay."

Miles held out a business card for a seed company. "If I could have a few minutes of your time, Mr. Stryker."

Charlie led the way in to the living room. Miles glanced around, then looked at them. If she had to pick an emotion, she would say he was both nervous and scared. Neither boded well for his news.

"I understand you've already planted your fall alfalfa crop," he began.

"Last week."

"Unfortunately, the seed we sent you has developed a problem. It's technical so I won't get into the details right now. Suffice it to say that it's poisoned."

Charlie blinked. "What?" she asked, bad-seed references running through her head.

Miles kept his gaze on Clay's suddenly unreadable face. "It has to come out, Mr. Stryker. As soon as it germinates. And not just the seed. The soil, as well. It's been contaminated. I brought specific instructions with me, along with information about our insurance. We will, of course, cover the cost for removal and returning your farmland to its previous condition. We're going to get this right. It will just take a little time."

Charlie leaned against the back of the sofa. "It all has to go?" she asked.

"Yes," Miles told her. "Along with eight inches of topsoil. I'm very sorry."

Clay hadn't said a word. He stood there, not moving. *Taking it all in,* she thought sadly. Watching his dream be destroyed before it had even begun. First the burial site, then Nate and now this. He must feel like his Haycation dream was cursed.

"Hand it over," Clay said.

Miles gave him the paperwork and Clay walked him to the door. When the other man was gone, Clay looked back at Charlie.

"I need to go deal with his," he told her.

"Are you okay? How can I help? I want to do something."

He looked resigned. The next words came out slow. "I'll be fine. We'll get this fixed and then I'll plant a new crop next spring. It's not important. Not like I was feeding people."

"Clay, don't. You have a great idea. The Haycations are going to work out. This is a setback."

"A hell of one," he muttered. He leaned in and kissed her cheek. "I'll be in touch."

He left. She didn't try to stop him—not sure if she should. While she knew that offering comfort was part of the dating relationship, she wasn't sure about anything beyond that. Should she have insisted he stay and

talk? Forced him to verbalize what he was feeling? She
was figuring out the girlfriend thing as she went and
not doing that great a job, she thought grimly.

She did believe that too much was coming at Clay
too fast, which could send him to a bad place. What she
didn't know was how he would act when he got there.
Or what it would change about them.

"I'VE NEVER known anyone who lived in a hotel before,"
May admitted. "It seems so decadent."

Dominique poured tea into the cups and then set
down the pot. "If I were to buy a house, I would need
staff. Someone to clean and do the cooking. Someone
else for the yard. This seemed easier."

May smiled at her. "You don't cook?"

"I don't like to cook. The food here at the Lodge is
good, so why not let them take care of the details? With
a suite, I have all I need. Meals are delivered and house-
keeping takes care of everything else."

They were seated in Dominique's suite at Ronan's
Lodge. She'd ordered afternoon tea for herself and her
guest. *Not just a luxury,* she thought with a sigh as she
passed over a plate of cucumber sandwiches. *A necessary stand in the battle of civilization over chaos.*

"I don't mean to pry," May said, "but isn't it expensive to live in a hotel?"

Dominique took a sandwich for herself and placed
it on the delicate plate in front of her. The hotel had
lovely china for their tea service. Traditional and just
fussy enough to be feminine.

"Money isn't a problem," Dominique said quietly. "I did well in my career and I've been even more fortunate with my investments. I could live in hotels for three lifetimes and never touch the principal balance. But as I'm sure you learned a long time ago, money might buy security, but it doesn't buy relationships. Besides, I believe that me living in a hotel helps Charlie. It makes my time here seem less permanent and therefore she's less threatened by me having bought the dance studio."

"Impressive," May said, then sipped her tea. "Looking at it from her point of view."

"It seems to help."

Dominique had come to see that she still had a long way to go when it came to understanding the mother-daughter dynamic. But progress had been made. Charlie took her calls and reacted favorably when Dominique suggested they get together. It would be some time before they were truly close, but Dominique was willing to do the work. When she was around her daughter, she felt a sense of belonging she hadn't experienced since Dan had died. Her only regret was the years she'd wasted being so self-centered and foolish.

"You're doing well," May told her.

"I hope so. Once I started to understand what I was doing wrong, I was able to make progress." She smiled. "I do miss talking about myself, though."

May laughed. "That's why you have friends like me."

Dominique smiled and reached for a sandwich, but her hands shook a little. Were they friends? she wondered. That would be nice. She couldn't remember the last time she'd had a real friend. Someone who cared about her without being tied to her business.

"Rafe and Heidi are due home," May said, obviously not aware she'd said anything significant. "Their flight arrives late Friday. I'm thinking of having a football party on Sunday."

Dominique tilted her head. "What do you mean?"

"People come over to watch football."

"On purpose?"

"Yes, on purpose." May said the words with a smile. "All three of my boys will be there. Heidi, of course and Annabelle. I suspect Clay will want Charlie there. Glen wouldn't miss it. Why don't you come? You don't have to understand the game to have a good time. There will be plenty of food and you can hang with Charlie without there being any pressure."

Dominique liked the sound of that. *Hanging,* as May called it. Just being one of the group.

"Thank you. I'd like to bring something." She smiled impishly. "I've gotten to know the head chef at the restaurant. Her sister was a huge fan and danced for several years, so we have that in common. I'm sure she could come up with something delicious."

May laughed. "Bring dessert. I'm providing everything else. It's just easy finger food. Nachos, chicken wings and a few other appetizers."

"Perfect," Dominique said, thinking about everyone sitting around watching a game on TV. "Easy food means easy conversation. I see where you're going with that. Very sensible."

May patted her arm. "You haven't been around many families, have you?"

"No. I was always traveling or rehearsing or attending class. The world of dance is demanding. When I was on the road, the company had instructors travel with us so we wouldn't miss practice." She smiled. "When I know you better, I'll let you see my feet. Dancers' feet are not pretty. Between the broken toes, the bruises, the years of abuse, we end up with battered and twisted feet." She held out her leg, showing off her sensible pump. "All concealed under the finest leather."

"You worked very hard for your success."

"I did," Dominique said easily. "The effort was the easy part. Being away was difficult. When I was married, I desperately missed Dan. After he was gone, I couldn't seem to grasp he wouldn't be home waiting for me. I've never been so sad."

"That was a long time ago."

"I'll never stop loving him."

"I know the feeling. I lost my husband, as well. It took me nearly twenty years to find Glen." May's eyes glistened with unshed tears. "I never thought I'd be in love again. Certainly not at my age. But there he was and I couldn't resist him."

Dominique had heard that people could fall for someone else. She didn't envy them. No one could come close to Dan and missing him was better than loving anyone else.

"I take it you're not ready to start dating," May said

with a gentle smile. "I shouldn't introduce you to one of Glen's friends?"

"No, thank you. I've taken lovers a few times, but never enjoyed the experience. There's only been Dan. I was blessed to have him in my life. I've been blessed in many ways. My career and now I've been given a second chance with my daughter. It's more than enough for anyone."

CLAY HELPED RAFE pull the sofas around to face the big TV. His older brother straightened and stared at the big screen mounted on the wall.

"Nice," he said. "Just in time for the season."

"Because you watch so much football," Clay said.

"I could always do more. Heidi likes it and Dante and I always used to watch the game together. I need to keep up the tradition."

"So your partner doesn't sulk?"

Rafe grinned. "Dante would never admit to sulking."

"I should have taken a picture while you were gone. He's not a happy guy."

"I got that from his emails."

They shifted the coffee table and then brought in the kitchen table and put it against the wall. Their mother was going for more Super Bowl party than casual Sunday-afternoon game day, but Clay wasn't going to complain. Not with all the smells coming from the kitchen.

When they'd finished, Rafe glanced around at the big room. "It's good to be back."

"Didn't love Paris?"

Rafe grinned. "I loved being with Heidi. The city was less interesting. But she liked it."

Clay could have teased him about being led around by his nose, or his dick, but he was more envious than mocking. When he'd been married to Diane, he would have acted exactly the same. He'd gone to see Broadway shows because she liked them. He'd taken her shopping, visited museums. All to see her eyes light up as she enjoyed herself.

Charlie would be different, he thought with a grin. She would find pleasure in car races and hiking. He doubted she could make it all the way through a ballet or opera without wanting to kill someone. Qualities he found appealing.

"I heard about what happened with the seed and Nate," Rafe said, tossing him the tablecloth they were supposed to put on the table. "You okay?"

Clay's good mood faded. "No. I'm pissed and confused. First the graves, then Nate, then the seed. I'll admit the seed and the graves are just bad luck, but I'm the one who picked Nate. I went with experience over my gut and I was wrong. What gets me is that he was screwing around in town. I want to live here for a long time. I don't want parents mad at me because my farm manager has a thing for teenage girls."

"You handled it. He's gone. The situation is resolved."

"I still feel like an idiot."

"Next time you'll listen to your gut."

"Agreed. I keep waiting to find out how else I've screwed up. With the seed, I'm playing a waiting game. It has to sprout before it can be pulled out. Something about the toxicity. My schedule will get pushed back, which I don't like, but can't do anything about."

"No fall alfalfa?" Rafe asked.

Clay faked a punch. "Shut up."

"I'm being sympathetic."

"Yeah, sure you are." Clay told himself to shake off his mood. He was going to see Charlie. That was worth smiling about.

"Hey, I was going to send flowers."

"Are you two fighting?" their mother called from the kitchen.

"Who us?" Rafe yelled back.

"You two boys get along, you hear me? Charlie and her mother are joining us and I want you to make a good impression."

Clay thought about last night in Charlie's bed. She'd wanted to be in charge again—a circumstance he found he enjoyed. She was learning more and more about what she liked and what they could do together. Good thing he worked out regularly—otherwise her energy could kill him.

"Charlie, huh?" Rafe asked. "When did you start seeing her?"

"While you were gone."

"She's good people." His older brother frowned. "Don't screw with her."

Clay knew what Rafe meant and he liked that Charlie

had people to care about her. "She's important to me," he said, then he grinned. "And she can't get enough of me."

"Then you're a lucky man."

"I know."

"I can't remember the last time you brought a girl around."

"I was still a teenager when I headed to New York," Clay reminded him. "I did most of my dating out of town."

"We all liked Diane, but it's good you're moving on."

Clay nodded. With Charlie, there was a growing emotional connection. He knew her and respected her. He wanted her, but that was easy. They were good together. It wasn't love, but it was more than he'd ever expected.

They finished setting up the table, then went into the kitchen. Shane and Annabelle were collecting ingredients for nachos. Glen was in charge of the barbecue, where he would cook the wings. May had just put a large tray of stuffed mushrooms in the oven.

The old-fashioned kitchen was crowded and loud. There were plenty of "excuse mes" and "coming throughs." Still, it was warm and Clay knew he'd been right to come home and settle here. Sure, Nate had been a mistake, but he'd made it right. He'd already put a call in to Ty and they were going to talk about the farm-manager job.

He heard a truck in the driveway. "They're here," he yelled and went out to greet their guests.

He winked at Charlie but walked around to the passenger side where he opened the door.

"Hello, Dominique," he said, holding out his hand
and helping her to the ground.

"Clay." She reached back inside and passed him two
pastry boxes. "I brought pie."

"We love pie."

"Make sure you keep working out after you eat pie.
My daughter deserves a handsome boyfriend."

"Yes, ma'am," he said, taking the boxes from her.
"Mom's in the kitchen."

"I can find my way."

Dominique started for the house. Charlie came
around the side of the truck and winced. "That was
a little heavy-handed," she said. "Sorry. The parental
thing is new to her and she's still figuring it all out."

He grinned. "You do deserve a handsome boyfriend."

"You're in no danger of falling short."

"I might get fat."

"Not if you want to make it as a volunteer firefighter,
big guy. We'll test your physical prowess every year."

He leaned in and kissed her. "On or off the field?"

She leaned in, her mouth hungry against his. "I'll
come up with some very special qualifying activities."

"I look forward to that."

He shifted the pies to his right hand and cupped his
left behind her neck. Her mouth was insistent on his.
He nipped her lower lip, then slipped his tongue inside.
Heat burned through him, making him want more. She
grabbed onto his biceps, as if in danger of falling.

"How do you do that?" she asked with a whisper. "Make me want you with just a look or a touch?"

"Magic."

She rested her forehead on his and tried to control her breathing. "I'm thinking that might be it."

He straightened, then stroked her face. "We have good chemistry and you're..." He hesitated, wanting to say it right.

"Highly sexed?" she asked in a low voice. "Am I normal? Should I want you all the time?"

"Hell, yes."

She gave a strangled laugh. "I'm being serious."

"So am I. You're young and healthy. Enjoying sex is natural. From my perspective, you're smart, funny and you have a killer body. Should I be sad that you want to make love with me on a regular basis?"

"When you put it like that," she said, glancing toward the house, then back at him. "Do you think it's because I went without for so long?"

"Maybe, but you should have calmed down by now if it were just that. You have an active sex drive." He looped his arm around her shoulders and sighed. "I'm taking my vitamins. We should be okay. You know CPR, right?"

"I could so sock you in the stomach."

"You could. Or you could punish me later."

Her blue eyes brightened with the idea. "I like that. A little torture. You all naked and having to stay perfectly still while I lick you into submission."

Suddenly he wasn't laughing. The image stopped

him in midstride and he wasn't sure he was going to be able to take a breath anytime soon.

Charlie raised her eyebrows. "Wow. The power of suggestion."

"You're irresistible."

She turned to face him. "You are, too."

He dropped his hand to hers and squeezed her fingers, then led her inside. They still had the game to get through, but later he would remind her of her promised "torture." It was exactly how he wanted to end his day.

AN HOUR LATER they were ready for the kickoff. The L.A. Stallions were favored to win against the Bears. Clay sat on the floor, in front of Charlie. He leaned against the sofa, her long legs next to him, her bare feet pressing against his hips. Clay glanced around the room and realized, except for Dominique, the whole family was going two-by-two.

The teams lined up, prepared to start the game. The Stallions had elected to receive. The players got into position and the ball was kicked into the air. It went up and up, then came down, close to the sideline. Too close. Players surged forward and the L.A. Stallion cheerleading squad scattered to get out of the way.

One of the young women didn't move fast enough and she was mowed down by a Stallion player. Instead of following the action, the camera stayed on the cheerleader, who lay on the ground, her leg at an awkward angle, her eyes closed.

"That had to hurt," Charlie said. "I hope she's okay."

No one else spoke. The camera moved in closer and the cheerleader's face filled the screen. Rafe swore, Shane jumped to his feet and May clutched her throat. Clay stared, unable to believe what he was seeing.

"What is it?" Dominique asked. "Is this part of the game?"

"No," May said, her voice a whisper. "No, it's not."

"Do you know that woman lying there?"

"She's my daughter."

CHAPTER EIGHTEEN

EVERYONE WAS TALKING at once. For Dominique, the press of bodies, the frantic conversation reminded her of the few minutes backstage before a performance. She was oddly comforted by the frenetic energy, but knew enough to keep that thought to herself. Instead she hovered by May, wanting to help but not sure how.

She spotted Charlie talking to Clay. Clay shook his head and walked to May. Dominique hurried toward her daughter.

"This is all very upsetting," she said. "For the family," she added. "I didn't know her."

"Me, either," Charlie admitted, watching Clay speak with his mother who waited on hold on the phone. She turned back to Dominique and lowered her voice. "Evie, Evangeline, is the youngest by several years. She's not exactly close to her mom."

Dominique swung around to stare at May. "Now that you mention it, I don't remember her mentioning a daughter. But that's not possible. May is the perfect mother." She frowned.

Charlie surprised her by putting her arm around her. "Not with Evie. I don't know very much except she moved out when she was still a teenager and hasn't been back. I know Clay and Shane have kept in touch with her, but even they didn't know she was a cheerleader."

Dominique took that in. If someone as good and understanding as May could make mistakes, there was hope for everyone else.

May seemed to collapse a little. Glen held her close while Rafe took the phone from her and pressed it to his ear.

From what Dominique had seen, Evie had been put on a stretcher and carried off the field. She hadn't opened her eyes or even moved. The hit had been a hard one. Anything could have happened.

"Los Angeles isn't that far," Dominique said. "Someone could get a flight out of Sacramento and be there in a couple of hours."

"I'm sure that's what will happen," Charlie said.

May excused herself and left the kitchen. Dominique hesitated a second, then followed. She followed May into the guest room on the main floor.

"I'm sorry," she said, coming up to her friend. "You must feel awful."

May nodded, her arms wrapped around her midsection. "I can't believe what happened. I don't think she was moving. Did you see her move?"

Dominique stepped closer and held May tight. "Let's find out what the doctor has to say before you assume the worst. I've seen hundreds of injuries in my day, let me tell you. Modern medicine is a miracle. I'm sure she'll be fine."

May drew in a breath. Her whole body was shaking. "I didn't know," she whispered. "I didn't know what my own daughter was doing. I haven't spoken to her in years. Sometimes I let myself forget about her because when I remember, I know I was wrong. And I don't know how to fix that."

Tears filled May's eyes. "That's why I wanted to help you with Charlie. One of us should get it right."

"You can still get it right with Evie," Dominique said, enjoying being the one offering comfort rather than taking it. "She's going to need you now more than ever."

"What are you talking about?"

"She's been hurt. She needs her family."

Dominique remembered an idiot stumbling into her while she was leaping into a grand jeté, knocking her off balance. She had crashed to the ground, feeling as if several bones had snapped. All she'd been able to think was how much she'd wanted Dan. He, of course, had been with Charlie. Dominique had been on tour, in London, painfully far from home. She'd recovered. She'd only missed three performances. But the sense of vulnerability had stayed with her. If Evie was seriously injured, she would want to be with those who loved her.

"You think I should go to her?" May asked.

"Of course."

May shook her head and took a step back. "No. She doesn't want me. I'll send her brothers. She likes them."

"You're her mother."

"You don't know what I did. I can never take it back."

"Whatever it was, I did much worse and Charlie has

forgiven me. She needs you, May. This is your chance to be there for her."

Clay walked into the room. "I just got off the phone with the local air-charter company. Finn can fly us to L.A. right now. We're meeting him at the Fool's Gold airport in fifteen minutes. The flight will take just over an hour. Annabelle and Heidi are going to work the phones and get in touch with Finn's office. They'll radio him when we find out where Evie is and we'll land as close as we can." Clay's eyes narrowed. "You coming, Mom?"

"Of course she is," Dominique said, giving her friend a little push toward the door. "Go on. The rest of us will take care of things here at the house. Make sure one of you calls us and lets us know how she is."

May glanced between them. "All right. Yes, I'll go, too. You're right. I need to be there."

She stepped into the hallway. Dominique expected Clay to follow, but he surprised her by walking over and hugging her. "I see a lot of potential in you, Mrs. Dixon," he said, then kissed her on the cheek.

Five minutes later, May and her sons were gone. Glen had driven them to the airport. Heidi and Annabelle were working two cell phones, trying to find out where Evie was. Charlie walked over to her mother.

"That was unexpected," she said. "I hope Evie's okay."

"Me, too." Dominique looked at her daughter. "I quite like your young man."

Charlie smiled. "Me, too."

"I WOULDN'T do that if I were you," Shane said.

Clay paused in the hallway. "You scared of a girl?"

"She's not a girl. She's our sister, and, yes." Shane glanced back toward the downstairs guest-bedroom door. "You think you can do better? Go ahead."

Evie had been in the house two days. In the end, Rafe, May and Shane had been the ones to fly out to get Evie. Clay had stayed behind to get the room ready and order any medical equipment she might need for her recovery. May and Shane had delivered her while Rafe had stayed behind in Los Angeles to take care of loose ends.

Evie had spent the first twenty-four hours in a somewhat drugged sleep. The doctor had said that was the best thing for her. Now she was awake and had Shane running for the hills.

"You're kind of an embarrassment," Clay told his brother as he pushed past him.

"We'll see how long that cocky attitude lasts," Shane called after him. "She's going to eat you for breakfast, little brother."

"It's two in the afternoon."

Clay knocked once on the partially closed door, then stepped inside.

Evie lay on the hospital bed he'd rented, her leg elevated. A cast covered her right leg from ankle to midthigh. She was pale and thin. Her long honey-blond hair was spread across the pillow. She didn't bother to look at him when he entered but he knew when she did, her eyes would be green. Different from her brothers and her mother—a reminder of the mysterious man who was her father.

"You scared Shane," he said by way of greeting. "Impressive."

"Go away."

"Sorry, no. I'm the entertainment portion of your visit."

The guest room got plenty of sun. Big windows let in light that sparkled on the hardwood floor. The regular bed had been moved out to make room for the one he'd rented. There was also one of those hospital-style tables on wheels. Crutches leaned against the wall, although as far as he knew, Evie was doing her best to avoid getting up. That included eating and drinking. Her untouched lunch was still on the tray.

He sat in the chair by her bed and took her hand in his. She had long fingers. She was built like a dancer—small boned, lean and elegant. But since he'd last seen her, she'd gone from fashionably trim to bony.

"Are you eating at all?" he asked.

"Not today."

Not recently from the looks of things. "Evie, hey. It's me. What's going on?"

She turned her head so she could look at him. The complete lack of emotion in her eyes cut him way more than anger. "Go to hell."

"Are you in pain?"

"Do I need to be in pain not to want to be here?" She deliberately pulled her hand free of his hold and turned away again.

"You know you were hurt, right?" he asked, wanting to make sure she understood what had happened.

"The cast on my leg was a big clue, but thanks for the clarification."

"You're in Fool's Gold. In Rafe's house."

That got her to look at him again. Now irritation flashed in her green eyes. He figured it was better than nothing.

"I have a fractured leg, not a head injury. I know where I am. What I object to is being here at all. You had no right to drag me here without even asking me."

He wanted to point out that technically he hadn't been part of the dragging team, but didn't think that would facilitate communication.

"You're injured. You should be with your family."

"And that's you?"

"Sure. We talk." He knew he stayed in contact with her more than anyone. "Why are you taking this out on me? I didn't even know you were a cheerleader. Why didn't you tell me?"

"When was I supposed to do that?"

"We're on the phone every couple of weeks."

"Right. Those meaningful calls. 'Hey, sis, it's me. How are you? Need any money? Great. Gotta go. Love you.'" Her mouth twisted. "Not much of a chance to share the personal details you're suddenly so interested in."

Clay wanted to say it wasn't like that. Except he knew it was. When he remembered to call Evie, the contact was brief. From her perspective, meaningless. A duty call.

"Tell me about being a cheerleader," he said. "I want to know."

She motioned to her leg. "Does it matter? I'm not going to be back on the squad anytime soon."

"I'm sorry."

"Me, too."

He didn't know how to help or what to say. "Evie, you're my sister. I care about you."

"Then get me out of here. Take me anywhere that isn't near Mom or anyone else I know. I'll recover in peace."

"You're going to need help. The fracture isn't deep, but it's tricky. Then you'll have physical therapy. Mom wants to drive you."

"I'd rather never walk again."

Clay's instinct was to defend May, but he knew better. Her relationship with Evie had always been difficult. Not just because of the mother-daughter thing but because May had always felt guilty about her one-night stand a few months after the death of her much-loved husband. Evie had been the result.

Clay had been too young to understand what had happened. All he knew was that one day he had a baby sister. As he was the youngest brother, he'd been the closest to her. A sad state of affairs, he realized, thinking about how much everyone else had ignored her.

He knew this wasn't the time to tell his sister that Rafe and May were packing up her apartment and moving her things to Fool's Gold. She would be healing for a couple of months and everyone had decided she would be better off closer. Not that she would appreciate the decision.

"I'm sorry," he said, aware the apology was lame at best and insulting at worst.

"You're just being a guy." His sister sighed. "You can't help it. I miss Diane."

"My Diane?"

Evie nodded. "She called me a lot and we would talk. She remembered my birthday and sent presents. Silly stuff, but it was nice." Her expression momentarily softened. "You so didn't deserve her."

"I know. I never understood what she saw in me."

"She loved you a lot."

"I loved her, too. I was very lucky to find her." He risked taking Evie's hand again. "Speaking of significant others, is there someone I should call? Anyone who's going to be looking for you?"

"No. There's no one."

The stark loneliness in those words made his gut twist. Evie was in her mid-twenties. She should be having fun with friends, falling in and out of love. She shouldn't be alone or cynical. She shouldn't hate her family or want to be anywhere but with them.

He swore under his breath. "I'm sorry," he said. "What the hell happened between us?"

Evie slowly, deliberately, pulled her hand away. "You didn't want me. None of you did. I was never a part of this family and each one of you made sure I knew it.

So don't get all surprised and righteous now that I don't want to have anything to do with you."

Clay wanted to tell her that she was wrong, only she wasn't. About any of it. The four of them had been a unit and Evie the odd man out.

"I love you, Evie."

She closed her eyes. "I'd like to sleep now."

It wasn't the shouting match she'd had with Shane, he thought as he stood. But it was just as destructive. She'd taken him down with little more than the ugly truth.

He walked to the door and paused. Realizing there was nothing else he could say, he walked out.

CHARLIE HONEST-TO-GOD didn't know where to look. She'd been called out to some truly horrific accidents, had pulled bodies out of burning buildings and been present at the birth of a baby. None of which had prepared her for the Fool's Gold Firefighter calendar shoot.

There were good-looking guys everywhere. Twelve in total, in various states of undress, styling and um, oiling. Yes, one overly plucked woman in her forties walked around with a bottle of oil and rubbed it over the exposed flesh of the models. And there was a lot of exposed flesh.

Charlie wasn't sure if she should enjoy the view or make her escape. Clay was supposed to join her, but he'd phoned to say he was running late and she should make herself comfortable. Charlie didn't think that was possible.

A low stage stood in front of a backdrop of a barn.

Lights with upside-down umbrella things were all around. There was a fan, lights on the floor and several props including a saddled horse. She couldn't figure out the best place to stand, let alone where to look. She was pulling her truck keys out of her pocket when the back door of the studio opened and Clay strolled in. Charlie surged toward him, eager to find some small measure of comfort or even protection.

"You're here," she said. "Thank God. This is a nightmare."

He grinned, then pulled her close and kissed her. "Miss me?"

"Yes. This is not my comfort zone."

He glanced around, then looked back at her. "You'd rather be fighting a fire?"

"Of course. I understand fire. This is madness."

"It's a photo shoot."

"You say that as if I've been to twenty."

He put his arm around her. "That's my girl. Speaking her mind."

"It's the only mind I have. How are you? Evie get settled okay?"

His good humor faded. "She's here, but she's not happy."

"She's hurt. That's got to be upsetting."

"I think she's more pissed to be around us than she is about the broken leg."

Charlie knew a little about the family dynamics. "She'll come around."

"I'm not so sure. We're all guilty of not making an ef-

fort. I should have been there for her. More than I was."
He shook his head. "One more place I've screwed up."

"Don't say that. Evie could have tried, too."

"Why would she bother?"

"Because in the end, everybody wants to connect.
Look at me. I'm getting along with my mother and who
would have thought that was possible?"

Clay touched her face as he stared into her eyes.
"You're right."

She sighed. "Those words never get old. Want me to
talk to Evie? Do you think it would help?"

"Maybe when she's feeling better. Right now she's
pissed at the world. Especially the part where the Stryk-
ers live." He glanced around. "Okay, let's talk about why
we're here. Can I answer any questions?"

"Aside from when can we leave? No."

He chuckled. "Want me to introduce you to any of
the guys?"

"No, thanks. I already have my own handsome su-
permodel. One is all I can handle."

"Good." He took her hand. "Because this relationship is exclusive."

She stared at him. "You're kidding, right? You're not
seriously worried about me being attracted to someone else."

"Why not? It could happen."

"Have you looked in the mirror lately?"

His dark gaze settled on her face. "What does that
have to do with anything? Cheating isn't always about
appearance. It's about how you feel. Are you happy?

Are your needs getting met? I meant what I said, Charlie. This is an exclusive relationship for me. I hope it is for you, too."

She had to consciously keep her mouth from falling open. "You're worried about me wanting to see someone else?"

"I want to make sure we're on the same page."

"We are," she managed, wondering if the situation with his sister was bothering him more than he was letting on. While Clay was more insightful than the average male, he was still a guy. How could he think she would want to be with anyone else? He was the one who brightened her day and made her—

The truth could be a bitch, she thought as self-awareness slammed into her. The reason she wasn't interested in looking at another man had nothing to do with appearance, as Clay had suggested, and everything to do with emotion.

She was in love with him. Wildly, desperately, madly in love with him. Somewhere between the laughs and the sighs, she'd given her heart. Just like her friends had warned her could happen. Talk about being a complete idiot.

"Charlie?"

"I'm fine," she said. "Just wrapping my mind around you worrying about my fidelity."

He leaned close. "I know what a wild woman you are in bed. If word gets out, you'll have all the men in town begging."

"Then we won't tell anyone. I had that ad going out in the paper, but I should probably rethink it."

"We're ready," the photographer called. "Jeremy, you're up."

Jeremy, a tall, well-built man, walked onto the low, wide platform. The photographer talked with him for a couple of seconds. Jeremy nodded. Without warning, he stepped out of his boxer shorts and handed them to an assistant.

Charlie nearly choked as she immediately looked away. "He's naked."

Clay frowned. "Sure. The shots themselves will be family-friendly, but to get some of the sexy poses, you have to be naked."

She glanced at the ground, then at the lights, before staring directly into the model's eyes. "That information doesn't make him any less naked."

"You're embarrassed."

"I don't know him. I don't want to see his you-know-what. It's Tuesday. I avoid that sort of thing midweek."

Clay pulled her close. "Penis," he whispered. "We're all adults. You can manage the word."

"Shut up." She shoved him.

He laughed and grabbed her hands in his. She stared into his eyes, knowing she would happily spend the rest of her life getting lost in him. All of him. Not just the pretty bits, but the man inside. The heart and soul of him.

To her right, a light exploded. She jumped and turned. The photographer lowered the camera he'd pointed at the two of them and shrugged. "Sorry. Great shot. Couldn't help myself."

He turned back to the model. "You know what? Let's put that plaid shirt on. With the hat."

Someone handed the model the shirt and hat, which he put on. Although he left off his boxers.

"Really?" Charlie asked. "He doesn't want to put on pants?"

The back door of the studio opened and Gladys and Eddie entered. The two old ladies got an eyeful of the model as he turned. Gladys put a hand to her chest.

"Someone get me a chair," she said. "I'm going to faint."

Charlie groaned, then glared at Clay. "This is your fault, isn't it?"

"I thought they'd enjoy watching the shoot. And, frankly, this is a great distraction from everything going on out at the farm."

"If either of them has a heart attack because of this, you are in so much trouble."

He gave her a quick kiss. "Let me get them settled. I'll be right back."

Charlie nodded. When Clay stepped away, Charlie went looking for the photographer's assistant.

"He just took a picture of me and Clay," she said in a low voice. "Any way I can get a copy of that?"

"Sure. No problem. Give me your email address and I'll send you a file."

"Thanks."

She wanted to have the photograph for later. In case

things worked out...or even if they didn't. Proof positive that she would find something special with the right person. No matter what, she would always have the memory of Clay.

CHAPTER NINETEEN

"YOU'RE STILL SULKING," Shane said cheerfully as he walked into the kitchen.

Clay glared at him over his cup of coffee. "I'm not sulking. I'm assessing my options."

"I'll admit you've had a few setbacks with the Haycation idea, but you're moving forward."

"Not today."

His brother patted him on the shoulder. "You might want to check out your land."

Clay glanced at the clock. It was barely eight in the morning. Charlie had kept him up late the night before and he was only halfway through his first cup of coffee. "What are you talking about?"

Shane leaned against the counter and grinned. "I don't want to spoil the surprise. North end. The acres that had the alfalfa."

Something Clay didn't want to think about, but had to face, he thought as he grabbed his truck keys and headed out. He drove to the north end of the property only to find a couple of old guys, some farm equipment and several trucks of what looked like dirt.

Last week the alfalfa had sprouted. The seed company's insurance had arranged to have it dug out and the top eight or ten inches of soil hauled away. Clay had avoided the area ever since. The earth left behind looked as if it had been through a war. He wasn't sure of the next step and hadn't had the heart to call and find out.

Clay parked and got out of his truck. One of the old guys waved and started toward him.

"You must be Clay," the man said. He was eighty if he was a day, all wrinkles and bright, alert eyes. His coveralls were threadbare but clean. His boots were probably as old as Clay. "I'm Bernard. That there is Ernie." He grinned as he motioned to his equally geriatric friend.

"Okay. Nice to meet you. How can I help you today?"

Bernard guffawed. "A nice way of asking what the hell we're doing here, right? Well, I've got a grandson-in-law who lives down in Bakersfield and Ernie's youngest is in Stockton. We heard what happened and put out a call." Bernard motioned to the trucks. "Best topsoil money can buy." He winked. "I got a real good deal for the insurance company, not that they deserve it. But I'm old-school. Why pay a dollar if you can get it for a dime, I always say."

Clay looked at the trucks. "You brought me dirt?"

"Topsoil."

Bernard slapped him on the back. Clay nearly went flying. The old man was stronger than he looked.

"You need to get something planted before winter, son. Ernie had a strain of legumes we'll be putting in later. They'll do fine over the cold months. Come spring, you plow 'em under and give them a season. Next fall, get your alfalfa planted. It puts you behind, but trust me. This way your land will be good as new."

Clay had been doing research and talking to some agriculture experts at UC Davis. But he hadn't been able to rent the equipment he needed. Fall was a busy time in the farming community and he hadn't gotten his order in soon enough.

"You're with the insurance company?" he asked.

"Hell, no." Bernard's mouth straightened into a disapproving line. "There's not enough money in the world for me to work for the bloodsuckers. I have an orchard on the other side of the vineyards. Ernie has the farm on the west edge of town. We've been working the land since God was a boy."

Bernard glanced at the clear sky. "We'll get a good day's work in. Trust me, son. By the end of the week, you'll have a plowed and planted field."

Clay didn't understand. "If you're not with the insurance company, why are you doing this?"

Bernard slapped him again. This time Clay was able to brace himself in time. "You're one of us. Okay, you're a slick city kid, but that'll fade. In a few years, you'll be able to tell anyone who asks that you're a farmer. Salt of the earth." He gave a wink. "Saying you're a farmer makes the ladies hot. Trust me. I've been milking that line for years."

"Good to know," Clay said, a little confused by Bernard and his folksy wisdom. "Just to make sure I understand, no one asked you to help? You're just here?"

"Sure. Look, kid. There isn't one of us who hasn't had to deal with the same mess. You'll be fine. Ernie and I can answer any questions you might have about whatever it is you want to grow. In the meantime, how about I teach you to drive that baby there."

He pointed to the large piece of equipment. It was the size of a small house and looked complicated. Clay grinned. "I don't know what it's called, but I want one."

"That's the spirit." Bernard waved at Ernie. "Let's make the magic happen."

NINE HOURS LATER, Clay walked toward the house. He was exhausted. Bernard and Ernie had worn him out. They were still going strong, talking about some movie they were going to watch on pay-per-view, joking with each other and coming up with some surprisingly dirty limericks. He wanted to be just like them when he was in his eighties.

He stopped at the back door and pulled off his boots. He'd been calf-deep in mud as he'd learned the ins and outs of prepping a field and then planting.

Still in his stocking feet, he walked into the kitchen to find Mayor Marsha, a couple of the old ladies from the city council and Dominique milling around. There were cakes and pies on the counters, a pot of coffee going and plenty of laughter. The latter came to a stop when he walked in.

His mother greeted him with a quick hug. "They showed up just after lunch," she whispered. "We have casseroles in the refrigerator and freezer. There's a guy watching the news who wants to talk to you."

He started to say he had no idea what she was talking about when the mayor moved toward them.

"I have some names for you," she said, handing over several business cards and a sheet of paper. "Contractors, mostly. A man who does restoration work and two companies for the pool."

Clay took the papers. "What pool?"

The mayor smiled. "We were thinking it would be nice to have another community pool. We'll need to work out the details, of course. But we can coordinate it. Share the expenses. We'll provide the lifeguards and insurance, if you'll take care of maintenance. That sort of thing."

"A pool?"

"By the vacation homes." Mayor Marsha spoke as if that information would help. "For your guests and the town."

"Okay," he said slowly. "We should set up a meeting."

"I agree." She pointed to the other business card. "After you talk to Milo about his donation, you'll want that number."

"Donation?"

"Talk to Milo." She motioned toward the living room.

He had no idea who Milo was, but if he was anything like Bernard and Ernie, Clay would like him. He nodded at the mayor and walked down the short hallway.

A man in his sixties stood when he saw Clay.

"You must be Milo," Clay said.

"I am. I heard about your Haycations. Great idea. Tourism with a twist. We welcome their dollars." Milo, a big-bellied guy with graying hair, rocked back on his heels. "I have a carousel. One of those old-fashioned ones with the painted horses. It needs a lot of work, but it used to be a beauty. You can have it, if you want."

"A carousel?"

"For your guests. All I ask is you pay to get it delivered here. And fix it up."

"Because it used to be a beauty?"

Milo beamed. "Exactly."

A carousel? There was plenty of room and it would be an interesting attraction. He glanced down at the card in his hand. One of them was for a guy who did antique restorations. Now he knew why the mayor had given it to him.

"We like what you're doing," the older man said. "Fool's Gold takes care of its own. You're one of us now."

"I'm starting to get that."

Milo sniffed. "Someone put on Eddie's chili. I'm going to get a bowl before I head out. Coming?"

"Be right there," Clay told him.

Milo disappeared down the hall. Clay stared at the

cards he held and thought about the pool and the carousel. The support shown. It hadn't just appeared. Someone, somewhere had said something. He had one guess.

Charlie.

"You're responsible," Clay said.

Charlie watched him anxiously, not sure if he was mad or not. It was about eight on Saturday night. The day had been warm, but the evening was cooling off. There was a light breeze that promised to be a stiff wind by morning. She was halfway through her twenty-four-hour shift and normally a visit from Clay would be a highlight. But she wondered if she'd overstepped any lines in their relationship.

They sat out on the patio behind the station. The rest of the shift was inside, watching TV. Charlie clutched her can of diet soda.

"I've been worried about you," she admitted. "First the bones, then Nate, then the alfalfa. It was so much. Your idea is great and I didn't want you to get discouraged. So I might have said something to a couple of people."

"More than something," he said, reaching for her free hand.

"You're not mad?"

He smiled at her. "Why would I be mad?"

"Because I butted into your new business."

He lifted her hand and lightly kissed the back of her

knuckles. "No. I'm not mad. I'm a little overwhelmed. Do you know about the carousel?"

"I've heard rumors. You interested?"

"I want to see it first, but maybe. Mayor Marsha gave me the name of a guy who does restorations. I'd want to work with him so I can do future repairs myself. The pool idea is interesting."

"Summers can be hot here. The tourists would like a pool."

"We could go skinny-dipping."

She was torn between the mental image of him naked and climbing out of the water and the idea that the pool wouldn't be built for some time. So an invitation to go skinny-dipping meant they would still be together.

Love was a bitch, she thought, as her heart gave a little shimmy of happiness at the thought of more time with Clay. Because if it were up to her, she would be planning time together into the next century. She had a feeling she'd inherited more than her physical strength from her mother. She might have also inherited a heart that could only love one man. But that was a problem for another time.

He continued to nibble along her fingers. As she was on duty and there were a half-dozen people in the building behind them, she let herself enjoy the sensation without having much in the way of expectation. Although if Clay suggested meeting her at her place after her shift, she would happily agree. Of course that wouldn't be until the next morning.

"They brought casseroles," he said as he lowered her hand to his lap. "Dozens of them."

"We're a town that likes to feed people."

"The chili was good." He turned to her. "Thank you. I know you talking to people was your way of saying you believe in me. That means a lot."

"Happy to help. And you're right. I do believe in you."

"It's nice to be more than a piece of ass."

She smiled. "You've always been that. Although it is a very nice—"

The alarms went off. She was out of her chair and moving before the sound even registered. As she ran into the building, she heard the loudspeaker calling out the address. Before the announcement had finished, she was jerking on her turnouts.

Olivia appeared at her side. The captain was pale, her eyes wide.

"It's the warehouse," she said, as they both grabbed helmets. "The one on the edge of town. My son told me that teenagers have been hanging out there. It's a party place."

Charlie swore. Teens partying usually meant alcohol. It also meant acting stupid. With the nights getting colder, the kids could have started a fire to stay warm. Or because they thought it would be fun. Old buildings and flames didn't go well together.

They ran to the engine. "I told him not to go there,"

Olivia said as she took the right-hand seat. "What if he didn't listen?"

Charlie didn't have an answer. The engine rumbled to life. Before she pulled out, she saw Clay and rolled down the window.

"Phone dispatch and tell them to call in the trainees. You'll be in charge of them. Stay out of the way and help where you can."

He nodded once, then took off toward the phone. She hit the siren and drove out into the night.

CLAY STOOD ON the sidewalk, momentarily immobilized by the rage of the fire. The warehouse was a block long, about three stories high, wood construction with a brick facade. Most of the windows were boarded up.

The flames were everywhere. Coming out the roof, shooting from the few openings that hadn't been covered over. Smoke rose into the night. It wouldn't take long until there weren't any visible stars, just thick, black smoke that stole oxygen and blinded those inside.

Once again, the sound shocked him. The roar of destruction, the crash as parts of the building collapsed. Snaps and screams filled the night as the structure fought against the inevitable.

"Go set up the monitor over there," Captain Fargo yelled.

Clay wanted to go help, but knew he would only get in the way. He stayed back by the engines, pulling out hoses when asked and keeping the growing crowd far enough away.

He didn't know if word had spread in the small town or if people could see and smell the massive fire. Either way, the two observers had grown to a crowd of fifteen or twenty.

One woman ran toward him. She was blond and frantic, her eyes wide, her cheeks wet with tears. "My daughter's in there," she screamed. "She's at the party. You have to help her."

The captain turned. "Get her back," she yelled. "Keep them all back." She started toward the building, then stopped. "How many teens?"

The mother sobbed. "I don't know. Eight. Maybe ten. Oh, God. Tell me she's okay."

Clay grabbed her around the waist and pulled her clear. "If you get in their way, they can't help."

He half led, half dragged her to the sidewalk. The other volunteer trainees showed up and he organized them into keeping the civilians safely away from the fire.

Several police officers arrived. He talked to Chief Barns, telling her how long the fire department had been there. More equipment pulled up as the two alarm grew to four. There were only five stations in Fool's Gold. He heard a policewoman say a call had gone out to nearby communities.

Smoke and sparks filled the air. Bits of embers landed on the sidewalk. Firefighters with axes and air packs disappeared into the building and later reappeared. Minutes later, a tall firefighter hurried out, her arms around two teenagers. The paramedics moved in to help them.

Clay studied the firefighter, noting the familiar number on her helmet. *Charlie,* he thought, relieved. But once the teens were safely with the medics, she turned and, with another firefighter, disappeared back into the inferno.

Time crawled. More kids appeared. Two were carried. Clay watched the warehouse, waiting for Charlie to reappear. He told himself that she wasn't alone. That she would be fine. This was what she did, who she was.

The ground moved. For a second, he thought they were having an earthquake. From behind him, he heard screams. He glanced back at the warehouse. The roof seemed to shimmer and dance then slowly, so slowly, folded in on itself. The outside west wall disintegrated.

Smoke and dust and debris rose like a living creature. The sounds faded until there was only the beating of his heart and a primal scream. *No!*

He was running before he knew what had happened. Running, determined. Because Charlie was still in the building. Charlie was in danger and he had to save her.

Someone yelled. He heard words, but they didn't penetrate. Someone grabbed him. He pushed the arms away. He was nearly there. Heat blasted him; he couldn't breathe, but that didn't matter. There were more arms, then he couldn't run. He was being held in place.

Rational thought returned and with it came fear. The cold kind that rose from his bones and made it impossible to move.

"I swear to God, I will knock you unconscious myself," the captain told him. "Stay the fuck here."

Clay nodded because he couldn't speak. He stared at the building, making deals with God, offering all he had. His life, his soul, everything. If Charlie would just be okay.

Embers landed on his shirt and burned through to his skin, but he didn't move. Water continued to flow onto the burning building and the smoke gradually turned from black to gray. Firefighters raced in and out of the building, dark silhouettes against the devil's handiwork.

Then he saw her. One second there was only smoke and steam, the next she was walking out into the night.

Relief kept him in place as firmly as fear had done. He watched her, grateful and terrified at the same time. Because knowing she was alive wasn't enough. He had to find a way to always keep her safe. She was… She was…

And then he knew. He'd never bothered to protect himself from Charlie because he didn't have to. They were friends. Lovers. But not in love. Never in love.

But sometime in the past few weeks, she'd worked her way inside of him. Into his heart. She'd become important. He loved her.

Charlie walked over to the medics and pulled off her helmet. He knew right away that she was fine. He caught scraps of conversation and heard her arguing that she hadn't been anywhere near the collapse. That she was fine. No one listened.

He returned to the growing crowd and helped keep order. By midnight the fire was out. By two in the morning, the cleanup complete. All nine teens were safe. Three had been taken to the hospital but were expected to make a full recovery. Sometime close to three, he drove back to the ranch.

He parked, but instead of going inside, he walked out to the corrals and stared at the night sky. He was cold, smelled of smoke. There were probably holes in his shirt from the embers. He might have a few burns.

None of that mattered. What he couldn't wrap his mind around was how it had happened. How had he fallen in love again? He'd assumed he would only love Diane for the rest of his life. There wasn't supposed to be anyone else. He couldn't do it again. Give his all and then lose it. He wasn't that strong.

Which meant he knew what came next. What he had to do.

Charlie was resilient, he told himself. Capable. In the end, he couldn't hurt her. Not really. She had survived worse. And so had he.

CHARLIE PARKED IN her driveway and told herself she really had to get out of her truck and walk to the house. Once there she would collapse. Her bed was waiting;

she'd already showered twice at the station. A good day's sleep and she would be healed.

It had been a hell of a night. The fire, set by teens lighting a fire in the warehouse, had destroyed the structure, but no lives had been lost. They'd been on the opposite side of the building that had collapsed. Apparently the old saying was true—God did look after children and fools. Last she'd heard, the couple of kids taken to the hospital would be released later today. The other buildings in the area had been protected. What could have been a disaster had ended as well as could be expected.

She climbed out of her truck and started toward the front door. Movement on her porch caught her attention. She saw Clay stand and walk toward her.

Instantly her exhaustion faded. She hurried toward him, wanting to see him and touch him. Right now she didn't even care if they made love. She just wanted to feel his arms around her and spend some time in his company. If that led to the wild thing, that would be good, too.

"Hey," she said when she stopped in front of him. "I heard you did good last night. Olivia said you got a little worried when that section of roof caved, but you took care of the crowds and stayed out of trouble."

"She's lying," he said, his voice oddly flat.

"What do you mean?"

"I thought I'd lost you."

The words should have made her do the happy dance,

but there was something in his voice. Make that something that *wasn't* in his voice. There was no energy, no
drive. It was as if they were talking about whether or
not to wash the car.

"What's wrong?" she asked, her stomach tightening
as something very close to dread washed through her.
"What happened?"

She waited for him to laugh and say he was fine. For
him to pull her close and kiss her. She would settle on
gentle teasing, as long as he said everything was fine.
That they were fine.

"I don't want to do this anymore," he told her, his
dark gaze unreadable. He motioned to the space between them. "Us. The relationship. It's over."

She'd spent much of her life protecting herself, emotionally. Now all that training took over. Raw pain cut
through her, but she didn't blink, didn't flinch, didn't
say a word. She felt her face stiffen, shifting to a kind
of shield where no expression showed. Her hands stayed
loose at her sides, her legs continued to support her.

The only outward sign that anything was wrong was
her chin rising slightly.

"All right," she said calmly.

"I wish you the best," he said. "And I'm sorry if this
hurts you. I'll tell everyone you dumped me. You know,
so there aren't any questions."

She wanted to point out that questions wouldn't matter. Not when she didn't have answers. She wanted to
scream that she didn't understand and then ask why he

was doing this to her. What had changed? Why was today different than yesterday?

For the first time in her life, she wanted to beg.

Instead she asked, "Anything else?"

He shook his head and walked away.

She watched him go. Waited until he'd gotten in his truck and driven away. When she was sure he was gone, was sure he couldn't see her anymore, she sank down onto her knees, her face pressed into her thighs, her body shaking, her hands pressed against the cement walkway. Tears soaked her jeans as she let the pain wash over her.

She had no idea how long she stayed there, crouched and in pain. After a while, she felt gentle hands brush against her back. Heidi and Annabelle urged her to her feet, then helped her inside. Once she was seated on the sofa, she covered her face with her hands and sobbed until there was nothing left. Nothing but a future without the man she loved.

CHAPTER TWENTY

"YOU DIDN'T HAVE to come back," Dominique told her bodyguard. "I called the agency and released you from your contract. You're free to go protect someone who actually needs your services."

Justice prowled the living room of her suite, as if confirming no danger lurked. "I wanted to say good-bye."

She laughed. "Hardly. We only worked together a few days. You're not here because of me at all." She tilted her head. "So what brings you back to Fool's Gold?"

His gaze settled on her face. "There's someone I might want to see."

"Someone? Or a woman?"

He stopped in the center of the room. "A woman."

"Tell me about her."

One corner of his mouth turned up at the corner. "I don't think so."

"Ever mysterious."

"It works for me."

"But she is here. The woman you're afraid to see."

"I'm not afraid."

"What's her name?" Dominique asked.

He hesitated so long she didn't think he would tell her. But he finally spoke. "Patience McGraw."

Dominique raised her eyebrows. "She's a hairstylist here in town. A lovely young woman. Former girlfriend?"

"Not exactly. I knew her a long time ago. When I was young."

The story was getting more and more interesting, Dominique thought. "You grew up here?"

"I lived here a couple of years when I was a kid. I doubt Patience remembers me."

"You're not the kind of man a woman forgets."

"I wasn't a man back then."

"Still. I suspect you were memorable." She smiled. "I'm stating a fact, not flirting."

His expression relaxed. "I know. I'm not your type."

"So about your friend Patience. Now what?"

"I have to leave on an assignment. She has a life. I shouldn't bother her."

"I doubt she would see you as a bother. You should speak to her before you go."

He shook his head. "I have to go to South America now. For a job."

Dominique wondered why he was waiting. Fear? Anticipation? "But you wanted to see her one last time before you left?"

He shrugged. "Maybe."

"Which means yes. So you'll see her and she won't see you. I hope you don't change your mind about coming back. You need some time in this town. It will heal you."

"Who says I need healing?"

"Anyone can see it in your eyes."

His gaze narrowed. "I liked you better before you were insightful."

"Now you're lying. I'm much more interesting these days. I don't know why it took me so long to pay attention to other people. They're endlessly fascinating. So flawed, but determined."

He walked over and kissed her on the cheek. "Goodbye, Dominique. It was a pleasure."

"I hope I see you again soon."

He only nodded and walked to the door. He let himself out.

Dominique stayed on the sofa, thinking about what she would do with her day. She needed to make a visit to the dance school. Being around the students was so refreshing. A few of the girls had actual talent. She should talk to the parents and make sure they had plans to continue their daughters' dance education. There was also a—

Someone knocked on her door.

She rose and crossed the living room. "Did you forget something?" she asked, opening the door and expecting to see Justice.

Instead, Charlie stood there. Her daughter's face was pale, her eyes red and swollen. She looked as if she'd been crying. Worse, she seemed almost small.

Without thinking, Dominique held out her arms. Charlie surged forward and let herself be held.

CHARLIE CURLED UP on the sofa as best she could. Sometimes being tall was a pain in the ass. Right now she wished she was small enough to simply disappear. She fought feelings of shame, along with a sense of being broken in such a way that she would never heal.

She knew she'd been a fool and that she had no one but herself to blame. But that didn't take away the hollow ache inside. The pain she felt with every breath. The loss that was so big, it threatened to swallow her whole.

Dominique sat beside her on the sofa, angled toward her. She didn't speak or ask questions. Instead she passed tissues and plied her with single malt Scotch. It might only be eleven in the morning, but Charlie was well on her way to being drunk.

After Heidi and Annabelle had helped her inside, she'd cried until she had nothing left. Halfway through her explanation of what had gone wrong, she'd realized she needed to see Dominique. Annabelle had driven her over. The true measure of a friend, she thought. Doing what was right for the other person.

"It's Clay," Charlie said at last, wiping her eyes with a balled-up tissue and wishing she could stop crying. "It's over."

Dominique squeezed her hand. "I'm sorry."

"I don't know what happened. I thought we were doing fine, but then this morning, he ended things. He said he didn't want us to be together anymore. That it was over." More tears fell. "I don't know w-why."

Charlie fought the sobs, but they won. She bent at the waist, clutching her arms around her middle, trying to hold in what was left of her heart.

"I loved him, Mom. I loved him so much."

Dominique reached for her and held her tight. She didn't offer reassurances or say anything stupid like "you'll be fine." Instead she simply offered physical comfort without judgment.

Eventually Charlie was able to catch her breath and straighten.

"It's my fault," she whispered. "Not whatever went wrong. I have no idea about that. But loving him. He was too good to be true, you know? Too perfect."

"It's never wrong to love someone," her mother said. "You're a wonderful woman. He was lucky to have you and a complete jackass for letting you go."

The unexpected words made Charlie smile through her tears. "Thanks. That's so nice."

"You're welcome and I'm right. Ask anyone."

"Not Clay."

"Why would you want the opinion of a jackass?"

"Good point." Charlie blew her nose. "I have to tell you something and I need you not to judge me. Okay?"

Dominique nodded. "I promise."

Oddly, Charlie felt as if she could trust her. "Clay and I weren't dating at the beginning. After the rape, I couldn't imagine being with a man. I dated some, but

I could never bring myself to be intimate. It was easier to avoid men, so I did."

Charlie talked about how she'd decided she wanted to have a child and that her friend, Dakota, had suggested Charlie needed to heal herself first. That to be the best mother she could, she would need to be whole. While therapy was an option, Charlie wasn't that patient and she'd decided to find a guy to help her get over her fear of physical intimacy. She'd chosen Clay.

"I'm impressed you had the courage," her mother told her. "Continuing to hide would have been much easier."

"Tell me about it," Charlie said. She drew in a breath and gave a brief recap of her physical relationship with Clay.

"Once he got me, um, back to normal, I thought it was going to be over. But he said he wanted us to continue to see each other. Like we were dating. I believed everything was fine until this morning. When he told me…"

The raw agony returned, as did the tears. She tried to steady her breathing without breaking down and was nearly successful. Once again her tiny mother held her as if she would never let go.

"It hurts," Charlie whispered. "It hurts so much."

"I know," Dominique said quietly.

They hung on to each other. Charlie tried to calm herself. To accept that this level of pain was her new normal. Others had survived much worse. Didn't everyone have to get over a broken heart?

But rational thought didn't help and she was left with

the knowledge that she might love Clay forever. Much as her mother had loved her father over a decade after his death.

"I could have Justice hurt him," Dominique offered.

"Who?"

"Justice. The bodyguard I hired. I have his number. I could call him and have him take care of Clay."

Charlie managed to slow the tears enough to smile. "That's great, Mom, but I'll pass."

"It might make you feel better."

"If beating up Clay was going to help, I'd want to do it myself."

Only she couldn't imagine wanting to do anything but hold him. To be close to him again, feeling his body against hers.

It wasn't just that, she realized. She wanted to talk to him. Hear his voice, laugh at his jokes.

"He has a really good sense of humor, you know," she said, her voice slightly strangled. "When we were first talking about having sex he teased me about the photos I'd seen of him. He said they'd enhanced his 'package.' He's like that. He can make fun of himself. But when the conversation is serious, he's totally there. He cares so much, about his family, about…"

About Diane, she thought sadly. *The woman he loved.* Was that what had happened? Had he guessed her feelings and been upset by them? There had been a tacit understanding between them. They were dating, but not supposed to get serious.

"He knew," she said slowly. "He figured out I fell in love with him. That's why he left."

Dominique cupped Charlie's face in her hands. "Don't be ridiculous. That's a stupid reason for Clay to leave. Besides, if he's all that you claim, and he thought you were in love with him, he would have been a whole lot more gentle about how he left. If you ask me, whatever is going on is happening in his head alone. Maybe he has started to care about you and is feeling guilty. Maybe he's actually a bastard and this is what he does. Whatever it is, you are not to blame. You didn't do anything wrong."

Whether or not they were the truth, the words felt good, Charlie thought. Supportive.

"Thanks, Mom," she said.

"You're welcome. Now wait right here. I want to get you something."

Dominique rose and walked into the bedroom. Charlie hoped she wasn't going to return with an inspirational book. Right now that was the last thing she needed. But instead of reading material, her mother returned with a small key chain.

"I have a very nice apartment with a view of Central Park," Dominique said, handing over the keys. "I would suggest you go there and see for yourself."

Charlie stared at her. "You're sending me to New York?"

"Sometimes getting away is the best solution. You'll have time to think without worrying about running into him. Or people looking sympathetic. I can tell you from personal experience that sympathy is the worst."

Charlie wanted to say that her home was here, in Fool's Gold. That her friends were here and her job. Except the idea of running had a certain appeal. There would be no explanations. She wouldn't have to talk to anyone. She could curl up and lick her wounds. Gain strength. Then come home.

"I do have vacation time owed me," she said slowly. *Weeks of it,* she thought. She'd always loved her job too much to bother with time off.

She reached out and took the key. "Thanks," she said.

"You're welcome. I'll call and tell my doorman you're coming. Now let's go online and find you a flight. If you're flying out of Sacramento, I'm not sure there's a direct. Hmm, I'll call the air-charter company May used."

"Mom, I'm not taking a private plane to New York."

"Let's find out if they can do it. If not, they can fly you to San Francisco and then you can get a direct flight there." Dominique touched her arm. "You're my daughter. I love you. I want to take care of you."

Charlie stood and pulled her close. Her tiny mother went easily into her arms. She was so small, Charlie had the sense she could crush her like a twig. Yet there was a strength in Dominique. Something Charlie had to hope she'd inherited.

"YOU DID IT," Shane said, standing with Clay at the edge of the freshly planted fields.

"It wasn't me," Clay said. "Bernard and Ernie did all the work."

"Is it just me or do they make you think of Bert and Ernie?"

Clay managed a chuckle. "Sometimes. Assuming Muppets age." He studied the land that had been through so much. "Disaster averted."

"I heard about the carousel," Shane told him. "Going to take it?"

"I haven't seen it yet. Maybe. I like the idea of it." More important, Charlie had liked the idea of it.

Damn. She was in his head. He hadn't realized that when he'd ended things. Not that it would have changed his mind, but he might have been a little more prepared. He thought about her constantly, missed her. Needed her.

"Rafe and I decided you have to eat all the casseroles made with tuna," his brother told him.

Clay managed a chuckle. "Sure. That won't bother me. I've eaten worse."

"Evie's looking better."

"She's up and around."

Still not talking very much and avoiding their mother, but healing.

"Rafe still hasn't told her he closed up her apartment," Shane said.

"That'll be an explosion."

Shane drew in a breath. "You okay?"

There were other questions buried in the couple of words. And a simple answer.

"No."

"Want to talk about it?"

"No."

"So I should let it go?"

"Uh-huh."

Shane shoved his hands into his jeans front pockets. "Charlie's special."

"This is you letting it go?"

"I can't do that. You miss her."

"I'll get over it."

"I'm not so sure about that. You love her."

Clay turned to his brother. "How do you know that?"

Shane shrugged. "I know you. And I've just been through the same thing myself. My mistake was thinking I couldn't trust Annabelle to be the kind of woman I thought I needed. Turns out I was wrong. About her and about what was best for me. I think you're making the same mistake."

"No," he said flatly. "You don't understand. Your first marriage ended in divorce. The only reason I'm not with Diane is that she died. Otherwise, we'd still be together."

"But she did die," Shane reminded him. "Years ago. It's time, bro. You can't live in the past."

"I don't. That's not what this is about. I don't want to be with Charlie."

"Why not?"

At that moment, Clay couldn't think of a single reason.

"I thought you'd come around," Shane told him. "I guess I was wrong. Her leaving was for the best."

Clay stared at him. "Leaving? What are you talking about?"

"Charlie left yesterday. I thought you knew."

Charlie gone? "Where?" She couldn't leave. Fool's Gold was her home. She belonged here.

His brother shrugged. "I don't know. Annabelle didn't say." He drew his eyebrows together. "She's sure as hell not going to tell you, so don't bother asking."

Clay took a step and stumbled. As he righted himself, he knew her leaving was his fault. He'd driven her away.

"I have to get back," he said and started toward the house. He half expected Shane to follow, but his brother let him go.

Yet there was no peace in the long walk back. And when he walked into the kitchen, his mother was waiting.

"We have to talk," May told him.

"Mom, no."

"Fine. Then I'll talk and you listen." She moved close and put her hands on his shoulders. "I'm so proud of you, Clay. At what you've accomplished. Your modeling career and now the Haycations. You're a success. You found Diane and married her. She was wonderful."

He didn't know where the conversation was going but he knew he wouldn't like it.

His mother stared into his eyes. "Now you're being a complete idiot and she wouldn't be happy at all. Do you think avoiding caring about anyone else honors her memory? Is that what you learned from loving her? To never share your heart with anyone else? What a horrible lesson."

He flinched. "It's not like that."

"Of course it is. You think I don't know? I lived it, Clay. For twenty years I kept my heart under lock and key. When your father died, I wanted to die, too. But I had my three boys and you kept me going. Then I had that night with that man and I turned up pregnant. I was so ashamed. Humiliated. Evie was proof of my betrayal. That's how I saw her. Living proof of my mistake. So I held back from her. I was a cruel mother and I hurt my daughter. For years I was distant. I knew what she wanted, what she needed, and I wasn't there for her. My actions are my worst sin. I will regret what I did for the rest of my life. But that's nothing. The person who has to pay for my mistakes is my own daughter."

Clay ached for her. "Mom…" he began.

She shook her head. "Don't try to make me feel better. There's no point in it. Now my daughter hates me and she has every reason. I want to heal what's between us and I'm not sure I deserve a second chance. All because I closed my heart to the possibilities."

She picked up a folder from the table and handed it to him. "This came today from your photographer friend. He thought I might like a copy. When I saw it, I knew the truth."

He opened the folder and saw a picture. It was the

one taken at the photo shoot, of him and Charlie to-gether. They were looking at each other.

She was so damn beautiful, he thought, taking in her blue eyes, the smile, her short hair all mussed because she'd been nervous and running her hands through it.

Then his gaze shifted to his face and he saw what his mother had seen. Love. It was so clear, it was prac-tically in writing. Even then he'd loved her. Had wanted to be with her. Only he couldn't because… Because…

"You're afraid," his mother said softly.

He put down the picture. "Terrified."

"It's safer to be alone. Easier. You can live a small, tidy life and never be hurt. There are no highs, but there aren't any lows, either."

Not a philosophy to make Diane proud, he thought. Or himself. Not what he aspired to.

His mother put her hand on his chest. "What a waste of a perfectly good heart," she said.

And he knew she was right.

"I don't know where she is."

May smiled. "I know someone who does."

DOMINIQUE MIGHT BE small, but she was formidable as she stared at Clay, her eyes snapping with the protec-tive instincts of a mother tiger.

"I should tell you this information why?" she asked. "You're the one who dumped my daughter. You hurt her, Clay. She wasn't crying…. She was sobbing. Her heart broken, her spirit shattered. You knew her deepest, darkest secrets. You claimed you wanted to heal her but in the end, you did more damage. So, no, I won't tell you where she is."

He stared at the tiny woman standing in front of him and wondered if there were any words to convince her. Because as far as he could figure out, she was the only person who knew where to find Charlie.

He thought about all the things he could say, how he could explain and realized there was only the heart-wrenching honesty he had learned from her magnificent daughter.

He drew in a breath, then dropped to his knees. "I love her, Dominique. I was wrong and I want to tell her that. I want to beg her to forgive me and give me another chance and I plan to spend the rest of my life convincing her I'm the one for her."

Dominique's stern expression remained unmoved. "Give me one good reason why I should trust you."

He swore silently. A trick question. He knew if he got it wrong, he was totally screwed. But what was the right answer? The one that would convince her that he—

And then he knew. No. Not him. His heart. Where the answer had been all along. But he'd been too blind to see it.

"You should trust me because Charlie loves me, too."

"I KNOW I said I'd leave you alone," Dominique said, her voice clear over the cell phone. "But indulge me."

"Mom, this is crazy."

"Agreed. And a cliché. But it will only take a minute."

"Why don't you come here?"

"Because there's something you need to see. Don't make me use my stern voice, Chantal."

Charlie gave a strangled laugh. "We wouldn't want that, would we? Fine. I'll meet you in Times Square at three o'clock."

"Take a cab. You don't know the subway system and I don't want anything to happen to you."

"I can handle myself on the subway."

Dominique sighed. "You're so stubborn."

"I get that from you, Mom."

"I know. It's a point of pride. See you at three."

"Okay. I love you, Mom."

"I love you, too, Charlie."

Charlie hung up the phone. She'd been in New York for three days and couldn't wait to leave. Sure it was a terrific city and her mother's apartment was spacious, bright and had views of Central Park. But none of it was Fool's Gold. She missed her friends, the town, the mountains and most of all, Clay.

Coming here had allowed her to catch her breath, though. She no longer cried all day. She'd even slept a little the night before. Maybe later she would order takeout and eat something. *Progress,* she thought. *Baby steps, but still, progress.*

She owed Dominique, she thought. Her mother had arranged for a private jet to fly her to New York. A town car had whisked her to the apartment. The privacy had allowed her to cry, to feel her pain and hopefully figure out a way to endure it until it faded.

Company wouldn't be a bad thing, she thought as she walked into the guest bathroom and washed her face. They could talk, maybe go out to eat. Being around her mother was actually kind of nice. Three months ago, she would have sworn she couldn't stand to be in the same room. Now she was looking forward to spending time with her.

She changed into a slightly less ratty shirt than the one she'd had on. She should probably put on better jeans. Dominique was always dressed so nice. But it would take more effort than Charlie could manage. Later, when they'd come back here, Dominique would guilt her into different clothes. She would face the issue then.

A little after two, she left the building and decided to walk. It was a crisp, clear fall day. The leaves had started to change and all of the city was vibrant with reds and golds, and pumpkins on window ledges and in doorways.

She went south on Broadway and saw the triangular shape that was Times Square. She walked toward the Starbucks. There was a large Sephora nearby, but it was the toy store that made her want to stop and look around. With so many of her friends having babies, toys were going to be a big part of her gift buying.

"Hello, Charlie."

The familiar voice caused her to spin until she found herself looking into Clay's handsome face. His eyes were warm, his mouth smiling. Her stomach flipped and her breath all rushed out. For a second the world seemed to tilt as she wondered if she was going to faint.

"What are you doing here?" she asked.

"Waiting for you."

Her mind was thick and uncomprehending. "I'm meeting my mother."

"No, you're meeting me. She helped me set this up."

Dominique wasn't in New York? "I don't understand."

He took her hands in his and stared into her face. "I'm sorry. I'm so sorry. I was wrong and selfish and I hurt you. I didn't want to. I wasn't thinking about you or anyone except myself. I was scared, Charlie. So damned scared. That fire. You could have died."

She didn't know what he was talking about. Part of her wanted to hope but the broken bits hurt too much.

"I'm not making sense, am I?" he asked, then released her only to turn her gently. "Look," he said, pointing at the massive electronic billboard in Times Square.

The picture shifted. Lights went on and off, finally reassembling in a picture. A photo of the two of them, together.

Clay was beautiful, she thought, staring at the image of him twenty or thirty feet high. His face, his smile. Then she blinked, not sure she was seeing what looked like—

"I love you," he told her, standing behind her, his arms wrapped around her. "Can you see it? I should have realized it sooner. I should have known you'd get to me. I should have been prepared. But I thought I knew how love happened. I didn't know it was also something that could grow from friendship and respect. I wasn't looking, so I didn't see what was right in front of me."

He turned her toward him. "I love you, Charlie. I'm sorry I got scared, but I won't again. I'm here for you. I want to be with you always. I want to marry you and give you those babies you were talking about. Please give me a chance. Please say you still love me."

She stared at him, afraid to believe but knowing she would never let him take the words back.

"I'm a forever kind of guy," he murmured, right before he kissed her. "That's how long I want."

"Me, too," she whispered and pressed her mouth to his.

They were still kissing when the billboard lights changed to three words.

Marry Me, Charlie.

Around them the crowd started cheering. People were yelling.

"Did she say yes?"

"Are they here?"

"What did she say?"

"I'll marry him if she doesn't."

Charlie raised her head and laughed. "Sorry," she said, staring into his eyes. "He's taken."

Clay grinned. "You got that right. For always, Charlie."

"For always."

* * * * *

And watch for a special holiday story
set in your favorite town,
A FOOL'S GOLD CHRISTMAS